To: Dad

Love Charlotte

Christmas '93

A STILL AND ICY SILENCE

A
STILL
AND
ICY
SILENCE

by Ronald Clair Roat

Story Line Press

This publication was made possible thanks in part to the generous support of the Andrew W. Mellon Foundation, the National Endowment for the Arts, and our individual contributors.

ISBN: 0-934257-94-9

Published by Story Line Press
Three Oaks Farm
Brownsville, OR
97327-9718

Book design by Lysa McDowell

ACKNOWLEDGEMENTS
I very much appreciate Robert M. Pirsig's permission to quote from his *Zen and the Art of Motorcycle Maintenance*. Also, former students John Wells and Kristi Gorman tutored me on how aviation fuel is delivered and sold at America's airports. Carmen Golden and other residents of Mackinac Island advised me about their magnificent island. And, my friend Patricia Aakhus has provided friendship and counsel without which there would have been no Stuart Mallory to share with my readers.

As always,
for Ruth and Brittany

Snow swept past the window, advancing up the street toward the traffic light. I couldn't see where it went from there, but I could guess.

I drank some coffee, then, using my thumb, I scraped a line of frost about four inches long from one of the lower window panes and watched it melt where it fell on the office window sill.

I drank more coffee.

Only a few cars navigated the street. My car huddled on the other side, alienated in the white, darkening world of the early weeks of a Michigan winter. When I got out of my car an hour earlier, a drift started to appear on the hood. Now it stood half a foot deep.

I removed more frost with my thumb.

Down the street from where the storm headed a heavily dressed figure leaned into the wind and plodded up the sidewalk face down, glancing occasionally to the side to measure progress. Advancing from across the street, the visitor entered the small office building that I stood in but was probably going to the dentist downstairs.

Soon I heard the footsteps from the hall.

I had both doors open, so she came straight through the empty outer office into my room and unzipped a dark green winter hood and coat. The wind was still in her cheeks.

"Stuart," she said. "You remember me?"

She was slightly overweight and younger than I would have guessed from my window perch. She had closely-cropped dark brown hair and marks on her face where she normally wore glasses. Her attire leaned heavily to winter practical.

"I'm sorry," I said, and shook my head. She did look a little familiar. After a while, most people look familiar.

"Can I sit down?" she said.

"Certainly." I moved a cardboard box from the client's chair and set it on top of another box on the floor.

"That's a long walk," she said, freeing her arms from the green corduroy coat and sitting heavily in the chair. "I left my car up the street at the drug store. Wasn't sure where you were."

"Coffee?"

"Ah huh," she said.

A long plastic bag of foam cups jutted from one of the cardboard boxes. I took one and poured coffee into it. She reached for it before I could ask about cream or sugar.

She sipped her coffee. I sipped my coffee.

"Some weather, huh?" Still the conversational wizard.

"I'm Danny Goodman's daughter, Sandra," she said. "You probably don't remember me, but you visited Dad once a few years ago, and he said some nice things about you after that."

"I remember," I said. "You were in high school. You were visiting Danny for a few days. Something to do with music."

"I was probably on my way to music camp at Interlochen," she said.

"I remember. A saxophone player." I eased around

my desk and sat down. I pushed the chair back so I could continue to gaze into the storm and watch Danny Goodman's daughter, too.

"I don't know if you've heard, but my dad died last night," she said.

I leaned forward to peer between the boxes. The chair squeak seemed loud.

"Tell me about it."

"He died in his bed. In a fire. Whole house came down."

"I'm sorry to hear that," I said. "Had he moved to Toledo or was he still here?"

She turned to see me peering at her between the boxes. "I've lived in Lansing for the last two years. My husband works at Olds. My last name is now Jensen. We're here because, well, I wanted to be closer to Dad after his heart attack."

"I didn't know."

"There's no reason you would know," she said, sipping her coffee. I emptied mine and put the cup on the window sill. I reached over to play with the frost, but it was out of reach.

"How much do you know about my father?" she said.

"Enough," I said.

"Probably enough to wonder about the fire," she said.

I nodded, then got up and refilled the coffee cup and glanced out the window. I said, "I know Danny hadn't worked the straight and narrow road for a long time."

"Dad was an arsonist," she said. "We both know that."

The wind beat on the windows. One glass pane rattled. I could nearly feel the heat being sucked from the room.

"You moving?" she said, waving one hand around the room of cardboard boxes.

I nodded.

"This is what's left of my detective business," I said. "I start a real job in a week or so. I need to empty the office before the lease expires."

She stood up.

"Then I've caught you just in time," she said.

CHAPTER 2

Sandra Goodman roamed through the office, peering at the boxes, trying not to snoop. I let her.

"The police told me Dad must have fallen asleep with a cigarette and caught the mattress on fire," Sandra said.

"He smoked a lot," I said. "It could have happened." She sipped her coffee and looked through a cardboard box.

"Hard to believe anyone could sleep through being burned to death," she said.

I watched her move from box to box trying to figure out what she wanted me to do. She pocketed one of my business cards, then she stopped at a box of books, selected from the top a dog-eared, green paperback copy of Robert M. Pirsig's *Zen and the Art of Motorcycle Maintenance*. She opened it at the blue marker.

I recited, "'This is the ghost of normal everyday assumptions which declares that the ultimate purpose of life, which is to keep alive, is impossible, but that this is the ultimate purpose of life anyway, so that great minds struggle to cure diseases so that people may live longer, but only madmen ask why. There is no other purpose. That is what the ghost says.'"

"You know that by heart?" she said.

"A few words here and there."

She closed the book quietly and put it back into the box.

"Stuart, I think somebody killed my father. I want

you to find out who did it."

"I'm not an investigator anymore."

"You are right now," she said, looking around the office.

"I'm a retiring private detective, a broke private detective, a private detective with a lot of creditors." Sandra picked up her coat and removed a thick envelope.

"I have money," she said.

"I don't want your money."

"It was Dad's money; money he gave to me and said to put away for a rainy day." She looked outside into the screen of snows. "That's close enough." She removed the folded money and dropped it with a thud on the desk where I could see it between the two big cardboard boxes.

"I can recommend someone, someone very good," I said.

"Hear me out," she said, looking down at a hefty wad of suspect $20 bills. "You are the only private detective I know. I can't trust the police to do this right, and I can't trust the fire department to do this right. I can only trust someone like you. So hear me out. Then if you want to recommend someone, you can, and I'll go."

I glanced at my watch. I had to call Patty within 30 minutes to arrange lunch.

"There's almost $10,000 there." She glanced at the desktop.

"You keep it," I said. "You'll need it."

Sandra stood and looked over the near box. "Dad and I were not very close, especially after Mom died and he went to the drugs, but when he had the heart attack we moved up here so I could be around if he needed me. And we got closer. Dad said he quit drugs and arson, and I never saw any more of them and he was getting to be almost human. I was about to have him over for Christmas, the first time in years. And then this."

Her lip began to quiver just a little. She focused somewhere deep into the storm outside and leaned most of her weight on the desk.

"Some bastard robbed me of whatever we could have had together," she said. "I want to know who he is."

She picked up the wad of money and plopped it directly in front of me. Stuck in the rubber bands was a note with her name and telephone number.

"Find out who killed my father," she said.

"You keep the money," I said, reaching for it to return it. "Buy something nice with it for Christmas."

She took two steps back from the desk, putting some distance between her and the money.

"Stuart, this is the least I can do for my dad now," she said. "Let me do this."

"I'll give you a receipt," I said.

"No receipts," she said. "That money isn't really there. I never actually had it."

"Sandra, you will find something better to spend it on."

Her face continued to be a blank. "There's more where that came from," she said. "And I'm spending it on my father. If it keeps you in business long enough to find his killer, then, well, that's where it belongs."

"What makes you think someone killed him?"

"My Dad? Killed in a house fire?" Sandra picked up her heavy coat.

"Do you have any idea who would kill him?"

"Nope," she said. "I know he had enemies, but he never hurt anyone. I mean, he burned things, but he didn't hurt people."

"Let me give you a ride to your car," I said, standing.

"It's only a block," she said, pushing her arms into the coat sleeves. "And this time it isn't against the wind."

I came around the desk where she was preparing for winter. "Was he working?"

She thought about it. "He said he was."

"Did he say who he was working for?"

"He said last weekend he was working for Stone," she said.

"Stone?"

"That's all. Stone."

"Doing what?"

"He didn't say," she said. "He figured I shouldn't know."

"Probably not something clean, like flipping burgers or sweeping hallways of a grade school."

She nodded.

I thought some more. "Did your father have any friends I could contact."

"He mentioned only one, a guy named Freddy," she said. "Freddy something or other. I think he lived in the same building."

"I'll call you," I said.

She stopped putting on clothes. "Don't tell Jack,

my husband," she said. "He didn't know I had that money, and he detested Dad. Jack wouldn't understand. I hadn't yet figured out how I could have gotten Jack to accept my dad for Christmas. I won't have to now." She pointed at the stack of bills. "Leave a message at the number on the slip."

"I don't think I'll be able to do much for you."

"You're not working for me," she said. "You're working for Danny Goodman, and he thought you were a real terrier."

I helped her with her scarf.

"If I find out he died in an accidental fire, then I'll have to end it there," I said.

She put her heavily gloved hand on my arm. "That's about all I can ask, isn't it?"

Then Danny Goodman's daughter went through the doors and out of sight. I watched from the office window as she disappeared in a swirl of snow.

A lawyer answered when I called Patty Bonicelli, and he said that she would not be difficult to find. He was right.

"Court's closed today," Patty told me. "The judge didn't get there. Bailiff got stuck. The parking lot is full of snow. But Patty Bonicelli got there."

"You probably welcome the chance to catch up on all that research in your fancy law library," I said.

"Sure. Aren't we supposed to do lunch?"

"Let's do lunch."

"Let's not," she said. "Let's you pick me up and we'll go to the grocery store and then we'll go back to my place and drink hot cocoa and eat lunch and wonder if the world's coming to an end."

"I'll be there in 15 minutes," I said.

"More like a half an hour," she said. "I know you're good, but you're not that good."

* * *

It took longer. I needed 10 minutes to array myself in winter apparel and another 10 minutes to get the snow off the car and still another 10 to free the car from the snow embankment the city plow shoved against it.

Once in motion, my expedition to the small office building Patty's law firm calls home was comparatively easy. The car radio blitzed me with reports of the mounting winter crisis. Two people were known dead from heart attacks and exposure. The weather— even for Central Michigan—finally became an emergency for the schools and they closed. Michigan State University officials might close the campus for only the third time in its history.

There was one bright spot. The legislature had recessed.

A four-wheel drive Ford pickup plowed the law firm's parking lot as I arrived, but I nosed in long enough to get Patty's attention. She stood in the doorway in black soft leather boots and a gum ball grape colored overcoat. An oversized black beret covered one ear and half her forehead. The pickup driver glanced at her at each pass.

Spotting me, she pressed toward my car. I got out and helped her with the 50 pounds of papers she was carrying. Once inside with the doors shut and the seatbelts buckled, we kissed, then we headed back to the almost impassable streets.

"Where's your car?" I said.

"Tucked safely away in its garage," she said. "I took the bus. Now they've stopped running too."

"Which grocery do we want?"

"Let's just go home," she said. "The refrigerator is full and the cupboard is full and you'd think we'd find something to eat in there."

It took nearly 20 minutes to cover the one mile to her apartment. I followed her in, carrying her books. We stomped our feet as we entered, then took the elevator to her fifth floor apartment. She told me to make myself comfortable and disappeared.

I grabbed the cordless telephone on my way to the armchair in front of the picture window. I dialed the detective section and asked for Lt. Maddox.

"You told me you were leaving the business," said Maddox. "So this must be a social call."

"I'm calling about Goodman," I said.

"A tragic story."

"Odd Goodman would die in an accidental fire in his own bed."

"That got a few heads itchin' down here, but that son of a bitch had no friends in this department. If someone burned him, maybe they did the public a favor."

"Did he die in the fire or later?"

"As I understand it, he was carried from the building by two firemen who beat the collapse of the building by seconds. Channel 6 has film, I hear. But he was already very dead and very much a crispy critter. This doesn't sound a bit like a social call."

"Autopsy?"

"That's the law, even for a maggot like Goodman,"

Maddox said. "I haven't seen the results. You can get those yourself."

"May I assume by your clinically objective attitude that you don't see any evidence of foul play."

"Nothing," he said. "It was an ironic accident. Remember, he wasn't just a penniless old man—burned out old man, if you'll excuse the phrase—who met a proper end while poring through *Penthouse* in a sleazebag room at the end of a clean and socially significant life. No, he was Danny Goodman."

"I hope you remember me more fondly."

"There's still time for you, so let's hope so," he said. "This has been a load of fun, this talking to you, but I've got to go and deal with real crime. If you are into this, make it your last case."

"Probably will be."

I put the cordless phone down and exchanged it for the VCR remote control. Signs of the times. I tuned into Channel 6 five minutes before the noon news.

Patty came in. She still had on her black tailored skirt with the pleat in the front and a silk long sleeved blouse in a color she called "oatmeal" and a black Harris tweed blazer. She handed me a cup of steaming hot cocoa.

"We have several choices," she said. "I can put together a salad from tuna captured from nets filled with dolphins because I haven't thrown the stuff away yet."

"Nope," I said. "Not a tuna kind of day."

"My thought, too," said Patty, stretching out on the couch and positioning her still-booted legs into my lap. "We can thaw some steaks, or have a ham sandwich, or make a pizza."

I ran my fingertips along the nylon on her legs. "The sandwich sounds good," I said. "I'd be glad to put together a salad to go with it."

"You can make both," she said. "You do so much better than me."

"OK."

"I heard you talking," she said. "What's up?"

I told her about the visit and about my chat with Maddox.

"So, you going to do it?"

"Yeah," I said. "I guess I will."

"Even though he was what he was?"

"Strange observation coming from a lawyer," I said. "You, who would defend any scumsucker who needed it."

"Not all scumsuckers."

"Well, Goodman wasn't always a scumsucker, and even when he was, he had a noble side. He had limits. He burned things down, of course, but he didn't fire Ernie Harwell or sell guns to the Iranians or own a thrift savings and loan."

"How did you come to know him?"

I got up and started to head for the kitchen. Patty followed.

"I was trying to find the cause of a fire four or five years ago and I bumped into Goodman," I said. "He helped."

I positioned myself so I could see the TV as I made the sandwiches.

"I'll be right back," Patty said and headed for the bedroom.

The TV news appeared. I worked on the salad while I listened to authorities from the governor to the night desk clerk at the Okemos Fire Department urge people to stay home. Many streets were impassable. The city road crews were working on the main arteries, but the wind was packing north-south roads full almost as quickly as the plows opened them. Most government offices had closed, as had many businesses.

Then the weatherman told us that the snow would end before sundown. Arctic cold would follow.

The station then turned to a series of at least five commercials for everything from soft drinks to the familiar furniture close out sales to pre-Christmas bargain sales.

Patty came back in blue jeans and a heavy sweater just before Channel 6 began to show tape of Goodman's house fire. The tape showed three firemen wearing oxygen masks hurriedly carrying a lifeless, darkened figure from the house. Behind them a wall collapsed inward, then the roof buckled and fell in.

Moments later a newswoman in a bright red coat and white mittens pointed at the part of the building where Goodman had lived—the side which collapsed first—and said he was dead when he arrived at Sparrow Hospital. No one else apparently was home at the time, and the owner of the building was not yet known.

Then we watched a commercial for laundry detergent showing a busy modern woman tackling raspberry stains, and two other "messages" about stereotypical farmers solving the world's problems through agricultural herbicides, an interesting holiday commercial grouping.

Patty began to harvest sandwich materials from the refrigerator.

"So, what will you do first?" she said.

I chopped some onion and tossed it into the wooden salad bowl. "Probably go look at the burned house."

"In this weather?"

"Sure. Keeps the crowds down. Even during the holiday."

"I'll go with you," she said.

"You have other work to do."

"We'll have time to do that tonight."

"We?"

"Yeah," Patty said. "I'll explain it later."

CHAPTER 3

Goodman had lived in one of a row of uniform houses that were placed side to side like bricks on Lansing's near east side to shelter the growing flocks of autoworkers. The structures went to seed about 40 years later, just before global economics discovered the American auto industry. Unlike some brick and mortar neighborhoods closer to the inner city, this neighborhood failed to attract enough yuppies to rebuild it.

Pushing along Pennsylvania we found Prospect, but we could not drive on it. The city would plow it by June. We continued to Michigan Avenue and nosed the car in behind a delivery truck and figured out what to do next.

"You stay here with the engine idling and stay warm," I told Patty. "No point in both of us trudging through this to see a pile of rubble."

"I'm going with you, kid," Patty said. "You won't store me in the car."

"OK."

We got out and reconnoitered under an antique street-light in front of a long closed neighborhood dry cleaners. It had stopped snowing, but the wind remained much with us. Maybe worse. We put our backs to it.

Glove in glove we crossed the street. We avoided the drifted sidewalk and pushed our way up the center of the street between two long lines of cars now stranded in the storm. Some wouldn't move for days. Some probably hadn't moved for weeks. And then I wondered how Goodman got around town, and whether he had a car.

Patty indicated the long line of cars to our left with a sweep of her arm. "They probably miss having a Mallory around," she said.

"What?"

"If they had a Mallory, their cars would be running."

"And they would be broke," I said.

Within two blocks we came upon what was left of the building Goodman had lived in. Only the north wall remained intact. The other three had essentially caved in. The rubble had just begun to collect some snow, indicating it had taken this long for the fires to become completely extinguished. The scene had no crime-scene yellow tape stretched around it.

We walked to the front of the building and stood there with our backs to the wind. The paint on the home next door had blistered, probably from the intense heat. Upstairs next door a woman watched us from her window encircled in tiny blue Christmas tree lights. I offered her a wave, but she remained at her post without seeming to notice us.

"She would have had a great view," I told Patty, pointing toward the woman.

Patty waved at her. The woman backed slightly out of sight.

What was left of the house was chiefly a pile of wooden rafters and walls, mostly burned. Some of the wood was encased in ice, undoubtedly the frozen water from the firefighters' efforts.

"Stay here a minute," I said, then worked my way around to the west side where Goodman's room would have been on the second floor. I kept my eye on what I might be walking on in the snow, remembering that when I was a child in Western Michigan that I had the habit of stepping on boards with nails in them.

I still remember well the sight of nails protruding through the tops of my shoes.

I tried to focus on the rubble on top. What was on top might be Goodman's. Using footholds on wood debris, I worked my way to the rubble. All I could see was what looked like the remains of a suitcase and a hotplate. The hotplate still looked like a hotplate, but I had to recognize the suitcase by the wire frame inside. I picked up a loose two-by-four and began to pry it in between some layers to see what was behind the suitcase.

"What're you looking for?" said Patty who had followed me and now stood a couple feet behind me.

"Be careful where you step," I said.

"I was," she said. "You be careful. You could fall into that pile the way you're doing that."

I pried some more, staying at the board's end and holding it high in the air.

"Very creepy," she said.

"Nervous?" It was difficult to pry the wood and see beneath it, too.

"No. Just seems a little strange. A man burned to death here last night. Now we're out here in arctic conditions rummaging through the debris. Death ought to carry more importance."

"It is important," I said. "That's why we're here."

"I suppose." Patty began to smack her hands together to fight off cold or boredom. Perhaps both.

"What's that?"

"What?"

She stooped to get a better look at what was under the section of roof I had pried up with the two-by-four. I could barely hold the board up.

"Hold it up higher," she said, moving to get a better look.

"Stay away from there," I said. "I can't hold it much longer."

"Oh, stop complaining," she said, reaching into the charred wood and pulling at something. She backed out quickly.

"Can't get it," she said.

I eased the roof down and picked up a shorter board and handed it to her.

"Now, as I lift the roof, you stick this in there as far as you can. I'll get a better position and lift the roof again."

She nodded and got into position.

In three tries we had the roof high enough to see under it. We squatted side-by-side in the blowing snow looking into the rubble.

"What did you see?"

"The mattress," she said. "At least the corner of it. Doesn't look very burned to me."

She was right.

"Remember much from your courses on arson?" I said, pointing at the mattress.

"We should see signs of where the fire started," she said. "I guess it could have started in the mattress, but it would make sense that the whole mattress should have been consumed."

"I don't know," I said. "It could have started there,

then worked its way to curtains, to the wall, and then elsewhere. The rest of the building would burn much faster than the mattress, which is thick and needs more time to burn right. It probably doesn't prove much."

"Still, it seems odd we're looking at the source of the fire and it's still here."

I nodded. The mattress was no longer on the metal bed but more toward the center of Goodman's room. Elsewhere under the collapsed roof we could see clothing, magazines, a couple of cans of food with the labels burned from them. I could see a pair of pants, half destroyed and encased in ice, still wrapped around the back of a chair which was now crushed under the roof.

I looked around for another board and found one partly nailed to a roof truss. It pried lose easily. I liked it because a nail jutted from its other end. I jammed it into the crevice and hooked it around the pants. It took several tries to remove the pants from the chair which was entrapped between the roof and what it fell on. It took another two cautious attempts to drag the pants out of the house.

The pants contained the stench of a garbage fire. I rolled them into a small roll and turned to go. We'd examine them later. We held hands to steady one another as we worked back to the street. Patty led, using our tracks from our way in.

Near the trees at the street I nodded toward the house next door. "Let's check on the lady in the window," I said.

* * *

Four grizzled apartment buttons protruded near the front door. I doubted any worked, but I figured numbers 1 and 2 were downstairs.

"Let's go in," I said, trying the door.

It was not locked and barely fastened to the building. As expected, apartments 1 and 2 were at either side of the front door. We walked noisily up the narrow set of wooden steps to the second floor. I picked out the apartment to the side where it would have seen the fire and knocked.

I heard nothing.

Patty untied her hood and pulled it back to release an abundance of long brown hair. This time she knocked and said, "Hello in there." I would open the door for such a voice.

After a few seconds someone walked across the creaky floor and opened it far enough to see us.

"Good afternoon," Patty said. "I'm an attorney. This is a private detective who's been hired to check into the fire next door. Could we come in for a minute or two?"

The woman thought about it, nodded, and unlatched the security lock. She stood behind the door as we entered.

"Thank you very much," I said, handing her one of my business cards. "I'm Stuart Mallory. This is Patricia Bonicelli."

The room was small, but long. It was about eight feet wide and at least 15 feet long and had an unusually low ceiling. One of its two windows faced next door. The woman stood much as she had in the window, against the wall with her arms folded but with

my card so she could read it. She wore a stylish pair
of jeans professionally faded, slashed, and destroyed
in the factory. A heavy sweater hung from her shoulders.
On an honest day she would be a brunette, but today with her hair pulled back she was basic blonde.
A high forehead accented her face and she held her
lips together in a thin grimace. She was very short
and I would peg her at 30.

"The police seem to think it was an accident," I
said. "Guy named Dan Goodman, the one who was
killed in the fire, fell asleep with a cigarette and caught
the building on fire. Is that what you've heard?"

The woman nodded.

"Were you here during the fire?" I said.

She nodded again.

"I would very much like you to tell me what you
saw," I said.

She looked out the window, presumably at the pile
of rubble, then back at me. She glanced at my card
again. She also looked at the rolled up pair of pants I
carried. I hadn't realized how powerful its odor was.

"You saw me remove these from the building," I
said.

She nodded again.

"He's not a thief," Patty said. "He's a very good
detective. He'll examine those back in his office."

"I was asleep," the woman said in a deep Kentucky
voice and nodding toward the chair in front of her
portable TV. It was near the window. "I fell asleep
watching the news. Then I heard someone downstairs
yelling about something. I got up, and all over the
ceiling here were yellow and orange flames from next

door. The reflections, I mean." She indicated with her arm. "Then someone pounded on the door and said we should leave the building because it might catch fire."

"Did you?"

"I put on my coat and boots and went downstairs. We didn't actually leave the building, but we were near the door and we could've left if we'd wanted to. It was very cold."

I joined her near the window so I could see her view.

"Who came to get you out of here last night?"

She nodded toward the floor. "Guy downstairs," she said. "Don't know his name. He's the only other person in the building. Collects the rent each week. Sort of manages this one and the two next door."

"Including the one destroyed?"

She nodded.

I looked out the window to illustrate my point. "Did you know Mr. Goodman, the man who was killed?"

She shook her head.

"But you could see him from here," I said. "Real close."

She nodded.

"Did you see him last night?"

She nodded.

"What did you see?"

"Am I gonna have my name in the paper?" she said. "I don't need no name in the paper. I got a personal life."

"I'm just a private detective," I said. "I'm not a city police officer, and I'm not a newspaper reporter.

A private investigator." I could have mentioned that I didn't have her name either.

"Like Stryker?"

"Yes, like Billy Lee."

"I liked Stryker," she said. "Yeah, I saw Danny last night. He came home about 9:00, right between programs." She grinned. "He sat in there just out of sight for a while. I could see his knees. Then I saw him get up, stand a moment, then answer his door." She pointed to her door.

"Is this building the same as the one that burned?" Patty said.

"Yeah, but backwards," the woman said. She flipped her hands around in a circle to illustrate.

"So this room would be the same as Mr. Goodman's," I said.

She nodded.

"Did you see who was at the door?" I said.

She shook her head. "Next time I looked over, the shades was pulled."

"Was the light on?" Patty said.

Nod.

"Did you happen to glance out after the fire started, before you ran downstairs?"

She thought about it. Steam hissed from a pipe at the far wall.

"Was the light still on?" I said.

She shrugged. Somehow I saw progress in it.

Patty was reading the woman's name off a magazine address label. "What is your name, please?"

She shrugged. "Terri Krug," she said, and spelled it. "My husband and I ain't living together no more. His

name is Bobby Krug, and he lives 'round here somewhere." She shrugged and glanced at Patty and me.

"Only a few more questions, Mrs. Krug," I said.
"Do you know another fellow who lives next door,
some guy named Freddy?"

She shook her head. "I've seen 'im," she said. "But
I don't know 'im. I think he's lived here longer than
most a us. Longer than Mr. Goodman."

"Do you know his last name?"

She shook her head as if in thought.

"Have the police talked to you about this?" I said.

She shook her head. "I don't want my name in no
paper," she said.

Patty said, "Do you have a telephone number where
we can reach you?"

More shakes. "They come and disconnected it," she
said.

Patty stood up. "Thank you, Mrs. Krug," she said.

"Yes," I said. "You've been very helpful." I shook
the woman's hand and found it cold.

Chapter 4

The sun crouched low at our backs, generating that bright golden light particular to winter evenings with snap in the air. Its brightness splashed over the snow-covered scene before us making it almost painful to view. We rode on a carpet of little squeaking sounds made by tires compressing snow.

We were driving to Patty's apartment.

"I once had an art instructor who said that light didn't exist in nature," Patty said.

"If you painted it, nobody'd believe it," I said.

"That's probably what he meant, but he didn't say it right," she said.

At her apartment building, someone on a small tractor with a big snow blower on the front was cleaning out the parking lot. He was an expert. He let the wind do half the work. Some people try to fight the wind, forcing themselves to double their efforts to get the job done. I parked the El Camino in a spot just cleaned. As Patty ran inside out of the cold, I got Danny Goodman's pants and a blue plastic tarp out of the trunk and followed.

Inside, she said, "On the table. Tarp first."

I did as I was told, then pulled up a chair and looked to see what I had. I carefully unrolled the trousers and stretched them from one end of the tarp to the other. The waist was at my right and I turned there first. From one front pocket—almost destroyed by flames—I removed a small, black comb, a two-inch blue jackknife, a BIC lighter, and a $1 bill.

The other front pocket contained some loose change

totaling 77 cents and five keys on a small ring. Two of them were well-worn Ford car keys. The others looked like door keys of one sort or another. I assume one was his room key, but I didn't want to sort through the rubble to find out.

"Those trousers stink," Patty said as she walked by. A whiff of coffee fell from her wake.

"Would you prefer I take them out to the farm and look at them there?" I said.

Patty was in her bedroom already.

I turned the pants over and looked in the back. I was in luck. Danny Goodman's wallet was still there.

I put it aside to empty the other, but found nothing but lint.

"You could probably never get to the farm in this weather," Patty said, drifting by again. This time she gave me a kiss on the cheek. "Still stinks, though."

I looked at the wallet. It contained a wad of folded money, anchored by 12 $20 bills. It totalled $261. The pockets contained Danny's driver's license, a pocket-size photo of his daughter and family, another of a woman who might have been his wife before she left him, and a Mobil credit card. Even his wallet traveled light.

Patty sat down.

"So, what do we have?"

"Not much."

Her eyes darted from object to object. Then she picked up the BIC lighter between finger and thumb, careful not to touch the rest of it.

"No fluid," she said, closely examining the container. She flicked the BIC three times. Nothing happened.

"Humm," I said.

"Humm," she said. "Doesn't prove anything."

"Interesting, though."

"When you smoked, did you put your lighter back in your pants pocket, or keep it with your cigarettes?" she said, thinking about it. "I kept the two together."

"Actually, I think I probably would have left the lighter in the pants. The cigarettes were in the shirt pocket. That's how boys do it."

"Girls are different."

"Yeah, I know."

Patty disappeared into the kitchen.

I examined the pant legs and found nothing interesting. I picked up the other end and ran my finger through the cuffs. The right cuff produced nothing, but the left cuff dropped a small pile of sawdust, partly toasted by the house fire.

"Humm," I said.

Patty brought in two cups of coffee. She put a box of Ziploc freezer bags near the table edge.

"Got it figured out?"

I told her what I'd found. She could see what was on the table.

"You got squat," she said.

"I got sawdust," I said. "And an empty cigarette lighter."

"You got a wallet, too," she said. "Don't you, at least when you are home, take your wallet out of your pocket when you go to bed? I've seen you do it."

"Sure," I said. "But Danny Goodman is not, or was not, Stuart Mallory. He might not have gone to bed.

And I'm not sure he changed his pants very often. Who knows? Tomorrow I'll visit the coroner and find out what he was wearing."

I began to put the various goodies into the plastic bags, keeping things in the same bags as they were in pockets. Probably wasn't important anyway. I wrote the contents and locations on the write-on labels. It didn't take long. Patty watched.

As I finished, I said, "Just like downtown."

"Could you take those pants somewhere," Patty said. "They're beginning to take over in here."

I rolled them up and rolled them into the tarp and headed for the door.

"Take your coat, stupid," she said.

I did. Outside it was dark and still. The wind had died as though it too had to find someplace to hide on such a glacial night. It took me about two minutes to get the back of the El Camino open and the pants stowed properly and back into the lobby. In those two minutes my face began to freeze.

I could still smell the burned pants as I entered the apartment, but I could tell it was lessening.

"I find the visitor interesting," Patty said from the kitchen. "Set the table."

"So do I," I said. I got the placemats out of the pie safe. The plates and silverware were in the hutch. "Then again, you can have a visitor even on the day you die."

I also was considering the lowered shade in Goodman's room. I was sure it meant nothing. But then, it was just one more thing.

* * *

Patty gave the dining room light rheostat a quick twist and flooded the oak table with light. I removed the dinner dishes and she dumped her material into several stacks in the center. I brought two cups of coffee and she sat on one side and pointed to the opposite chair.

I sat down. I tried to do it as though I thought of it first.

Patty held her hands over the spread material as if emphasizing the size of it.

"What we have here is a massive accounting problem, in a way," she announced. "My client is the former line supervisor of Midway Aircraft, some outfit out at the airport. He's been accused of stealing money or selling gas on the side."

"Criminal theft?"

"Don't interrupt me," she advised, pointing in my general direction. "Midway agreed to let me take a look at all the gas receipts and gas logbooks for the past three years—the last two of which are the years in question—and photocopies of their accounting records for these receipts." She indicated the several piles with her right hand.

It was a lovely hand.

My fingers started to tap.

"What we have to do, you and I, my able assistant, is account for all of this, to double-check, to compare the accounting records with the actual receipts, and see what we come up with."

Patty started to arrange things, probably figuring out where to start. She grabbed the sheets and began to shove piles of receipts with red rubberbands around them in my direction.

"May I speak?"

"You may," she said.

"What specifically does Midway accuse him of?"

She found what she was looking for. "Well," she said, "Midway's owners say he stole about $7,000 in gas, or stole the money he got for the gas, all over the past two years. My client says that's ridiculous. What would he do with all that damn gas, anyway? He doesn't have an airplane himself, and most people pay by credit card or check anyway."

"Midway says that something's missing and he's at fault. So they fired him."

"No," she said, still arranging materials to suit her needs. She dropped a pencil on the floor and went looking for it. "He got mad and quit."

"He probably thinks it now looks bad."

"Precisely," Patty said, returning with the pencil. "We have to clear all this up before he can get his job back or have any credibility to get another. Now, let's get started. Grab that pile to your left there and start reading them so I can identify them and check them off."

The rubberband broke as I removed it and went flying out of sight into the living room. It unleashed a pile of receipts—called "tickets" in the business—which were in no particular order.

"I wonder what 'avgas LL100' is, anyway," Patty said, reading her accounting sheet.

"Low-lead aviation fuel with a 100 octane rating," I said, starting to sort the tickets by date.

She put down her sheet and studied me.

Patty said, "You used to fly."

"I did," I said.

Patty studied me from the corner of her eyes.

"It's been, what, 15 years?"

I nodded.

"Do you miss it?"

"Sure."

"Do you still think about it?"

"I think about it every waking hour of my life," I said.

"Really?"

I nodded. "I probably land an airplane on some runway in my head several times a day," I said. "Especially when I'm driving."

She grinned and leaned back. "Want to fly again?"

I was sorting the gas tickets by making piles by dates from left to right. I was losing track during the questioning.

She snapped her fingers. "Flyboy."

"I can't afford it."

Patty caught on to what I was doing and could see it would save us some time. She grabbed a pile of receipts and started arranging them by dates.

"I don't know a damned thing about this, but what do you have to do to get back in? Do you have to take the training all over again? What?"

I shook my head with calculated disinterest. "It doesn't matter."

"This isn't like you, Stuart," she said. "Stop making me pump you with questions. Talk to me."

I put the receipts down and looked at Patty. She looked at me.

"I love to fly," I said. "When I was a little kid, I noticed every plane overhead. I watched them as far as I could see them. I can still see some of them almost as clearly as the day I first saw them. They made such powerful impressions on me. My parents have candid shots of me pointing to the sky and saying 'airpane.' Eventually I learned to fly at MSU."

"So, how many years has it been? Certainly before I met you."

I shrugged my shoulders. "I gave it up because it represented so much of what I hated about 'nam, generally the military. I suppose it's been long enough now to forget. But I can't afford it now anyway."

"So you fly in your head."

"Fuel's cheap that way," I said. "And I don't bend anything I can't fix. Can we work on these receipts here?"

She retrieved her papers. "I don't know," she said. "All this makes me sort of jealous and excited. I saw that glint in your eye, that smile on your face as you talked about flying. Wish I could put that kind of smile on your face."

"You do," I said, "and you will later if we can prove your client isn't a thief first."

"You think so?"

"Sure," I said. "We can prove he isn't a thief, you and I. We're good."

"Not that," Patty said. "The part about the smile."

"We're good at that, too."

CHAPTER 5

It was still very dark outside when I got up. I made coffee and showered. I rummaged through the refrigerator until I found enough for breakfast and began to make it. While it was starting to sizzle I called my office answering machine. Nothing.

I had the *Detroit Free Press* spread across the counter and was reading the opinion page when Patty made her initial appearance. She stood there in stocking feet and nylons and slip. I got up and dropped the scrambled eggs into the still hot grease and poured the pancake batter into the electric skillet.

Patty kissed me slowly and delicately on the lips.

"Good morning, knight errant," she said.

"Good morning, counselor," I said.

She dressed for the legal system's battles. I dressed for the mean streets.

Patty looked at the set table and the frying eggs and almost-ready-to-be-flipped pancakes.

"I know," I said. "Pancakes go straight to your hips."

"Yup."

"Not to worry. It's 25 below out there. You'll burn it up before you open your office door."

"That cold."

I flipped the pancakes. They would be among my best.

She returned looking more like a lawyer and sat down. I served. We ate. The sun began to splash a little light on the eastern horizon.

"I thought about it," she said. "It'll be a little difficult, given the weather and all, to check on the underground avgas tanks."

I ate some pancake. "True," I said.

Before we went to bed and put grins on one another's faces—twice—we began to see a pattern in the gas losses. Each month about 300 gallons of 100LL would disappear. Some months more, some months less. I suggested the underground 100LL tank had sprung a leak. She said her client had mentioned the possibility.

"Another fine breakfast," she said. "I knew there was a reason I let you carry my books."

"I thought it was my razor sharp wit."

"Your what?"

She ate some eggs and bacon.

"So, what are you doing today?" I said.

She thought about it. "Some meetings, some phone calls, and probably all screwed up because of the weather," she said. "And you?"

"Out to the farm, change clothes, plow the driveway, and then take those car keys and see if they fit anything on Prospect. Check with the medical examiner. Talk to the manager of that building next door. You know, details."

Patty began to run her finger gently over the top of my left hand as it rested near my plate. She studied it. "It being Friday, perhaps we can spend the weekend at the farm," she said. "Burn a couple fires. Pet Basil. Break in some new mistletoe."

"It's a date."

She shoved herself from the table. "Good," she said. "You drop me at the office on your way home."

We scooped the dishes off the table and put them into the dishwasher and cleaned the pots, then prepared for the arctic blast outside. I told her to give me a five-minute headstart to warm up the car. She didn't argue.

Outside the air almost instantly froze the inside of the nose and began to threaten the eyes. Everything seemed brittle, including the car door. The vinyl seat was as solid as steel. The car's engine turned over three times and rumbled to life and began to purr. In about three minutes Patty ran out and climbed in and we hit the road.

Lansing was catching its stride again. Hard to keep a northern city down even at more than 20 below. The streets weren't crowded, but traffic was usual for 7:00 a.m. Patty climbed out at her near downtown office. I walked her into her office, then headed out toward the Lansing Airport and home.

The radio told me that a woman had run out of gas on I-96 and spent the night in the car. She was being treated for frostbite at a local hospital. They can't treat them for stupidity. Keep the tank full in the winter. The schools remained closed, but the legislature had resumed its efforts to save Michigan from encroaching rust. The governor, the radio told me, was back at his desk trying to mix austerity and economic growth.

I passed the airport in a different mood than I had in years. I kept glancing at the twin-engine commuter climbing into the western sky, wondering what the pilot was thinking, what an airplane's dashpanel looked like today, and whether I could still fly.

At the farm I got a real break. Since my driveway was almost straight east to west, the wind had blown it clean. It left a drift about six feet deep on the east side of the house, though.

Basil greeted me at the door and asked me, as a cat can ask, where the hell I'd been. I wandered through the house to make sure everything was still there. No windows broken. No pipes burst. Lucky again.

I changed clothes but stayed with the winter theme. No time to don loafers and slacks. I took the .38 out of the drawer and clipped it to my back belt and covered everything with a thick rag wool sweater. Ready to work.

Basil complained about the lack of food until I met his need.

"Patty will be here tonight," I told him. He ignored me.

Just as I opened the back door, the phone rang. I considered ignoring it, but I answered it instead.

"Sgt. Phillips, LPD," the voice said. "Lt. Maddox wants to meet you at the medical examiner's. The county road commission just pulled a woman from a snowdrift. Frozen solid. Maddox wants to know why your card was stuffed in her pocket."

CHAPTER 6

The sergeant was waiting for me at the medical examiner's door.

"The lieutenant's not here yet," he said. "Take a seat."

"Mind if I do a little public record business while I'm here?" I walked past him toward the examiner's inner office. The sergeant said nothing.

The examiner's chief investigator was there, pulling on a well worn Winston. The sign on his desk, Ron Conley, Investigator, peeked out from under two pounds of photocopied reports. He looked up as I came through his open door. He'd been reading the *Detroit Free Press*.

"Mallory," Conley said. "Heard a nasty rumor you were out of the business."

"I was."

"Not any more."

Conley examined me through very tired eyes and a two-day beard. His mustache was eschew. He picked up the paper again.

"Danny Goodman," I said.

"He's dead." He moved to the sports section.

"What killed him?"

Conley must have stumbled over a captivating report about the Detroit Pistons. Finally he said, "Didn't think that was any secret. He burned to death."

"Simple as that?"

He put the *Free Press* down and looked around the piles on his desk. He picked up one report and handed it to me.

"It's incomplete," he said. "Some people to interview, a few details to nail down, some tests to get back." He returned to the sports section.

"Can I have a copy of it?"

"Keep it. I made one too many."

I read through the first page. No surprises in the details of the fire, what there were of them. I was on page two reading about the preliminaries to the autopsy when there was a door shut hard out front and men started to talk.

Conley said, "Now maybe my 48-hour shift is over." He lighted another cigarette.

Maddox poked his head in while Phillips stood in the hall.

"Ready?"

Conley circled his desk and shuffled deeper into the building. Maddox signaled me to follow, pivoting as he did so and moving smartly down the hall with his starched coat swishing behind him. Phillips followed all of us. We went into a room where one body was covered by a light blue sheet of plastic.

Conley pulled the sheet back revealing a woman with a deep gash in her upper left leg and some abrasions on her face and hands, probably obtained after death. I imagined the wounds to look like what happens to frozen beef when you cut it with something heavy and sharp. Her face dripped with condensation much like a glass does when it contains ice cubes. Terri Krug wore the same clothes she had on when I interviewed her in her apartment yesterday.

"County plow hit her," Conley said. "Driver saw an arm sticking out of the snow and swerved. Too late. Hard to swerve a four-ton snow plow."

I said, "How long had she been dead?"

"Last night, early," Conley said. "That's the best we can figure. She was frozen as solid as a chuck roast when they brought her in here."

"Should've used a microwave to thaw her out," Phillips said.

Maddox looked at me. "He's really a good cop," Maddox said. "He's just an insensitive slob sometimes."

"Seen enough?" Conley said.

Maddox glanced at Phillips and me, then nodded. Conley put the sheet back.

"So, when do we get the report?" Maddox said.

"I'm going home," Conley said, already on his way through the door. "They'll do her as soon as she thaws."

"Any ideas?"

"No bullet holes, no knife wounds, no cut wrists," Conley said. "Hard to tell so far. But the plow didn't do it."

"That's all right," Phillips said. "The PI will tell us who did it."

I stopped and looked at Phillips and gave him a little less room than he needed going through the door. He tried to ignore me. Maddox led us to a small room the examiners used to interview people. I finally took off my coat and so did Maddox. Phillips stayed in the hall and drank some water from a fountain.

"Well?" Maddox said.

"Her name is Terri Krug and she lives, or lived, next door, upper floor, to the building Danny Goodman used to live in. I talked with her yesterday afternoon."

Maddox thought about it.

"What'd she say?"

I summarized the conversation. I told him every-thing. After all, if Maddox began to view Goodman's death as something other than an accident, my job was more or less over. And if it was homicide, I had to tell him.

"That's not much," Maddox said.

"They unraveled Watergate with less."

He looked at his watch, then brushed something off his left sleeve. "Yeah," he said, "but they were reporters. We're just cops. We don't know shit."

I stood up. "Well, somebody damned well better unravel this one. You might think Danny Goodman died pleasantly in his sleep, but I'm beginning to think someone arranged it. And now the only witness I talk to is in there thawing on a table."

"I'll get someone over to her room to go through her place," he said.

"What's the point?" I said. "She's already dead. And if she was a witness, she only witnessed the murder of a scumbag arsonist."

"Easy, Stuart."

I was on my way outside the door.

Phillips leaned against the opposite wall looking at nothing in particular.

Maddox said, "Why don't you accompany Sgt. Phillips to the office where he can get an official statement from you."

Phillips cleared his throat. "Someone else will have to get it. They'll be cuttin' her up shortly."

Conley suddenly appeared with a down jacket and thick gloves and looked a little like Dr. Zhivago. People were entering the building behind him, probably what composed the next shift.

From somewhere down the hall came a voice, "Show time." Phillips trotted off after it.

Conley just nodded and headed out the back door.

Having finished with my coat, I was working on my gloves and heading generally toward the door.

Maddox said, "Where you going?"

"To work."

"One more thing, Stuart," he said. "You know any reporters at the *State Journal*?"

"Sure," I said. "A couple. If you want a free yard sale ad or something, reporters can't help you much."

"Don't be cute. I'm a little pissed at you. I know damned well you put him up to this. Guy called late yesterday and asked me all about Danny Goodman."

"Who?"

"I don't know him, but I've seen his name once or twice," he said. "You put the bastard up to it."

"Who was it, and what did he ask?"

Maddox was studying me.

"You know damned well."

I began to button my down jacket and prepare to leave. "Look, we've known each other too long for this."

"That's why you did it."

I headed for the door. "Nope."

"Make sure you go straight to the office and make a statement," Maddox said. "I'll be there waiting."

"Who called you?"

"Guy's name is Sayre," Maddox said, heading for his unmarked car.

Never heard of him.

* * *

A small traffic jam near the active construction of
the new Riverside Mall at the edge of the central business
district caught me as I tried to slip through town.
City leaders heralded the mall as the savior of downtown
Lansing. Even the governor and the legislators were
waving flags about the mall. They told us that holiday shoppers will be flooding the place next year during
the Christmas rush bringing millions of dollars to the
revitalized downtown.

Most of the owners of existing businesses were still
restraining their enthusiasm. So far, the mall gener-
ated chiefly traffic problems all the time and dust in
season.

I drove straight to Prospect Street and although the
city had opened one lane right down the middle of
the street, there was no room to park. I left the car
on Michigan Avenue again and walked back to Prospect Street. I tried Danny Goodman's keys in every
Ford-made vehicle on the street. They fit the third
one, a late '70s full-sized Mercury two-door. It wasn't
locked, but it would take three men an hour to dig it
out.

Pushing snow from the foot of the door, I got in
and looked around. Although the police might soon
take charge of this case, I wanted first crack at the
man who killed whoever got in his way.

The glove compartment contained a few state maps
and one map of Lansing. I took the city map. There
were two Marlboro regular butts floating in a sea of

gray in the ashtray. I left them.

On the seat was a pair of military gloves with inserts and an ice-scraper. I could see nothing in the backseat except two paper bags and some wrappers from McDonald's. Pushing my hands between the seats and the seat-backs I found nothing but dust. I got out and looked under the front seats. The tire iron was under the driver's side, and so was a small automatic pistol. I put it into my pocket. I'd look at it when the neighbors couldn't jot down my every move.

Under the passenger's seat were three used fast food napkins, a parking sticker for the Water Tower in downtown Chicago dated two months ago, and a tourist map of Mackinac Island. The trunk held a spare tire and a tool box with the handle broken off. I sorted through it and found nothing unusual and nothing to tell me who killed him. There was a little sawdust on the trunk floor.

It was getting cold standing out there.

With the trunk closed, I went up to Terri Krug's house and knocked on the manager's door. No answer. I knocked again. Still no answer.

So I went back to the car and then to the police station. Maddox waited in his office.

"Take the long way here?" he said.

"I stopped to get fitted for a new suit," I said.

He nodded. "Good thing this is your last case," he said.

"Who's taking the statement?"

"You in a hurry?"

"Gee, there's been a couple of murders, lieutenant," I said. "Seemed a good idea to look into one or the other of them, sort of try to find the bad guy. That might reduce the odds of him doing it again, or so the theory goes."

I started to leave.

"Detective Wilson will take your statement," Maddox said. "He's the bald one in the corner."

I sat beside Wilson and explained. He glanced at Maddox and began to take notes as I talked. Then he cranked some paper into an IBM Selectric and banged out a statement. The whole operation took about 12 minutes. Maddox wandered over when Wilson seemed to be closing in toward my signature.

"I want to see you before you go," he told me, leaving before I could reply.

I signed the statement and went back to Maddox's office. He was reading a report with his back to the door.

"Close the door," he said.

I closed it quietly.

"Sit down."

I stood.

"Please," he said.

I sat down.

Maddox swung around and looked at me. I looked at him. He grinned. I grinned.

Maddox said, "I've been in a shitload of trouble over the years having been friends with you."

I shrugged.

"Obviously, we'll take a good look at this woman's death," he said. "It has every sign of homicide."

"Difficult decision," I said. "She could have just stepped outside, having forgotten the severity of the weather, and wandered to Holt, all the way across town—four or five miles—before falling prey to the cold."

He ignored me. Perhaps it's a virtue. "And if what you say is true, it might have something to do with Danny Goodman's death."

"Seems likely," I said. "Very likely."

"Your license still in order?"

I nodded.

"Gun license in order, too?"

I nodded again.

"You returning to the business?"

I shook my head. "Once this becomes a full homicide case, my job's done. Right?"

"Sure," he said.

"Besides, the license isn't good for much longer. My bond dries up in three weeks or so."

I got up and got lost momentarily in the scene outside the window. Three birds were fighting over a scrap of something—perhaps fat—and were tearing it to shreds on a roof ledge next door, probably burning more energy than the food would deliver. It was a desperate season out there.

"Before you forget it, drop off Goodman's pants so we can have a look at them," said the lieutenant, turning to some paperwork. "You never know. Maybe an active cop can find something."

I went down the stairs outside Maddox's office and opened the trunk, which was easy. Someone had forced the light weight steel lock on the El Camino, and the only thing I could see missing was the pair of pants.

CHAPTER 7

By the time Maddox's detectives let go of me it was nearly lunch time. I called Patty from the same pay phone a person uses for his one phone call after he is arrested.

"Is food all you think about?"

"How about Clara's?" I said.

I could hear her thinking, almost as though metal parts were clicking into place. "Sure," she said. "Fifteen minutes. Nothing is happening when it is supposed to down here anyway, and I have some news to talk to you about."

"So do I."

I took my time getting there. The sun had come out, investing a lot of light on the downtown Lansing area. A man on a street corner—a poorly dressed vagrant of unknown origin—reminded me of a similar scene in Saginaw when I was a boy and the family was driving through the downtown area on the way to relatives for the Christmas holiday. He stood there, chin out, at the edge of death, in what is supposed to be the happiest time of the year in the richest nation in the world.

I went up to Patty's office and could see her talking on the phone through the partly opened office door. She gave me a signal showing her impatience. A few minutes later, while I thumbed through a copy of the *Wall Street Journal*, she dashed out and led me into the hallway.

"Let's get away before the phone rings again," she said. "No one wants to drive today. Everyone wants to do his business on the phone. Have you ever had three conference calls in a row?"

"Tough to remember the last time it happened to me," I said, opening the downstairs door for her.

"The hell with you, Mallory," she said.

Once in the car we headed to Clara's. I told her where and how Terri Krug was found. I tried not to be flippant or indelicate, but I told her what I knew.

"Oh, Jesus," Patty said.

I navigated through the Michigan Avenue traffic and turned at the railroad tracks. I nosed into a place near Clara's front door. Frigid weather cuts down on the competition for the best parking spaces.

Patty was visibly shaken. She looked out the side window, then through the windshield, then outside again.

"We killed her," she said.

I listened to the car running a moment.

"We didn't kill her," I said. "But someone thinks she told us something important, or could have told us something. Maybe she did."

"We killed her by talking to her," Patty said. "Someone saw us."

"Or heard about us."

"Jesus," she said. "I guess this means someone killed Danny Goodman."

"Yup," I said. "Let's eat."

We got out. Patty deliberately exited the car slowly. I walked around the car to help her out and remembered that I hadn't yet mentioned that someone stole Goodman's pants out of my car. That could wait.

Clara's is the former passenger train station, and it

opens into what was the main lobby. Now closed booths awaited at each side with party seating toward the tracks. The waitress put us into one of the booths and stuck menus into our hands and left us to think about things.

The waitress seated four women who giggled and smoked cigarettes in the booth opposite.

Patty the attorney was back.

"I talked with my airport client," Patty said. "He says all you have to do is get a physical and something called the biennial flight check, or review, or something like that, and you're back in business."

"Beats me," I said.

"Says there's a list somewhere out at Midway of local doctors who give physicals," she said. "I thought we would drive on out there and get some names and get you checked out."

"I can't afford it."

"My treat."

"Patty," I said.

"It'll be your belated birthday present," Patty said.

"You already gave me a birthday present, adorned with black balloons and a sympathy card."

"That was last year on your fortieth," Patty said. "Then this will be your Christmas present."

"But you said you already bought my Christmas present."

"Not this one I didn't," she said. "Besides, this is my treat, too. I want you to take me flying. He told me about this Mile High Club, and I want to be a member."

"Your client told you about that?" I tried not to

look around the menu.

"He certainly did," she said. "Why hadn't you told me about that? I have to learn it from a client, for God's sake."

"Stay away from him," I said. I put the menu down.

"He's cute," Patty said, staring into her menu. "But not that cute. I want to earn my membership credentials with my sweetie."

The waitress returned with water glasses and coffee cups. We ordered. The waitress went away.

"Someone stole Goodman's pants from the back of the car," I said. I sipped coffee and told her how I discovered it and how Maddox felt about my incompetence.

Patty looked across at me with eyes which still suspected she had helped lead an innocent woman to her violent death.

"You'd better find that killer," Patty said.

"After lunch," I said.

* * *

I dropped Patty at her office and headed straight out to Holt to take a look at the spot where Terri Krug was found. It took about 15 minutes to get there, and it was easy to find because the snow was all cleared away and there was a police yellow ribbon sort of laid over the snow. No one was there, and the traffic was light enough for me to stop and pull to the side without fear of causing an accident.

It was an isolated spot. The nearest home to the west was not far, but it was down a slight grade and out of sight. To the east an old farm house huddled among a group of old, thick pine trees. The only windows in this direction looked frosted shut.

I tried to picture the scene during the night. Whoever brought Terri Krug here must have stopped along the road, then tossed her high on the bank of snow, perhaps hoping she would fall to the other side.

Perhaps she did. Perhaps she was still alive when he did that, and alive enough to crawl back to the top of the snow before she froze to death.

The scene was not difficult to picture, but it was hard to stomach. Standing there in the road, I wanted to look over my shoulder to make sure I was alone. The evil crawled around out there in the silence.

I got back in the car and headed to my office. Over the night the plow had coerced the snow from the street to the curb parking lane. I managed to find a small spot a block away behind a stranded old LaSabre and squeezed my car in by jockeying back and forth. Maybe I could free it by May.

The one-block jog to the office was crispy. In twenty yards my eyes began to solidify. In another twenty the wind cut through the pant legs. I moved quickly after that, wishing I had prepared better.

I felt at home in the office, despite the boxes. I moved the boxes from the desk and piled them to the side. I fired up the coffee pot, then called the number Sandra Goodman Jensen gave me and left a message. I settled into position at the desk where sunlight surged through the window and there I studied the autopsy report.

Danny Goodman was still wearing his underwear when he died. He'd eaten about three tacos with a cola drink a few hours before his death, and he would have died from lung cancer in a matter of months. His ulcers might have started to bleed heavily and killed him first. His fingers had no telltale sign that he'd fallen asleep with the cigarette still in his hand. He died of toxic smoke inhalation and suffocation while still flat on his back. There was no evidence of a struggle or that he had moved once he fell asleep, the report said.

But a section of Goodman's body along his left arm and the same side of his face had received third-degree burns. In fact, a chunk of his arm had broken off while being carried from the building. And Goodman was still alive when his left arm received that burn.

I stopped reading and looked about my office. I needed some distance form the reality of the report. Then I looked at my own arm, wondering what kind of pain Goodman had to endure.

"Jesus Christ," I said.

That arm was presumed to have been nearest the wall, according to the report of the fireman who carried him from the building. No part of Goodman's body touching the mattress had burned. Otherwise, his body had first-degree damage and was covered with ash.

I poured some coffee and listened to the faint sound of the dentist's drill downstairs. It made me think of Dustin Hoffman in *Marathon Man*. Dentists must loathe that movie.

I jotted the fireman's name into my notebook, adding it to a growing list of people to find or talk to. So far it also included "Freddie," the apartment manager, Sandra Goodman, and Bobby Krug. Much of it depended on how far I wanted to take this.

I pulled Goodman's pistol from my jacket pocket and examined it on the desk. It was a .32 caliber automatic and it had only two rounds in the clip. I made a note of the serial number and that it apparently had not been fired recently, then put it away in a lockable filing cabinet.

The phone rang.

"This is Sandra," she said.

"Thanks for calling so soon," I said. "I have some good news and some bad news, and I'll give it to you in that order, OK?"

"Sure."

"It would appear the police are now beginning to suspect your father was murdered and might soon investigate it as such."

"You say 'might' as if you're not sure," she said.

"That's the bad news," I said. "A woman I spoke with last night, Terri Krug, someone who lived next door and occasionally saw your father through her window and through his window, was found frozen in a snowdrift this morning."

"Dead?"

"Very."

"I don't understand. Is there a connection?"

"That's the point, Sandra," I said. "There's just too much coincidence, and I don't have to explain coincidence to you. So far as the cops can tell now, she wasn't shot to death or stabbed to death, but she was already dead when the snow plow hit her."

"Oh God," she said. "I'm sorry."

There was a little silence between us.

"I think someone killed her because someone learned she talked to me," I said. "Someone thinks she told me something, or thinks she could tell me something. Whatever it is, it must be important. Two people are dead."

"What'd she say?"

"I'll give you a full report when this is over," I said.

I didn't want to tell her that Terri Krug might have been the last person to see her father alive, except for whoever killed him.

She hesitated. "If the police start investigating this, then it's over, for you anyway."

"Hardly," I said. "Somebody killed Terri Krug because of me, and I want to find that person."

"But you're not responsible."

"I am responsible," I said. "She should have grown old and had grandchildren and died quietly pulling weeds next to a trailer in Florida, years from now. But she talked to me, and somebody killed her for it."

She started to say something, then changed her mind.

"And someone stole a pair of your father's pants out of my car today. I removed them from your father's room yesterday, or what was left of the room. I'm still in this, like it or not."

"Thank you, Stuart," she said.

"Sandra, I don't deserve your thanks, and I don't want it," I said. "In fact, I'll remove one day's pay from the money you gave me and give it back."

"You aren't working for me anymore," she said. "You're working for my father, and his neighbor lady."

I heard the *Lansing State Journal* hit my inner office

door and decided to change the subject.

"I found a set of car keys in your dad's pants that fits a car buried in the snow on Prospect," I said. "You might want to check with the cops about it."

"He didn't have a car," she said. "He lost his license a couple of years ago."

"I doubt that would keep him from driving, Sandra," I said.

"He took a bus every time he came to see me," she said.

I changed the subject. "Have you scheduled the funeral?"

"No funeral," she said. "He'll be cremated."

We let that one hang there a second or two without saying anything. I could already hear Phillips joking about it.

"Listen, Sandra, pretty soon the Lansing police will be at your doorstep, probably asking the same kinds of questions," I said. "You don't have to tell them you hired me, but you can if you need to."

"I know," she said. "And I won't. They'd wonder how I'm going to pay you."

"No," I said. "They probably wouldn't."

CHAPTER 8

Sandra Goodman promised to drop by the office and leave the most recent photo of her father she had. I needed the photo for some legwork. She didn't want me to come near the house.

While waiting, I called Patty's office and was told she was at the courthouse in conference with a judge.

Then I called someone at the Michigan State Police headquarters in East Lansing to find out who owned the car that Danny Goodman had keys to but Danny Goodman's daughter said wasn't his.

"Got a printout of it right here," the clerk said. "Busy day for this car."

"Lansing PD?"

"Lansing PD."

"Good to know somebody's working the case," I said.

"Frederick S. Samuelson, DOB 9-27-40," the clerk said. "Lives on Prospect, but I suspect you know that."

"Yep."

"Got to run. Nice chattin' with you. Oh, by the way, we got a new instructor in here. Going to teach some basic courses for us. A retired sheriff from Hamlin. He mentioned you the other day."

"What was the tone of that reference?"

"Just curious."

"His name is Emery Frost," I said.

"That's the guy."

He hung up.

I wrote the information about the Mercury into my notebook. So far I didn't see much in the notebook.

I called the fire department and left a message for the fireman to call me back. He might even do it.

Forty minutes later a short man with a long cigarette hanging from his mouth and a *State Journal* and a large brown envelope in his hand came through the door.

"You Stuart Mallory?"

"Yep."

He walked to the desk and handed me an envelope and the newspaper. I opened it and found a photo of Danny Goodman inside.

"She says you're to pay me," he said. "Meter says $15. The newspaper is yours, anyway."

"Glad I don't have to pay for it. Again." I got out a $20 bill and told him I wanted a receipt. He got out a dog-eared receipt book and scribbled something on the top one and tore it out. I gave him the twenty and told him the rest was his, too.

"Thanks," he said, glancing at Goodman's photo laying on the desk. I let him. You never know where it will lead.

It led nowhere. He left.

I still had an hour or so of daylight if I used it right, so I assembled my notes and mittens and coat and headed for the door. The phone rang. I took off the mittens and answered it.

"They haven't disconnected your phone yet," Maddox said.

"Rent's still paid up, too."

"I called you because, as you know, we are critically short-handed down here, and we're only marginally competent at full force anyway. We just had a meeting here in the detective section, and we are just so delighted that you are on the case that we'll pass this along to you, without obligation, just hoping that you'll unravel this case and spare us further public humiliation." .

"Cut the shit," I said.

Maddox shuffled some papers at the other end.

"Your friend, Danny Goodman, was loaded with D's, or dilaudid," Maddox said.

"Only vaguely heard of the stuff," I said.

"You mean you've never heard of it, right?"

"No, I mean I have a vague recollection. Familiar, but not at the tip of my tongue."

"You're gonna shake our confidence in you, Mallory."

"To avoid further damage, I'll buckle. What is it?"

"A painkiller. Narcotics tells me it's probably the most powerful painkiller around," Maddox said. He spelled it for me. "Certainly the most powerful stuff on the street. They use it for cancer victims and burn victims."

"Seems appropriate."

"That's supposed to be my line," he said. "Anyway, he was loaded with it. Probably felt nothing at all. I'm told you can take a few milligrams of this stuff and watch your own mother cut to pieces by an ax and not even get interested."

"Injected or oral?"

"Pills are normal. We've got some boys down there now digging around in the rubble looking for more. Could have taken the stuff himself."

"Someone could have given it to him," I said.

"Either way."

"What about Terri Krug?"

"We've got the lab looking now," he said. "Helps to know what you're looking for. Might save some time."

"Where do you get this stuff?"

"It's all over the street, Mallory," he said. "You're losing touch. Let me explain. Even no-goods get cancer sometimes, and some of those no-goods manage to get it prescribed for them, and instead of taking it all they stretch it out a little and sell some of it. It gets a pretty good price."

"Hard to suppress the capitalistic instincts," I said.

"Especially among the poor."

"Speaking of the woman, what killed her?"

"No change, so far as I know. So far, I think they figure she froze to death."

"No witness, no evidence, no explanation what she was doing there."

"Nope. Gee, when we stumble over some information on that, I'll make sure Phillips types it up and runs it right down to your office. Or do you have a FAX machine?"

"Doesn't go with my office motif."

"Seems like everybody's got one of the fucking things these days. We've got one right here in the detective section. God knows what's being FAXed out of here to people like you."

"Maybe I'll rent one just for this case."

CHAPTER 9

I had the *State Journal* spread across my desk for no more than three minutes when I knew how I'd fill the rest of the afternoon. According to the front page, one of the latest victims of the recent arctic blast was the developer of the downtown Riverside Mall, Stone, Inc.

Maybe it was Goodman's "Stone." It sounded about right. I bundled up better than I had earlier and walked to my car and headed downtown.

The story said the recent heavy snow and sub-zero temperatures had damaged the yet-to-be completed center building of the downtown mall, probably setting the project back another month. This, the story noted, followed heavier than usual fall rains and problems with labor unions.

When you see the word "problem" linked with labor unions, you can frequently identify the core of the issue. The workers want more money, and the owners aren't anxious to give it to them. A tractable labor union isn't earning its keep, but a "problem" union means it's at least trying.

I parked the El Camino between two delivery trucks and headed for the largest construction office trailer, the one painted a nice powder blue with "Stone" in six-foot medium blue letters on the side. One could hardly read the word. Stone probably paid big bucks for that logo. I went inside.

Two women were on the phone. Stacks of paperwork surrounded them, much of it in boxes. A fan of a powerful electric heater worked nearby, pumping warm, dry air through the room.

One of the women hung up her phone. A sign on her desk said "Staci."

"Can I help you?"

"I need to see Mr. Slater," I said with all the quiet humility I could muster. I needed to work on it.

"Leon Slater is pretty busy this afternoon," she said with plenty of sugar. About four lumps worth. "Can I tell him what this is about?"

"Sure," I said, stepping a bit closer. "I'm here about, well, I'm a friend of the family, and I'm here to get his personal effects."

"Pardon me?" she said, stirring up a breeze, batting her sweeping eyelashes involuntarily.

"Oh, I'm sorry. I mean Daniel Goodman," I said. "I'm a friend of the family, and I'm here to collect his personal things. He's dead, you know. There was a fire."

Staci got up and came around the desk. She was dressed as though she intended to depart after work for Boyne Mountain Ski Resort. The ski gear was breathtaking on her, although I tried not to notice. Such an observation wouldn't complement my pretense.

"Let me check with Mr. Slater," she said. "Can you wait a minute?"

"Sure," I said, watching her disappear down the central hall to my left.

I waited. I listened to the furnace. Somewhere a telephone rang, and somewhere people were smoking cigarettes. I tried to breathe it in as it had been two years since I quit.

"If you'll take a seat," said Staci, returning from

her mission, "Mr. Slater will try to help you in a minute or two." Three lumps.

Staci slid around and took her seat in a very polished way. She would be difficult for most men to ignore for very long. I suspect she knew it, too.

Five minutes later Staci picked up her intercom and told me to find Leon Slater on the second door on the left.

"Oh, thank you," I said. "This could be very important to me."

"I hope he can help," she said. I rated it two lumps. Somewhere in the previous five minutes I had been rendered irrelevant. I'd work on that.

I walked into Slater's office and found a lean, balding man sitting behind a cluttered desk. He wore a sweater intended to be loose-fitting, but on him it needed to be a size or two smaller. Standing in the corner was a man about the size of Lake Huron in full-length insulated blue coveralls.

"Thank you for seeing me so quickly, Mr. Slater," I said, sticking out my hand. He gave it a quick jerk. "But this should only take a moment. I'm just cleaning up a few odds and ends for the Goodman family, what's left of it, and I'm here to collect his personal effects. Maybe his last paycheck, too, if you have it."

"I'm sorry," he said, "but my secretary failed to give me your name."

"Ah, Stuart Mallory," I said. "Family friend."

"Yes, Stuart," he said, standing. "That fellow behind you is Randall. He knows a lot about my business here, and perhaps he can help us."

Randall watched me very closely as he gave me a

handshake. It was firm without being an attempt to crush my hand. I think he could have crushed it without much effort, but he didn't need to prove anything to me.

"Well, Randall, can we offer this gentleman anything?" Slater looked hopefully to Randall. They were searching one another's faces.

"Leon, I've been on several jobs lately, I'm not sure who this Danny Goodman guy is," Randall said, turning to me. I'd give him one lump at best. He was trying.

"Can you remind Randall what Mr. Goodman does here, Stuart?" Slater said. "I'm afraid I certainly don't know any Goodman in our employ."

I looked out his window at the brick exterior of the new downtown mall.

I offered a small snicker. "I suspect your personnel records would show that," I said, trying to stay in role. "He was, well, he was a utility sort of person. He may have been serving as a security guard. You see, he never told me himself. I'm just a family friend. The family is too much in grief to handle these matters right now."

Randall's eyes grinned, but he didn't. Behind him on the wall was a large blow-up photo of the Mackinac Bridge as seen through a summer haze. In the foreground sprawled the business province of Mackinac Island.

"Say, that's a nice shot there of the bridge," I said. "You take pictures, Mr. Slater?"

Slater chuckled a little and Randall offered a conspicuous exhale. Maybe it was his chuckle.

"I'm not much at photography, Stuart," he said, wandering over to the photo. "That was taken by my sister Darelle, actually, from her cottage."

"Up at Mackinac?" I said.

"On the island," Slater said. "We have a home in Chicago near our headquarters. She recently moved to the year-around cottage on the island. I guess she likes it better there."

Kowalski shifted from one foot to the other a little faster than he needed to. His impatience was beginning to show.

"Must be nice up there," I said.

"It's lovely," he said, returning to a position behind his desk.

In the room's corner sat an architect's scaled mock-up of the Riverside Mall, equipped with two parking garages loaded with miniature cars and a clean Grand River flowing by. It looked formidable.

"That's a pretty impressive mall you have there," I said.

"Yes," Slater said, smiling. "Space for nearly 40 individual shops, anchored by two department stores, with a state of the art dome in the middle, mimicking the capitol's dome. A truly inspiring place for Lansing's shoppers to gather and enjoy their city."

"I think Mr. Goodman spoke highly of it too," I said.

Slater shrugged with his arms spread a little. Then he seemed to scratch his head. The picture of concern. "I'm afraid we can't do much for you, Stuart. I don't remember a Goodman among our staff, and I know all the security personnel. Perhaps if you can find out what sort of work he did for me—if he did anything for me—we can narrow things down and find what you need."

Randall cleared his throat. "He might have worked for another construction company," he said. "Have you checked around at all?"

I tried to look surprised. "That might be a good idea," I said. "I'll check around."

"That's right," Slater said, pushing me toward his door. "You check around. I'm sorry we could not be of more help. If we do discover that we can help, how do we get in touch with you, Stuart?"

I dug around in an inside pocket and pulled out a pen and made like I was looking for something to write on. From somewhere Staci could see my need and arrived with a small notepad of "From the desk of Staci" on top. I wrote my office number on it.

"Fine," Slater said, taking the note. "Perhaps we'll get back to you."

"Thanks, Mr. Slater," I said, looking past him at Randall. "You've already been a great help."

Staci guided me away. Slater's door shut.

"I sure hope he had what you needed," Staci told me. Two lumps.

I was buttoning my coat.

"Well, it certainly appears that he can help," I said. "Maybe Randall, oh, what's his name?"

Staci's smile faltered a little. "Randall Kowalski," she said, spelling it. No lumps for that one.

"Yes, Mr. Kowalski. He might be able to help."

She picked up her telephone and began to punch the buttons. "Good luck," she said. No lumps again. She was no longer trying.

Outside I fired up the El Camino and sat there a few minutes making notes on some of the things I needed to check. While I was there, Randall Kowalski came out from behind the trailer and walked down a line of cars and got into a full-size Ford Bronco. He pulled into traffic and headed north toward Michigan Avenue.

I wrote down his plate number, then pulled out three cars behind him. Within fifty yards we all stopped for the Michigan Avenue traffic, particularly heavy at this time on a Friday afternoon, despite the weather.

People were heading home, wherever home was.

Kowalski turned east on Michigan Avenue while the two cars in front of me held steady, their occupants probably in heavy discussion about the latest development on *The Young and the Restless*. Finally I got to turn and couldn't find the Bronco anywhere. I drove on quickly for a few blocks, checking the side streets, but he had disappeared.

* * *

I drove over to Prospect where a city plow was cleaning the street. I parked right behind two police cars parked behind Fred Samuelson's car. Two cops were looking it over.

I ignored them and tried the apartment manager again. He wasn't home. Then, with Danny Goodman's photo in hand, I went door-to-door to see what I could learn. I learned nothing in 30 minutes and went back to my car and got warm. Three police officers were sorting through the rubble of the destroyed house and they finally went to their cars to get warm, too.

As if from nowhere, Sgt. Phillips showed up at the driver's side window and motioned me to roll it down.

I did.

"An old gray-haired lady who lives in that bungalow over there says she saw a man earlier today open up that car up there, sort through the trunk, and then leave. You know anything about that?"

I pulled off the gloves and dug around in my pockets for the keys to the car. I handed them over to Phillips.

"I told you about them this morning," I said.

"No you didn't," he said. "I would have remembered. I don't like PI assholes who withhold evidence."

"This morning it wasn't a crime," I said. "I was the one who convinced you it was a crime, remember? Dump that bullshit on someone else. Not me."

Phillips disappeared behind me and then as quickly opened the other door, sat down, and closed the door.

"Woman up there in the house hadn't thought a thing about it until you showed up at her door a few minutes ago," he said, looking straight ahead over the dashboard. "Then she remembered you. If you hadn't fessed up to it, I'd have run you in. I just want you to know that."

Phillips offered me a stoic face.

I considered offering a compromise. "Until an hour ago I thought it was Danny Goodman's car," I said. "I found the keys in his pants pocket."

Phillips looked at the keys. "Probably isn't important," he said.

"Probably not," I said. "They're not the originals, just copies. Still..." I shrugged.

Phillips was thinking about getting out of the car again, but he clearly had no enthusiasm for it.

"They say each day we'll start gaining a few seconds of daylight now," he said. "Winter is officially here. I've always wondered why winter begins when the days actually start getting longer."

I said nothing. The sun was rapidly setting in a cloudless sky to the west. It would be another cold one.

"I knew Goodman when he was a fireman," he said. "It doesn't seem like a long time ago, I mean, it doesn't seem like long enough time to make a man go from being a pretty good fireman to being a goddamned arsonist."

"Maybe he was always an arsonist at heart," I said. "Just wore a fireman's uniform. They let him play with fires that way."

Phillips shrugged.

"I want to be the one to find his killer," he said.

"You probably will be," I said.

"I want you to back off, stay clear, stay the fuck away," Phillips said.

I turned off the idling engine and watched the men digging in the rubble. They were removing it piece by piece.

"I'm no longer on that case," I said.

"Good."

"I'm trying to figure out who killed Terri Krug."

Phillips had been removing his gloves, but now he began to put them back on, one finger at a time. Neither of us said anything. Finally I changed the subject a little.

"Anyone know where this Freddy Samuelson has gone to?"

Phillips nodded toward the fire scene. "They're trying

to figure out if he's in there, too, maybe at the bottom. What you want him for?"

"Talk to him."

Phillips opened the car and got out, allowing a snow squall to advance through the opening. "Remember what I said," he said, shutting the door.

I watched him go to the nearest unmarked car and tell a uniformed officer something. Then he got in and drove away.

The uniformed officer removed his left glove, then dug into one of his pockets. He pulled out a wad of tickets and began moving toward my car.

I rolled down my window.

"Restricted area," he said. "If you don't move your car, we'll ticket it."

I fired it up and headed up the street behind Phillips. Two blocks away we drove past Randall Kowalski's big Bronco parked at the side. No one was in it.

"Interesting neighborhood," I said to the dashboard.

Phillips turned west on Michigan Avenue. So did I, but I was heading to Patty's office.

CHAPTER 10

I knew the location of my driveway not because I could see it but because it had to be about midway between the utility pole and the mailbox. I aimed the El Camino at the space between and sliced through the mound of snow left by the plow. We hit it with a "whump," propelling a sheet of snow into our headlights.

"We'll never get out of here," Patty said.

Fish-tailing a little, the car maintained its momentum to reach the drifted-in ruts, then it gained some traction as I guided it to the barn. Behind us the ruts began to drift full again. I got out and opened the barn door and drove the El Camino inside. We gathered our groceries and closed the door and pushed our way through the backdoor into the house.

Basil greeted us and leaned against Patty's knees. Lucky cat. Then he passed her and headed for the almost closed door.

"Stop him," she said. "It's cold out there."

I let Basil outside.

"He'll be back in a few minutes," I said. "And be wiser for the experience."

"Heartless bastard," she said.

Patty headed toward the kitchen, probably to determine how desperate our food supply was. I went into the living room and opened the Woodstock woodstove. Lighting a wadded up piece of paper, I established a draft, then lit the already prepared paper and kindling. I watched the flame crawl ambitiously upon the paper, then I closed the door, leaving an inch of draft.

Patty turned on two living room table lamps and curled up under the knit Afghan. She watched me as I watched the growing fire through the stove's glass window.

"Call me when it's warm," she said.

"We won't get much heat for a while," I said. "Takes a while to warm up the soapstone."

"I know," she said. "You explain that every time."

I went into the kitchen and put the groceries away. I returned with two glasses of brandy. I eased myself down on the floor in front of Patty and handed one to her.

"You will get the bastard who killed Terri Krug," she said.

"Somebody will," I said. "Maybe me."

The fire began to seriously consume the larger log in the firebox, carelessly slinging rays of heat toward us, even through the cold stone. Patty's hand came down over my left shoulder, her fingers playing with my collar bone.

"I couldn't help thinking about it all afternoon," she said. "He must be an awful man. I get this feeling, you know, the feeling that you're actually dealing with a true fiend here. He sets fire to a man, then a few hours later kills a woman, then dumps her into a snow drift."

Patty slid closer to the edge of the couch and wrapped her arms around me.

"You be careful, you silly bastard," she said.

"Like my life depended on it," I said.

"Yeah," she said. "Like that."   She squeezed me again.

"Sometimes you seem to like me," I said.

"There are moments."

We kissed.

Basil scratched at the back door. I got up and let him in. He allowed me to scratch the side of his head for two seconds, then trotted straight to Patty's lap. I went to the front door and peered into the moonlit stillness. Dr. Zhivago peered upon a similar scene from the ice palace. In my case, my southern horizon was defined by twinkling lights from the apartments at civilization's border, which approached ever so slowly.

I added a splash of brandy to my snifter and a larger log to the fire. I closed the firebox door, but left the vent full open as the fire was gathering some sense of itself.

"Tomorrow morning we go to the airport," Patty said.

"How's that airport case coming?"

She set Basil on the floor, but he turned and began climbing the armrest.

"It's not that. I'm told there's a list of doctors on the wall out there who give the physical exams. We have to find you a doctor."

The brandy was pushing a glow into my face.

"We ought to give that some more thought," I said.

"I've thought about it as much as I intend to," said Patty as she rubbed Basil's head just behind both his ears. His eyes were closed in what must be ecstasy for a cat. "My treat. And please don't give me more shit about it."

I returned to the kitchen and turned on the oven, then took the chicken breasts out of the refrigerator and cleaned them up. I employed some salt and pepper and sprinkled some tarragon on them and slid the pan into the oven. I got two large potatoes washed and put them aside and went back and sipped my brandy.

For a moment I thought Patty had become mesmerized by the fire, but then I saw she was asleep. I put the Afghan carefully over her legs and feet, then took a seat almost opposite her. Brandy in hand, I watched the sleeping woman.

Five minutes later the phone rang. I caught it before the second ring.

"Stuart Mallory?"

I said it was.

"I'm C.R. Davis, fireman," he said. "You called." There was a lot of background noise, as though he was calling from a poolhall. Maybe he was. Unlike people from most walks of life, the majority of firemen are engaged in a variety of small business enterprises. They seem to have more time for it than members of the chamber of commerce.

"Thanks for calling."

"I tried your office, but you aren't there."

"Nope. I'm here. I'm looking into the death of the guy you carried from the building couple of nights ago."

"Danny Goodman," said the fireman.

"Yep."

"Not much to tell," he said. "Down here they say I should have left him in there."

"What was the condition of the room when you went into it?"

I could hear him thinking. "It was on fire, particularly along the outside wall. The fire had come up through the outside wall. There was a lot of smoke. Listen, what do you want to know?"

"Was there a chair somewhere in the room with a pair of pants draped over it?"

"Yeah, near the bed. I had to kick it aside to get to him."

"Was the door open or closed?"

"It was closed. It was one of four rooms I checked. I had to ax each door to get into the rooms. He was the only one I found upstairs. It was the only occupied room. Two of them had no furniture, as a matter of fact."

"Anyone downstairs?"

"No, all the rooms were empty."

"Empty? Nothing in them?"

"They had furniture and stuff, but they didn't looked lived in. Hard to say, though. There was a lot of smoke. I was looking for people, and that's all I was looking for."

"I know this would be hard to tell, but was he alive when you reached him?"

"I don't know," he said, thinking. "He didn't seem alive, and he didn't look alive, but I'm told he was still alive when they put him on the machine in the van. Then he died."

"You know where the fire started?"

"No I don't," he said. "I've been off a couple of days. I haven't talked to the guys here much since I got in. I don't really know."

"I could tell by the news footage that you did a

hell of a job," I said. "Getting out just before the house collapsed."

"Lucky," he said.

"Thanks for calling," I said.

"Yeah, sure. Say, listen, I had to talk to the district chief here before I could call you back, and he said to tell you to call the main office and go through channels from now on."

"Thanks for the tip," I said. "I'll try to remember that."

"Sure." We hung up.

I've never ceased to be surprised when someone hands you a piece of obvious advice about an obvious subject and expects you to receive it like news that Mars is inhabited. Golly, why didn't I think of calling the main office and be told to get lost?

I returned to the living room and slipped another log into the woodstove. It was pumping out heat pretty strongly now.

"Hey, flyboy," Patty said. "Come here and keep me company."

I went over and moved her legs so that I could sit down with her feet in my lap. Beautiful feet. I began to rub her feet, starting with a gentle massage. They say it eliminates all the day's stress.

"I smell something good," she said.

"My after shave," I said. "Nothing but the best for my sweetie."

"It's lovely, Stuart, but not that."

"Must be the wood smoke," I said. "Always does something for the air."

"You know what I mean."

I rubbed a little harder and began to work on the toes.

"I think I'm on to something," I said, and I told her about my visit to Stone.

"Stone, eh, right downtown," she said. "You'd think we would have noticed that sooner."

"It's not like something you've seen for a long time over the years, like the Frandor Shopping Center or the Oldsmobile Plant. He's a developer, probably out of town, and the letters are so large on the side of the trailer you can hardly read them. And the name is Slater, not Stone. I don't know why yet."

"You gave him your real name?"

"Seemed like the thing to do."

I watched the fire and watched the fire in Patty's eyes as she watched me and the fire.

"Does this mean that if you are right about all of this that they'll be hunting you down next?"

"Or you."

"Me?"

"You interviewed Terri Krug, too," I said.

"Well, are we next?"

I shook my head without much conviction. "I don't think so," I said.

The wind disturbed the front door.

"You lock the door?" she said.

"Always."

She got up and kept the Afghan around her. Like I had done, she peered out the window toward the city, then moved the shade aside and looked outside to the front. I reclined on the couch.

She returned to the couch and cuddled up next to me so that we could both watch the fire.

"I like it out here most of the time," she said. "You

know that."

"Birmingham girl," I said.

"Detroit."

"Oops, sorry," I said. "Detroit girl, can't feel safe unless the neighbors can hear you belch."

We cuddled some more. I moved my hands up under her blouse.

"I keep thinking about moving out here with you," she said. "But I keep coming up against the fact that my furniture just won't fit in this house."

"And there's room in the barn for only one of our cars," I said.

"Yeah, that, too, and I have the newer car."

"You can have the barn," I said. "My heap is getting old anyway."

"So you've told me," said Patty, unbuckling my belt. "Let's check it out."

"I meant the car," I said.

Under the blouse, my hand found what it was looking for.

"Get these off," she said, pulling on my pants. I did as I was told. I moved fast, but by the time I was done, Patty sat beside me with just her earrings on.

"There's more room upstairs," I said, kissing her shoulder and moving down to her breasts.

"But I'm not upstairs," Patty said. "We Birmingham girls like heat."

I managed to pick her up and lift her off the couch and set her reasonably gently on the woven carpet in front of the roaring soapstone.

"Warmer here," I said.

"Eeeewwoo baby," Patty said.

* * *

We had been talking about how our days had gone and were eating tarragon chicken and baked potatoes when I looked down at the piece of baked chicken and thought that Danny Goodman's arm probably looked a little like the chicken. It's a difficult thought to get out of your mind once it is there.

I put the chicken breast back on the plate. It wasn't a good time to tell Patty about what the autopsy said.

"While chatting with Leon Slater today, I saw the miniature model of the mall they're working on," I said.

"I've seen pictures of it in the newspaper or on TV," she said. "It'll be fun to shop there. It's close to the office."

"It looked like quite the building," I admitted, giving the chicken another glance. "Hard to imagine they could put all that stuff between Grand Avenue and the river. Or would want to."

"So what's wrong with putting the mall there?"

"Nothing, I guess," I said. "What we need, of course, is another mall."

"We always need another mall," said Patty Bonicelli, child of Birmingham.

"That's just the point," I said, taking a bite of chicken. "We don't need another mall. We already have plenty of places to worship free enterprise, and they are well attended, particularly on Sundays."

"A good reason to build another," she said. "Avoid crowding. Keep the corridors free, avoid crammed parking lots. Besides, you sound like a disappointed Christian."

"I'm not," I said.

"Good. I was getting confused."

"I'm just speaking to the irony," I said. "We speak of being Christians —"

"We don't."

"Yes, but the country does," I said. "But the truth is, we are spenders, consumers, worshipers of the power of money, slaves to what it can acquire, or what we think it can acquire."

I looked down to find my plate clean. Goodman's arm was barely a memory, and I hoped it would stay that way until I left the table.

"Stuart, have you been taking a flashlight to bed and reading Veblen under the blankets again?"

"That wasn't Veblen," I said.

"Nader then."

"Now there's the irony," I said, raising a finger in the air. "Ralph Nader is one of the religion's high priests. He champions consumption. That's the foundation of his ministry. But he preaches safe consumption, so that thy resources can take thee further on thy journey along the path of treasures. Nader's the Martin Luther of our time."

"You're on a roll on this," Patty said. "You can stop anytime."

"Nader bids us safe passage onto the land of Adam Smith."

Patty was still eating her chicken. She hadn't been distracted by Goodman's arm.

"What has this to do with the Riverside Mall?"

"Nothing."

"Good," she said. "I almost need to whip out my MasterCard or VISA to feel good again."

"Witness to the wicked," I said, grinning. "It will heal thee, bring thee into the fellowship."

She ate some more and was silent. She was losing patience with me.

"I suppose all this helps in your pursuit of the bad guys," she said.

"It does," I said. "It helps me understand why the town's leaders stumble all over one another to support such endeavors. You read that stuff in the paper, and remember that banquet we went to where the governor was affirming his beliefs in Lansing's economic development?"

"That was the bar's annual banquet, for God's sake," Patty said.

"My point exactly."

"In this culture, Stuart Mallory, we like free enterprise," Patty said. "We savor it. It's what makes the system work. It greases the wheels. It provides us the goodies we want, that keeps people working, that pumps life into the economy. It's the system the Russians are trying to jumpstart in their front yard these days. It's not perfect, but it works. So it spawned its own religion? Most religions grow from our needs to make sense of things."

"Simplistic analysis."

"Artless, perhaps, but devout."

"Heretic," I said.

"Heathen," she said, crooking her finger, telling me to join her. "Approach me and I shall heal you, wash your soul of this disorder."

I went over and got on my knees. She kissed my forehead very tenderly.

"Feel better?"

"Yes, I do," I said.

"Good," she said. "Then let's hear no more of it tonight."

I started to say something, but she laid her finger on my lips.

Probably just as well.

CHAPTER 11

The phone rang about 6:00 a.m.

"So, where's the car?" said Phillips.

"Car?"

"That Mercury parked on Prospect you had the keys for, Mallory," Phillips said.

"Somebody take it?"

"It's gone. I don't have it. The department doesn't have it. I figured you made copies of the keys and drove off with it."

"Thinking like that is probably what made you a sergeant," I said.

He hung up.

We stayed in bed another hour, waiting for the sun to come up. Then we joined it.

The wind died during the night, encouraging life to return to something near normal, despite the fact that the temperature was not likely to climb above a minus 15 degrees. At least the drifts would not return immediately. Patty made a big breakfast of eggs, sausage, and pancakes and piled it deep on the table facing the window overlooking the snow-covered cornfield to the north. I poured coffee.

"So," Patty said, "my client told me that the flight physical checks some different things than a normal physical. He didn't explain what kinds of things. Some sort of secret about it?"

I poured Michigan maple syrup—the real thing—over a stack of three pancakes.

"No secret," I said. "I suspect he just didn't know for sure."

"You're not answering my question," she said. "At least what I wanted answered."

Sometimes lawyers are tough to talk to.

I thought about it a little and worked on the sausage patty.

"Well, during my third or fourth physical—I forget which—the doctor had me stand up and extend my arms to my side and close my eyes. Then he told me to turn around two or three times, fairly rapidly."

I carved out a slice of pancakes and forked them into my mouth. Good syrup.

Patty began to glance up from her plate. Sometimes PIs can be difficult, too.

She said, "That's it?"

I drank an inch of coffee, particularly good stuff on a cold morning.

"Well, while I was turning I could tell his hands were real close to me because I kept bumping into them. I asked him if he was checking my armpits or something like that. No, he said, you'd be surprised how many people fall down when asked to turn around like that. He said people grow up not knowing they have a balance problem, probably associated with a clogged esthesian tube or something, and they find ways to compensate, like depending on their sight. He said a lot of people who are afraid of the dark tend to fall down during such a test, so he's ready to catch them."

I took a couple fork-fulls of fried eggs and added a little pepper to the remaining eggs.

"I'll bite," Patty said. "What's the dark have to do with it?"

"In the dark they have very little balance," I said.

"Of course, this first happens when they are young, and they develop a fear of the dark instead of knowing they have a balance problem."

"Ah ha," Patty said. "Makes sense."

"Anyway, pilots need their sense of balance," I said.

"I would hope so."

"Actually, they need it, although half the time it becomes their enemy."

I ate more eggs and enjoyed my dangling mystery. After all, she started it, I didn't.

"Why?"

"Well, you can operate a chopper, or a plane, of course, in such a way that you convince yourself that any direction is down, if sight doesn't tell you otherwise."

I straightened my arm and pointed toward the front door. "If that's down, then this way is up." My left arm pointed at the back door.

"Vertigo," Patty said.

"Precisely," I said. "Your sense of balance lies to you. If you follow it, then..."

"You crash."

"You crash," I said, "although it seemed that the operative phrase among pilots was crash and burn. One tends to go with the other."

"Nice image," Patty said. "Is that why you stopped flying? Crash and burn?"

"Nope," I said. "When Uncle Sam stopped buying the gas, I couldn't afford it."

We talked like that until all the eggs and pancakes were gone, then we washed the dishes. Outside the sun glared from the snow. The barn and fence looked

stolen from a New England Christmas card. Finally,
I got dressed for the arctic and went outside and got
the *Detroit Free Press* from the roadside box. Back inside we looked over the paper and finished the coffee and kept the fire going.

Great winter weekend morning.

"I have some work I have to finish today at the
office," Patty said.

"It's Saturday."

"I know it's Saturday, but I have briefs to write,
stuff to read. You know, lawyer stuff, but I'll do it
all after we go to the airport. We can get back together later. Besides, you should be out hunting down
the killer."

"Detective stuff," I said.

"Yeah, detective stuff."

"First," I said, "I've got to plow the driveway."

"I was wondering when you would get to that."

I stood and prepared for the arctic again. This time
I wrapped my head in two scarfs even after I put on
a hat. I went to the barn and pulled a blue plastic
tarp off the John Deer lawn tractor and got it going
with a little spray ether. I maneuvered it past my car
and into the driveway. The large snowblower on the
front end immediately bit into the snow, forcing the
engine into mild labor. It recovered on its own. I aimed
the blower to the north, to keep the driveway from
drifting again, and headed toward the road.

Twenty minutes later I eased it back into the barn
and covered it up.

Patty greeted me at the back door and used the
broom to sweep the snow off me, which had gathered from head to foot. I looked like I'd just crawled

from an avalanche.

"That's the main reason you live out here," she said. "You like playing with all the farm toys."

* * *

It neared noon when we pulled off Grand River Avenue and found a place behind Midway Aviation.

"I want you to do the talking out here, OK?" Patty said.

I offered her my best quizzical look.

"I shouldn't be out here, wandering around, looking like I'm snooping, at least until we get this matter straightened out with my client," she said, pulling her collar up high and her hat down low. "It might look bad."

I laughed. "It would look worse hiding yourself like that. Does anyone out here know you?"

"Just my client."

"Come on," I said. "This was your idea anyway."

Midway was housed in one of the older structures along the southwest corner of the Lansing Airport. To both sides of the relatively new headquarters building stood rusting quonset huts dating to the 1940s. Inside the main building we found two uniformed young men and a uniformed young woman talking about the fact they were waiting for a special snowplow to make quick work of the snow outside. The walls were covered with various bulletins and posters from the FAA warning pilots of various things that can go wrong, which are plentiful. Six cartoons cut from various magazines and newspapers were stapled into the wall along the edge of the counter.

"Can I help you?" the woman said.

"Where's your list of FAA physicians?"

She pointed up. "Upstairs. The stairs are down the hall to your right." She pointed. "It's on the bulletin board in there."

A lot of pointing going on these days.

Patty led the way upstairs. Four or five older men sat on the couches and chairs and drank coffee and looked out the window at the goings-on. A Mister Coffee sputtered in the corner.

Patty found the list quickly. "Here it is," she said, pointing at it. Of course.

There were about five physicians on the list. I dug in my pocket for a pen.

"Take Doc Mills over in Ionia County," said the man sitting with his back to the window. He was talking to us.

"He probably wants a real doctor so he can get a real physical," said the guy in the red corduroy shirt. "There's a guy over in East Lansing—I forget his name, but he's up there—and you can get in pretty quickly. He'll charge you $75, though."

"Mills costs about $30, and he's a good doctor," the first man said. "He does more than make sure you're warm and got a pulse, of course, but he don't go lookin' where he don't belong."

They both laughed. They were watching Patty, not me. I understood.

I jotted down both doctors' names and phone numbers.

"You just getting into flying?" the man by the window said.

I shook my head and stuffed the note into my pocket. "It's been a while since I've flown," I said.

"He flew helicopters in Vietnam," Patty volunteered.

They nodded, digesting that. One man got up and poured himself a cup from the Mister Coffee.

"Have your own plane or renting?" said the older man with the best view.

"I got a plane you can have half of," said Red Shirt. "The price is right."

"You don't want half of this guy's wreck," the first man said. "He's been trying to find some sucker for years." He turned to his friend. "This guy will know junk when he sees it."

The plane-owner shrugged. "It flies well," he said.

"Used to fly well," his friend said.

The third man spoke again. "What you aiming to reactivate? Commercial, instrument, multi-engine?"

"Think before you answer," said Red Shirt. "This guy's an instructor lookin' for business. Economy's been bad on 'im."

The instructor was pouring coffee into plastic cups and asking Patty if she needed cream and sugar.

"Black," Patty said. "For both of us."

He handed me a card. It said he was a CFI, certified flight instructor. He looked to have about ten years on me, maybe less. "I'm Henry Bretton," he said, extending a hand. We shook. I introduced myself and Patty, who winced just a little, but only a little.

"A private eye," Bretton said. "Never met one before that I know of." He was thinking about that.

"I want him to fly again," Patty said.

"Well, we can sure take care of that," he said, and he handed us two cups of coffee. "Let's go down to my office."

"Watch this guy," said the man at the window. "He'll have you signing up for all sorts of things."

We went back downstairs and into a small office with a nice view of a snowdrift outside.

"Ever earn your CFI certificate?" Bretton said.

"Yep, but I don't want to teach," I said.

"CFI?" Patty said.

"Certified Flight Instructor," I said. "Lot of people in the military eventually earn it."

"No matter," Bretton said, digging into a file drawer. "They've so increased the requirements since then they'd probably not let you take the first student off the ground today. You'd think people back then couldn't fly."

"I've had to sort of twist his arm to get him down here," Patty said. "Don't say anything to discourage him."

"You apparently didn't hurt him too much," Bretton said, looking at me. "He doesn't look like he's in a lot of pain."

He shoved a paperback book at me across the desk.

"It's a wee bit old," he said, indicating the book. "But it'll bring you up to date. Read it before you come back for the biennial."

I picked it up.

"And do come back," he said. "That book cost me two bucks."

* * *

It was around noon when I dropped Patty at her office, then drove downtown and parked the El Camino a block or so down from the Stone trailer. I walked to the work area gate about 40 yards this side of the headquarters trailer. I didn't worry about getting cold outside because I didn't figure I'd be there long enough to worry about it.

Four workmen came out of the construction area and carefully worked their way down the slippery path toward the street. I stepped inside the gate and showed them the picture of Danny Goodman.

"You know this man?"

They looked. Two continued to walk away. One continued to look at the picture. The fourth was at idle, sliding his feet back and forth on the icy walkway and whacking his thigh with a black steel lunch bucket.

"He looks familiar," he said. "He work here?"

"I think so," I said.

He shook his head. "Ain't seen him lately, I don't think."

They left toward their cars.

Two men were coming into the work area. I showed them the picture and asked my question.

"Yeah," one man said. "I've seen him. He looks older than this picture, though. He doesn't actually work on the crew, I don't think. He's a guard or something."

The other guy shook his head. He went back in.

I waited. Two more men came out of the building and headed at me. One was Randall Kowalski and he was walking faster than the other man.

"Stop messing around with my men," Kowalski said, still coming. "You're getting on my nerves." He reached for my shoulder. I was backing away slightly, into the snow to the side, waiting for his reach. I took his arm and weight and flipped him end for end. He landed beside the gate in a pile of crusty snow. His buddy stopped.

I pulled out the revolver and put it up against the side of Randall's head where no one from the street could see how cozy we were getting.

"Steady, Randall," I said. "You and I both know I'm not the weenie you met yesterday. Tell your buddy to go back inside so we can talk about Danny without being overheard."

He considered it. "Go back inside," he told the man.

The other man didn't move. "You alright?" he said.

"For Christ sake," Kowalski said. "Go inside."

With little enthusiasm the other guy turned and returned to the building. He watched from inside through a dirty window covered with chicken wire.

"Danny Goodman," I said. "Remember him now?"

"Fuck you," he said.

"That's not an answer."

"Best you'll get."

"What did he do here? Shine your boots? Follow you and apologize to everybody for your rudeness? Burn things?"

Kowalski didn't answer. He was working on sliding down the snow pile to get into a much better position to deal with me. He knew I couldn't shoot him here in front of all of Lansing.

I pressed the barrel into his temple.

"Fuck yourself," he said.

That was when the other two men arrived. They lifted me from Kowalski as though a crane hook had snagged me. Randall sprang to his feet and faced me, then tried to pry the pistol from my hand.

I wriggled and the two men held me more rigidly. I lifted both legs and planted them on Randall's chest. He staggered backward toward the gate, but didn't fall, catching himself on a gate post. He came at me again. I dropped to my knees and my weight managed to twist one of the men around in front of me. He was skidding on the heavily walked area and was losing his grip on me. It was very challenging to hold me while wearing gloves. I managed to swing one leg at him and it toppled what little balance he had left.

He went down with a "whack."

"Shit," he said.

Randall was back, casting a large shadow on the entire fight scene. I came up under him and he lost his balance again. I skittered across the ice toward the gate and lost my balance as I neared the gate. I tried to do as Kowalski had done, but I missed the post on the way past. I collapsed next to the curb in salty slush.

Several cars had gathered near the construction site, their occupants watching the disturbance. I smiled at a gray-haired woman in the nearest car, a candy apple red Buick Park Avenue.

Genteel sleuth.

Kowalski had picked up a scrap piece of two-by-four and was coming through the gate toward where I stood retiringly between the Park Avenue and the curb under a handsome City of Lansing Christmas street decoration.

"In front of these people?" I said, gesturing with a

sweep of my arm. "Besides, Randall, you don't want the police asking why I stopped by."

He stopped.

I brushed ice and slush from my coat and jeans.

"Stay away from this project and my workers," Kowalski said. "We understand one another?"

I grinned. "Yes, we do," I said.

Chapter 12

I drove to a North Side Subway and got a foot-long sandwich with lots of sliced onion and diced hot peppers and a Pepsi and then drove to my office to eat it. I looked forward to a humdrum Saturday afternoon at the office.

I got a parking spot within two blocks of the office. Things were looking up.

The answering machine blinked at me upon my arrival. On Friday evening, I received one disconnect and a call from the phantom reporter, the guy named Sayre. He left his number and no hint about what he wanted. On Saturday morning I received a call from the Midwest representative of the insurance company which owned the house Danny Goodman lived in. She left a number, too. Sandra Goodman didn't leave her number when she called.

I called the insurance company first.

"We heard you were out of business," Melody Price said. "You were going to work for some government office."

"Planning commission," I said. "It pays better."

"Then we heard you were sniffing around one of our buildings, looking for trouble," she said.

"Clues," I said. "I was looking for clues."

"We thought you might be looking for work," she said. "You know you have a standing offer to work for us."

"It's your dental plan," I said. "I can't work for an outfit with a dental plan like that."

Melody seemed to let it pass. "You're in a good

mood today," she said. "I can tell."

"Some guy just tried to beat me up, and in so doing, told me more than he wanted to tell me."

"I vaguely remember a communications theory class in college where I learned communication can take many forms, but that wasn't on the list," she said.

"A punch in the nose tells a guy a lot," I said. Stuart Mallory, communication theorist.

"I suppose," she said. "You represent the Goodman family?"

"Can't say," I said.

"Of course you do," Melody said. "Who else would you be working for?"

She was right, so I admitted it.

"Anyway, our interests are the same, except that you're representing an arsonist," she said. "The owner insured the building for replacement value, just as the underwriter most certainly advised him when he bought it, I'm sure. But we don't want to pay it. That place was a dump."

"Insurance morality," I said. "I love it."

"What?"

"It was either insured for replacement value or it wasn't," I said. "Either way, you pay something."

She shuffled some papers.

"Anyway, Stuart, we figured you'd be in for 10 percent if you could get us off the hook," she said.

"Ten percent of what?"

"Replacement value. About eighty thousand, give or take."

"There's something you're not telling me," I said. "The only way you can get out of this is if the owner burned it down."

"Or was negligent. Knowingly had a faulty furnace, bad electrical wiring, and so on. Whatever caused it. Just get us off the hook."

"Sounds like work for a real expert, someone who can dig around in the rubble and comprehend the significance of charcoal dust."

"That's probably true, but they're busy right now. December—especially this December—is a busy fire season. Besides, the authorities will do that, I hear."

I picked up my BIC and pulled out the notebook.

"Who owned it?"

"Stewart Meyers," she said. "He spells his name with the 'w'." She gave me his address, which fell somewhere west of Waverly Road and at least two rungs up in castes. "He's a real estate investment broker and financial adviser with offices downtown in the Wolverine Building."

I vaguely remembered his name from the *State Journal* story. "He the guy who's sort of point man for the downtown mall project?" I said.

"I don't know," she said, but she began to click some keys on a computer. I looked around on my desk for yesterday's *State Journal*. "Well, maybe. He shows up among those insurance policies."

"You have that policy, too?"

"Yup."

"Ah ha," I said.

"Talk to me," Melody said. "What do you know?"

"Got a company named Stone, Inc., in there too?"

"Sure," she said. "Old client of ours. Leon and Darelle

Slater, owners."

"Ah ha," I said.

There was silence. "Listen, Stuart, if you have something, spill it, or cease with this 'ah ha' stuff."

I took a big bite of the foot-long sandwich and a sip of Pepsi.

"Did you know that Danny Goodman was working for Stone?"

"You're shitting me," she said.

I let it hang.

"You know this for a fact?"

"When asked, Slater seemed a bit confused about it, of course," I said. "But a thug employee of Slater just threatened to beat me up if I didn't stop asking about Goodman down there."

"We could void his insurance right there," she said. "Employing an arsonist."

"You'd have trouble making it stick," I said. "Goodman was never convicted, and I doubt he was paid by payroll check. But Slater probably wouldn't challenge it in court anyway."

"Are you at your office?" Melody said.

"Yup."

"I'll get right back to you," she said, and she hung up.

I'd finished my sandwich and sorted through my mail by the time Melody called back.

"You have a FAX?" she said.

I allowed I was out of touch.

"You really ought to get a FAX," she said. "They save all sorts of money, even for an operation like your's."

"I'm going out of the business," I said.

She laughed. "Sure you are."

"The FAX."

"Oh, yes, I just held a little telephone conference, and we decided to put you on a retainer."

"I already have a case," I said.

"Same case, two clients," she said. "We'll wire you $1,000. That's $200 a day for at least five days. When you succeed, we'll send you the balance and your expenses."

"I already have a case," I repeated. "And I get more than that."

"It's your new courtesy rate," she said. "I'll have all this stuff sent to you by courier if you want."

I sighed. "FAX is OK."

"But you don't have a FAX."

"No, but I have a lawyer," I said, and I gave her Patty's FAX machine number. "Send it to me in care of Patricia Bonicelli."

I spelled it and she typed it into the computer. "You're still seeing her," she said.

"As often as possible," I said.

"Too bad," Melody said. "I was just thinking I ought to drop by the Lansing operations. I haven't been there in a long time."

I remembered. "It hasn't been that long."

"Too long," she said. "And the memories are still good."

Sandra Goodman wasn't there when I called. Neither was Sayre, the reporter. I left two messages. I also called Patty to tell her to watch for my FAX.

Then I went down the hall and cleaned the coffee

pot, then made some fresh coffee. While it dripped through, I propped my feet on the window sill and was thinking about the situation when the phone rang.

"We haven't found that Mercury yet," Sgt. Phillips said. "You know anything more than you told me this morning?"

I thought about telling him about the automatic I found under the Merc's seat, but I didn't like his attitude. So far, I'd never liked Phillips' attitude.

"I know nothing for sure," I said. "And so far, my guesses have not turned up much either. The only thing I've figured out is that I had this detecting business figured all wrong. I thought the normal work week was Monday through Friday, but here it is Saturday afternoon and I'm busier than ever."

Phillips wasn't listening.

"We've located Bobby Krug, the husband," he said. "He lives only three blocks away from where his wife lived. Seems he went out and got pretty drunk the night his wife disappeared. He can't remember a damned thing."

I said, "This will sound strange, but it would be good to find out that Terri Krug's death had nothing to do with me. Is her husband a suspect?"

"Everybody's a suspect," he said.

"Cut the crap," I said. "Is he likely?"

"Not really," he allowed. "We have no motive, and he seems genuinely distressed about her death."

I listened to my coffee drip.

"Is there anything more I can help you with, or should I jump in the car and drive around the South Side looking for lost cars?"

"I wake you up this morning?"

"Consider this my answer," I said, and I hung up. I hoped he interpreted it correctly.

The phone rang again before I could return from the coffee pot.

"This is Sandra," she said.

"I haven't been terribly successful in the last 24 hours," I said, anticipating her question. "The only thing I have is that I think he worked for Stone, the contractor building the new mall downtown."

"I've been thinking," Sandra Goodman said. "Maybe we ought to leave things well enough alone. Dad's dead, and nothing you can do will bring him back. Maybe we'll just stir up trouble and get hurt."

"Is this the same Sandra Goodman who braved a blizzard to hire a private investigator to find out who killed her father?"

I could picture her shifting the phone to the opposite ear.

"I've just had a change of heart," she said. "I'd prefer you just drop it."

"OK," I said. "I'll return your money immediately."

"No," she said. "You have to keep it. I have plenty of money. Just drop the case and keep the money. Don't come near my house. I'm sorry, Stuart. That's just the way it has to be."

She hung up.

It was just one piece of good news after another.

* * *

I called Patty to see how her day was going.

"I've got a FAX over here from that slut in Chicago," Patty said. "You've only been out of my sight for two or three hours and already you're smelling around Melody. She had the gall to write a cute little note on it saying we should do lunch sometime and have a talk."

"She could learn a lot from you," I said.

"She'll learn not to write cute little notes," Patty said. "I sent her one back that ought to tweak her nipple."

"Did you tell her about last night in front of the fire?"

"That's a thought," she said. "I'll send another."

"Other than Melody, I've had a busy day already," I said. "You ready to call it quits over there?"

I could tell she had cupped the telephone and was talking to someone else. "Hold on a minute."

I waited. As I waited, someone pushed a *State Journal* through outer office mail slot. Either that or a flat paper bomb.

"OK, I'm back," Patty said. "We're actually doing some good work over here right now. How about five o'clock, just like we originally agreed?"

"Three hours," I said. "A long time. Could I stop and get the FAX?"

"Sure, but I can have Frank deliver it," she said. "He's on his way home. There will be a small carrying charge, of course, which you'll pay tonight."

I was reading about Michigan State's football possibilities for the next fall when Frank, a law student research assistant in Patty's law firm, panted in and delivered the twelve pages of FAX from Melody. He pivoted and left, saying his car was double-parked.

I glanced outside and, sure enough, there was his little Isuzu squatting in the middle of the street.

It took six cups of coffee and an hour to read through Melody's insurance paperwork. Stewart Meyers was deeply into renting exhausted housing in and around Prospect. He formed partnerships with doctors, lawyers, dentists, and other mainstream American professionals to own and manage apartment buildings and houses forged into tenement houses. I presume he hitched their money to his financial wizardry since I had no indication he had money of his own. Likewise, Meyers was a financial planner for the new downtown mall and was a partner with the Slaters.

It was an impressive list.

On Prospect, he owned three houses. I pulled a map from a nearby cardboard box and spread it on the floor. I got a red felt tip pen from the desk and put a mark more or less where Meyers owned a house. Most were near downtown, and about two-thirds were east of the Grand River, on the opposite banks from the new downtown mall along the river.

As I skimmed through the addresses on the list of 19 exhausted houses, I found one street familiar. I found Bobby Krug's address in my notebook. Not surprisingly, he lived in a Meyers property.

"Gee," I said.

I picked up the phone and dialed Meyers real estate management office, also insured and on the list.

"Say, where have you relocated Freddie Samuelson?" I said.

"Who?"

"You know, the guy whose house on Prospect burned

down a couple of nights ago," I said. "We got some stuff to get over there by nightfall. Where the hell is it?"

"Just a minute," the clerk said.

I had nothing to lose. If I was right, I would be right. If I was wrong, then...

"He's down on Michigan Avenue now," the clerk said. "Above the pharmacy."

"Thanks." I hung up.

I looked it up on the list and marked it on the map.

Frederick S. Samuelson now resided on Michigan Avenue about four blocks from Prospect.

Using two thumbtacks from my desk, I hung the city map on the wall to assure myself that I was actually doing something. I got the last cup of coffee and leaned back in my chair and studied my handiwork.

The map's patchwork of red marks in the downtown area delivered the uncanny appearance of splattered blood.

CHAPTER 13

It was time to talk to Freddie Samuelson.

I locked up the office and tiptoed by the dentist's office downstairs from where high-pitched electric motor screeches emerged. Even on Saturday afternoons. The little office building no longer housed the robust established business traffic and instead it sheltered the up-and-coming and the down-and-out. I didn't know which group I belonged in, or the dentist for that matter. At least Patty, whose office used to be next door, was certainly no longer among the up-and-coming.

Outside the air actually felt warm. My face didn't freeze within one block, showing the temperature must be sliding up on zero's underside. Maybe winter's normal "January thaw" was just around the corner, appropriately in January.

I knew the general location of the pharmacy on Michigan Avenue, so I drove over there without hurrying. The place had recently been renovated. It now sported an ugly brown shingle facade along the front and the bricks toward the side street were army latrine green. It looked five years from demolition. We could hope so, anyway.

I parked on Michigan Avenue across the street and made my way through six lanes of moderate traffic to the side door which led to the apartment upstairs. Neither of the two broken mailboxes inside the ground floor door had a name.

At the top of the stairs were two doors. I didn't know which to pick. Sounds of a college football game came from behind one door, the one to the rear. The other door was silent. Light spilled from both.

I knocked on the one to my left, the one fronting on the alley to the rear. The football game narrative dropped in volume and soon someone began to remove several chains. Someone opened it far enough to let one chain still hold it.

"Excuse me," I said. "I'm looking for Freddie. Short, stocky guy. He just moved in here."

"Across the hall," a man's voice said. "Moved in yesterday."

"Thanks."

"And he's thin."

"Thanks again."

The door was shut and the locks were latched. In a few seconds I could hear the game again, too.

I knocked on the other door. No answer. I knocked again. Still no answer. I tried the door, but it was locked. I got out my tools of the trade and began to work on the single-cylinder dead-bolt lock, but I wasn't having much luck. The door was wedged pretty good in the frame and the bolt was probably wedged in there, too. Be hard to get it open even with the key.

Back outside, I stood at the corner long enough to know I didn't want to stand on the corner very long. I went into the pharmacy and lingered in the card section. I finally bought a candy bar and a bag of menthol eucalyptus cough drops and went back outside and got into the car. I started it up and parked it where I could watch the side door.

I turned the car off but left the radio on. Listening to the newest rock and roll, I began to feel old, so I went through the dial until I found a station with a

Philharmonic orchestra playing classic Christmas music. I left it on until some announcer with a British accent began telling me about the various instruments. I rapidly lost the little interest I had in the first place and turned it off. I popped a cough drop in my mouth and waited some more.

Ninety minutes and a handful of cough drops later I drove around the block looking for the Mercury, but I couldn't find it. Then I drove over to Patty's office, arriving at five o'clock on the button.

"Clara's," she said, getting in. "And step on it."

I did.

Three blocks later Patty said, "I smell eucalyptus."

"Cough drops." I explained the lead I had to Freddie Samuelson's apartment on Michigan Avenue and how I came to buying cough drops in my sleuthing through the pharmacy.

"Clever," she said. "Bet you fooled them all."

Clara's was not busy, it being too early for the Saturday night crowd. We got a nice booth opposite the tracks and ordered something Italian.

"I'm starved," Patty said as the waitress left. "It was too cold to walk somewhere for lunch, and then we thought we would order a pizza or something. We didn't, but I don't remember why."

"I'm sorry," I said. "I went to Subway."

"You bastard."

"You had a productive day, though," I said.

"Yup." She summarized her activities and we talked about a case she was handling defending the Bowman Center. Again the center was back in the courts.

"I had a productive day too," I said, and I told her

everything I could remember, including my little interaction with Randall Kowalski.

"You suspect him of something?"

"I suspect Goodman was working for Slater, and Slater doesn't want anyone to know that, and Kowalski works very hard at making sure Slater's wishes are pressed upon those he wants them pressed upon."

"And he's a big guy," she said.

"Barely fit into his Bronco," I said. "Part of him might have had to ride outside."

Patty sat back in the booth's shadows and was working on being quiet. Her eyes glistened, though, as they examined each person passing the booth. They examined me too.

"I apologize," Patty said. "I'm so hungry I'm a little paranoid. Shaky. I'd better be quiet until I have some food in me."

I selected a slice of garlic bread from the basket the waitress left and put fresh soft butter on it and gave it to Patty. She ate it rather quickly.

"Long time to go without food," I said.

She nodded in the shadows.

"So, do you have a physical appointment yet?"

"Doctor didn't answer the phone," I said, selecting bread for myself. "It's Saturday."

She nodded again.

"Let's go to a movie," I said.

"Anything in particular?"

"We could see *Dances with Wolves* or *Robin Hood* again."

"I'm always willing to watch Kevin Costner," Patty said. "Whatever he's in."

"I thought so."

* * *

On the way home from *Robin Hood*, we drove past the pharmacy where Freddie was supposed to be living. No light showed upstairs, and the Mercury was nowhere to be found. But it wasn't even 10:00 yet.

"You going to tell the cops about where to find Freddie?" Patty said.

"I'm not sure Freddie lives there," I said. "If I find him and talk to him, then, sure, I'll tell Maddox."

"You wouldn't want them talking to him first," she said as we drove up Grand River Avenue. "But you have good reason to believe you know where he is."

I nodded.

"That's sort of cutting a fine line, isn't it? I mean, keeping your license could balance on that sort of thing."

"You speaking as my lawyer or as my friend?"

"Both, for Christ sake," she said. "Answer my question."

"I'm going out of business in a few days anyway," I said. "The license just doesn't matter."

"OK."

"Besides, the truth is, I don't know Freddie lives there. Not really, not yet, anyway. I don't know what he looks like, smells like, talks like. I don't know if he survived the fire or was still living there or has left town or what."

I turned right on the road to the farm. Two miles to go.

"There are some things to speculate about, though," I said. "First, someone dropped by Prospect and drove off in the Mercury. I presume it is either an industrious but rather stupid thief, or, more likely, someone with a key."

"Such as Freddie."

"Right. Then there's the fact that Meyers' real estate management office responded rather positively to the name Freddie Samuelson and knew where he was. At least it appeared so."

"How did you come to check that, anyway?" Patty said.

I shrugged. "I don't know," I said. "Perhaps it's the subconscious, perking something up, something suspicious, something that didn't fit, or something that fit all too well."

"I understand," she said.

"Of course you do."

"The subconscious works within us all," she said.

"Yes," I said. "Especially in us private eyes."

"Lawyers, too."

"Yeah, probably. Another part of it is that it seems everybody lives in a Meyers property. That's odd, and there's probably a reason for that. Could be just coincidence, I suppose."

"But you don't believe in coincidence."

"Nope."

"Neither do I."

We drove some more. There's a pleasure driving in cold weather difficult to pinpoint. The car runs well. The traffic is lessened. The air is clear.

"My subconscious tells me that for two straight weekends we've stayed at the farm," Patty said. "Do I spot a pattern?"

"No, for the next two weekends, we'll stay in your apartment."

"Can't next weekend," she said. "I'm going to my sister's and then to my parents in Birmingham. You said you might go with me, remember?"

"I'd like to go with you and meet your parents," I said.

"It would be about time," Patty said. "They ask me about you often."

"Like, why are you running around with that no-good never-come-to-anything private eye, of all people."

"Something like that," Patty said.

"Makes me anxious to meet them."

"I think the Stuart Mallory I've learned to respect and love would melt their hearts," Patty said. "But they would have to meet him for that to happen."

"OK, I'll go to Birmingham. But what about this pattern? Two weeks after that weekend, then. Besides, this pattern idea was your idea. You can't hold this pattern against me."

"I'll find something to hold against you," she said.

We drove into the long driveway with relative ease, compared to the previous evening, and stopped in front of the barn.

I didn't get out. "You know, if I was a good detective, I would pack a sandwich and thermos and sit outside that pharmacy until Freddie showed up. I've taken the money, I should do the job."

"You know I'll understand if you do," Patty said from the right front seat. "Being honorable and doing the job you've committed to doing and all that integrity shit is part of what I love about you."

"And you put it so well, too."

"We could go in and make some coffee and make you something to eat—although God knows you ate enough buttered popcorn to hold you for awhile—and then you could take me home. I'll love you for ever and ever whether we sleep together tonight or not."

I thought about it. "And if I find Freddie and talk with him, I can come to your apartment and slip between the sheets later, and there won't be any weekend pattern we have to properly balance a couple of weeks from now. And we won't have to wonder if you'd love me for ever and ever. Yeah, I like that."

Patty grabbed me and kissed me on the mouth.

"God, I love it when you talk like that," she said. "Although I forgot about the cough drops."

Then she opened her door and headed for the house.

CHAPTER 14

When I drove Patty home, we drove past the pharmacy. Still no light. Still no Merc.

I parked the El Camino on Michigan Avenue again, this time facing east in front of a closed neighborhood meat shop, squeezing between a rusty pickup truck with a load of snow and a Japanese-make sedan also covered with snow. The location provided a good view of the pharmacy and its side entrance, and I could see almost a block up the side street. Sparrow Hospital loomed just a few blocks down the street, too. I hoped I would not get closer for at least a few years.

I turned off the engine and turned on the radio, sliding through the FM dial past today's music. Quickly I stumbled over Neil Young's *Helpless* and tuned it in. That ended all too quickly, though, but Bob Dylan's *All Along the Watchtower* followed. It was all making me think of another time. About a half an hour later I poured a cup of fresh coffee. I'd been thinking about cutting the caffeine in half, having been advised to do so by a physician I'd cornered in the late summer on a charge of writing fraudulent prescriptions. But every time I sipped a cup of the fully charged coffee, I decided to decide the issue later. Some things are hard to give up.

The disc jockey was engaged in nostalgia, meandering through music with little active audience out there. The DJ was dabbling in a little Eric Clapton about midnight when someone journeyed up the snow-packed sidewalk, fired up the pickup, and left, leaving me with a guitar my speakers could not handle. I started up my car and let it idle long enough to get my feet warm again. The snow on the hood quickly melted from the engine's heat, and in the rearview mirror I noticed the condensation cloud from the exhaust. I shut off the engine. A car without a cloud around it is less noticeable than one with a cloud. Probably says so in the detective manual.

I drank more coffee and listened to Dylan's *Forever Young* with relief and perhaps with a tear in the eye. I knew that if I died a minute later, at least in my mind I'd partly repaired the Dylan song that Rod Stewart had so recently damaged. Maybe I'd have to get the name of that disc jockey and send a thank you note.

I scraped frost off the side window so I could see the pharmacy.

About 1:30 in the morning a Bronco looking a lot like Randall Kowalski's Bronco drove past me and turned left, stopping at the side entrance to the pharmacy. It was difficult to tell how many people were in the Bronco, but one figure stepped out and went directly into the building. The Bronco sat at idle for a few moments, then U-turned in the side street and prepared to take a right turn back toward downtown Lansing.

His headlights swept past me as he turned. If he saw me, he didn't show it.

Freddie's lights came on, presenting me with a dilemma.

I started the engine and U-turned on Michigan Avenue, swinging in behind a Camaro where I turned on my lights. The Camaro's driver immediately hit

the brakes and eased toward the right, probably figuring I was a cop about to nail him for speeding.

I passed him gently.

The Bronco was in no hurry and it was easy to see.
I stayed more than a block behind him, not worrying
too much about losing him. He smoothly turned south
on South Cedar Street, then swung downtown and
drove into a workmen's parking area for the Riverside Mall. There was precious little traffic to hide in,
so I stayed well back.

Two men got out of the Bronco and went into the
nearest new building. From my distance, neither looked
familiar, but both looked big. Hard to figure them
both in the same Bronco.

There didn't seem to be any other activity around.
The workmen's parking area was virtually empty. Other
than the perimeter security lights, no lights showed
from the building. No construction supply trucks pulled
into loading bays. No cement trucks idled nearby.
No club-wielding guards waited to whack private investigators.

I waited for further developments. But there were
no developments.

I drove past the mall and went back to Freddie
Samuelson's apartment. The lights remained on. I parked
on Michigan Avenue again and walked across the wide
street and up to the apartment. I knocked on the door
and listened.

"Be right with you," said an anemic voice inside.

Expecting someone at two o'clock in the morning.

The door opened to a man very much like the voice,
a man in his 60s in need of a shave for the past two

days peering at me from eyes sunken into well-rubbed sockets.

"Who're you?" he said, half shutting the door.

"I'm Stuart Mallory," I said. "I'm a private investigator. We need to chat."

"Some other time," he said, swinging the door shut. He didn't have the strength to do it very quickly, and it was no problem to stick a hand out and push it back. I went in behind him.

"Hey, you can't come in here like that," he said through a dry voice carrying little enthusiasm. "I'll call the cops."

"Why is it that every time someone's in this spot he says he'll call the cops?" I said. "Please call the cops, Freddie. They've been looking for you since Friday. You'll save the city a lot of overtime."

Freddie stood at the door's side and thought about it. He wore his coat and boots and held his gloves and hat in his hands. Even a rookie could tell he was going somewhere.

Freddie stayed where he was, but he began to look around the room, figuring what to do next. If he had a telephone already, it was well concealed.

"Sit down, Freddie," I said. "We've got to talk about Danny Goodman."

"He's dead," he said.

"Everybody keeps telling me that," I said. I pointed at the worn couch and he hesitatingly went over to it. I locked the door before sinking deep into the worn easy chair between Freddie and the door. My knees almost came up to my chin.

"Sit, Freddie," I said. He did, but he would not

look toward me.

Freddie had gray, wiry hair cut short on the sides and was bald on top. It was in disarray and probably always was in disarray. His army surplus style long underwear jutted from inside his blue flannel shirt at the sleeves and neck. He held the gloves and hat in both hands and looked across the room toward what I believed to be the small bathroom.

"Tell me about Danny Goodman," I said. "He was a friend of mine."

At that he glanced in my direction, then shifted his focus toward the bathroom again. The room was sparse, containing only the threadbare furniture Meyers' company put there to call it a furnished apartment. A dusty dime store wall painting of ducks taking wing hung over the couch. There didn't seem to be anything in the room belonging to Freddie except a small worn suitcase under the single bed in the corner.

"Danny Goodman," I said again.

"What do you want to know?"

"Tell me about his last night," I said.

"I know nothing about his last night," Freddie Samuelson said. "I was lucky I wasn't sleeping in the building, too."

"Where were you?"

He put down the hat and gloves and unzipped his coat. I unbuttoned mine.

"Keep your hands out of your coat," I said.

"I lost everything I had in that fire," he said. "I wasn't even there. I don't know what Danny did on his last night. I heard he fell asleep with a cigarette and caught the mattress on fire."

"You don't believe that any more than I do," I said. "Someone killed him."

He said nothing, so I changed course.

"What kind of work do you do for Stone?" I said.

He shrugged his shoulders. "Nothing much," he said.

"What did Danny do?"

Another shrug.

"It's late," I said, extracting myself from the depths of the chair. "I'm tired. I'd rather not even get into all this anyway, so I'll let the cops talk to you and get this information. Then I'll read it in the *State Journal* in a day or so."

I managed to stand. Freddie did, too, picking up his hat and gloves.

"I gotta take a leak," he said and headed into the bathroom.

"Leave the door open," I said.

He shut the door.

I looked around the room. There was nothing to look at except the ducks. Then I heard a bolt slide into place on the bathroom door.

"What you doing in there, Freddie?" I said.

The bathroom was silent. I tried the door and it would not move.

"At the count of five, I'll kick it in," I said.

I counted. Then I kicked it in. It gave quietly to one kick, revealing an open window on the far side of the room. I reached it in two steps, hanging out the window, watching Freddie through the fire escape grates as he ran between the buildings toward the alley.

"Freddie!"

I stepped through the small window and put one foot on the ledge of the fire escape in time to hear it break free of the building and swing noisily from the rusty connections remaining.

Back inside, I rushed through the apartment and down the stairs. I broke for the alley, but when I got there I could see no one. Stopping to listen, I could hear only my heavy breathing. Freddie's tracks led down the alley away from the side street. I followed, looking between buildings as I went. His tracks became hard to follow because he quickly wised up. He began to run on the snow packed so hard it resembled ice. For me it was like trying to find footprints on rock in the dark.

At the end I could see no one or hear no one. I came back along Michigan Avenue and kept my eyes open, but the thin man was nowhere to be found. I pulled my coat tight and went around the entire block. Still no one.

I returned to Freddie's apartment to see what I could find. In the bathroom I forgave myself for not seeing the window because it was hidden from view by an ill-placed shower stall. I closed the window.

In the other room I opened Freddie's suitcase and dumped its contents on the bed. It contained three pairs of socks, one pair of worn work pants, two shirts, various pairs of underwear, a small bottle of pills, and a worn leather shaving kit. It contained all the equipment one needs for traveling light.

There was no label on the pill bottle, and the little pastel pink pills inside told me nothing.

I dumped all of it back into the suitcase and shoved it back under the bed. It stopped less than halfway under. I removed it and discovered the second suitcase hidden earlier by shadows and the placement of the first one. I hauled it out and dumped its contents on the bed. It contained the same kinds of items, but more of the same. Two newspaper clippings had been carefully folded and put into an envelope. I unfolded them and spread them out. They were about a Danny Goodman trial some years back.

I took a better look at the other items. They seemed bigger than the items in the first suitcase. If Freddie Samuelson put on the pants, he could invite two women along, too.

They were Danny Goodman's clothes, and the clippings were Danny's, too.

Chapter 15

Since there was no telephone in the room, I put the things back into the suitcase and stuffed it back under the bed and left.

There was a phone booth just to the side of the pharmacy door, so I used it to call the detective section. The sergeant who took the lengthy message told me he would get the message to Sgt. Phillips, if he was home. I told him I would watch over the unlocked apartment for 30 minutes, then I would go home, too.

I went back upstairs and took out the suitcase. I got the clippings out and sat down and read them. They were about the time the Eaton County Sheriff charged Danny Goodman with arson and lost the case in trial because the state's witnesses had even less credibility than Goodman. Goodman had kept the clippings for reasons known only to him. But he was probably like most of us when we get our name in the paper. We clip out the story, along with those of our neighbors' newspapers, and save it, sending a copy along to grandmother who will proudly attach it to her refrigerator door and tell all her friends about it.

Phillips arrived in about 20 minutes, knocking lightly on the door. It swung open with his knock.

"So, where's Freddie?" he said.

I took him into the bathroom and opened the window and noted the less than adequate fire escape. I told him about the brief one-sided talk with Freddie and how Freddie had gotten away. I told him about my effort to find him and about the suitcases.

"Jesus, Mallory," he said. "You had him."

"It's late, and I'm tired," I said. "Chew me out tomorrow."

He looked at me through tired eyes and it is possible he understood. "You say something about suitcases?"

"Yes," I said. "I think you'll find the contents enlightening." I showed him the pill bottle in the first and everything in the second, including the clippings.

Phillips was more interested in the pills. "We'll have to find out what these are," he said, putting them into his pocket.

"Won't you need a search warrant?"

"Sure," he said, patting his pocket. "We won't lose them, meanwhile."

Phillips went through the rest of the stuff. It took him less than five minutes to form the same opinion I had about the contents of the second case. That's when he used his hand-held radio to call for a patrol car to guard the room until he could get a search warrant to find what he'd already found.

"By the way," Phillips said. "The woman had the same drug in her that Goodman did."

"Dilaudid."

"Yup," he said.

"What are the odds that's what's in the bottle?"

He shrugged, then sat in the easy chair.

"Christ," he said, sinking.

"I'm going home," I said.

"Not until you tell me how you came to find Freddie here," he said. "You left out a lot."

"I got a list of Meyers' properties and called his office and someone there told me where he had moved,"

I said, relishing the brevity. I decided not to tell him about the Stone connection. I'd tell him later, if I had to.

He shook his head. "Seems simple," he said. "Someone fucked up or we would have been here first."

I handed him the Goodman clippings and headed toward the door. "Here, you can read these while you wait," I said. "You can figure out why Danny Goodman has been carrying them around for years, and why they're here instead of among the ashes on Prospect."

"I'll call you in the morning," he said. "Early."

"I know you will."

The air had chilled even more outside and it felt much like the night Terri Krug froze to death in Lansing's suburbs. The only traffic on Michigan Avenue was a police cruiser turning into the side street and pulling up behind Phillips' unmarked but obvious car.

The El Camino's seats were almost frozen solid again as I climbed in. I stuck in the key and waited for the slow groan of the engine. Instead, the car offered a high-pitched buzz and then the hood blew off with a "whump." That was followed by a bright flash as the entire front of the car caught fire.

I rolled out into the street and kept rolling for about 10 feet. I didn't know whether I was on fire, too, but the rolling would help. Behind me the front of the El Camino was engulfed in flames which had worked its way through the firewall and into the interior.

Two uniformed officers ran across the street toward me with a large fire extinguisher.

"What the hell," one said as he passed me.

The second officer aimed the extinguisher at the fire and opened up. He was gaining on the fire moments later when the extinguisher ran out of chemicals. That's when one of the front tires caught fire, dropping the car on its nose.

Phillips stopped at my side in the middle of Michigan Avenue and tried to catch his breath as he called the fire department on his hand radio.

"Yours?" Phillips finally said to me.

I nodded.

"Sorry," he said.

* * *

The sun hinted its eventual arrival as a Lansing police detective dropped me at the farm. I went inside and called Patty, dialing directly into her recording machine. I gave her a brief description of the night's events and said I was going to sleep.

And I did. I awakened to the smell of corned beef and potatoes and went back to sleep, not believing any of it. It was after 1:00 p.m. when Patty Bonicelli kissed me on the forehead. Twice.

"Arise, knight errant, and greet this beautiful day," she said.

I mumbled something.

"Corned beef, cabbage, potatoes, and various vegetables await," she said. "You barely have time for a shower." She kissed me again.

Then she was gone. Basil walked across the bed and stuck his wet nose on my hand a couple of times, then he was gone.

I got up and shaved, showered, and completed the usual bathroom ritual as quickly as possible, and went downstairs. Patty had the small wooden table spread out like a Sunday dinner with a basket of rolls in the center. A fire sparkled in the soapstone and the combined *Detroit Free Press/Detroit News* lay in the easy chair. A steaming cup of coffee sat on the end table.

"Good afternoon," said Patty from the kitchen doorway.

"I don't deserve you," I said.

"I know, but we can pretend you deserve me just for a day," she said. "It might be fun."

"Do I have time for the coffee?"

"Sure," she said. "I'll join you."

"You're just making sure I'll go to Birmingham," I said. "It's working."

She arrived a few seconds later with a full cup and sat at the end of the couch. She coiled her legs and feet and watched me sip my coffee.

"You're rather domestic today," I said.

"It seemed like a good day for it," Patty said. "When I got up, I missed you, then I saw the red light on the machine. It became a day to be domestic with my honey."

"Thanks," I said.

"I'm sorry about your car," she said. "I know how you depended on it and how reliable it had become. You can use mine for as long as you like as long as you drive me to work and back."

I twisted to look over my shoulder into the driveway in back. I could see her new bright red Oldsmobile Achieva two-door coupe poised in front of the barn.

"You brought it out of hiding," I said. "It'll get

salt all over it."

She shrugged. "I live in Michigan," she said. "It's time to toughen it up, get it ready to embrace life in the fast lane. Besides, I remember you telling me about all that galvanized steel in it."

I sipped my coffee. "Thanks for the offer," I said. "But I wouldn't survive a day in that car. Too red, too bright, too noticeable."

"The Simon brothers drove a red Camaro," she said.

"They always amazed me," I said. "They had no visible means of support, but they had a nice office, leased a luxurious apartment with waterfront, owned a small yacht, and bought a new red Camaro every year."

Patty shook her head a little. "GM doesn't sponsor you, though."

"Not lately," I said. "No, I have another idea, and perhaps we can get to it tomorrow. But I appreciate your offer. I know you mean it, and I love you for it."

"You'd do the same for me," Patty said. "In fact, you've done the same for me."

I put the newspaper aside and carried the coffee cup into the kitchen. There I got three generic ibuprofen pills and washed them down with the last of the coffee. That ought to kill the headache.

Patty began to serve the lunch, placing slices of corned beef and potatoes and cabbage on two plates facing one another. The sun burst through the window and splashed across the table. Maybe it would be a good day.

We sat down. I carved out a couple bites of corned beef and followed them with some potato.

"This is fantastic," I said.

Patty smiled. "Tell me about last night," she said.

I told her everything. I told her how Freddie ran off and how the police towed my destroyed car into the city garage to have a look at it. Patty listened intently to every word, convincing me I didn't deserve her.

"What did they find?" she said.

"The theory varies," I said. "We all stood there looking into the engine compartment, where everything that hadn't totally burned had at least melted. The going theory is that either the car selected that moment to have a gas line rupture and spray fuel all over a loose spark plug wire, or someone came along and arranged something similar. The results were pretty impressive, regardless. If I hadn't jumped out, I might be on my way to the University of Michigan Burn Center."

"If you were lucky," she said. "What do the police believe?"

"I think they suspect the latter," I said. "Hard to tell at this point, since only one mechanic took a look."

"And you?"

"I think Freddie or Kowalski or someone rigged the car to kill me," I said. "It made a strange buzz just before it exploded. That was the first sound it made, and I think that was an exposed hot, arcing wire standing in the way of spewing gasoline."

I finished my second—or third—helping of corned beef and pointed to the remaining cabbage. Patty shook her head. I put what was left of the cabbage on my plate and dug in.

"Wouldn't there still be evidence of some of that under the hood?" she said.

"Probably, if you know what you're looking for. All the wires were burned away, but the coil wire wasn't attached to the distributor. I could see that."

"How?"

"The metal connector end would still be clamped inside the top of the distributor," I said. "But it wasn't there. I looked and found it full of ashes."

Patty looked out at her car and back at me.

"Rather convenient for you that the insurance company hired you," she said. "That provided timely information, and a reason for you to be sort of investigating a murder."

"Yup."

"You didn't ask the insurance company for that, did you?"

"Nope," I said. "It fell into my lap." That reminded me of the money Melody was sending me. I made a mental note to check my answering machine. She ought to have wired it somewhere by Sunday morning.

"You lose anything important in the fire, like maybe a camera or a submachine gun or wiretap equipment?"

"Just the car," I said. "That was important. It's odd, but I took everything out of the car last week when it turned so cold. I didn't know what those temperatures might do to the camera and binoculars. Just lucky, I guess, though I did lose my Harry Chapin and Randy Newman tapes."

"You'll be lonely without them," she said with just a little patronage in it. "You can tape those over at my place again."

She began to pick up the plates and carry them to the kitchen. I helped.

"Let me wash," I said.

"I will," Patty said. "But first you read your newspaper, and then we'll climb into bed and see what happens."

"The newspaper can wait," I said.

CHAPTER 16

I was inspecting Patty Bonicelli's profile, running my finger down from her shoulder across her arm along the curving, soft line of her stomach and then up along the curvature of her hip. I finished with an exploration along her thigh to her knee and finally to her foot.

We were in bed, partly covered, and partly unconscious. She seemed asleep, but I knew she wasn't.

I began the same examination of her right breast.

"Such a gentle man," she said. "I like a person containing such power and such gentleness."

"How many persons do you know with such gentleness?"

She was quiet, then said, "I don't know exactly."

That's when the phone rang. I reached over Patty and picked it up. It was Maddox.

"You've lost your touch," he said. "And your car."

"My car's gone," I said. "But my lawyer assures me that I haven't lost the touch."

"We'd like you to look at some mug shots, if you can spare the time," he said.

"Today?"

"If it isn't too much trouble," Maddox said. "We know how inconvenient this investigation is for you."

I dropped Patty off at her apartment, promising to return as soon as possible, and took her Olds Achieva downtown to the police department. Phillips was not on duty. Maddox had a few books ready for me to examine. He even had another officer get me a fresh cup of coffee.

Cops probably understand what it is like to lose your car.

I spotted Freddie Samuelson—a much younger and fuller Freddie Samuelson—in the second book. Turns out he was actually Maurice Ludwig, released from prison in Illinois last year where he served most of six years for selling narcotics. Ludwig had been arrested five times, twice for arson, and still was wanted by the Chicago police for questioning in a downtown apartment building fire.

"Bingo," Maddox said.

We were sitting in Maddox's office where he was going over what the Chicago Police Department sent him by FAX machine.

"You had a hunch?" I said.

He shook his head. "Phillips had a hunch," he said. "You know, or you probably knew before you retired, that when you're a working cop you put bits and pieces of information together and you develop ideas. Sometimes these ideas leap beyond the available information to reveal patterns that others cannot see."

"Golly," I said. "I never knew that stuff."

"And you had him in your hands," he said. "We could have almost called Chicago PD and told them one of our very own private investigators had captured him."

"Give it a rest," I said.

The detective lieutenant smiled to himself as his eyes scanned the pages. He wore a blue blazer with a fresh light blue tie with dark red streaks in it.

"So, what do we do now?" He handed the package to me.

I looked them over quickly. "Do we have a plan, lieutenant?"

He shrugged. "It's Phillips' case," he said. "Let's let him decide. He went home a few hours ago, so let's wait until tomorrow morning. Meanwhile, maybe you can stir up Freddie again, or Maurice."

"Whoever," I said. "Actually, Maurice seems to fit him better. It would be helpful, too, if word did not get around that we know who he is until we find him."

"I agree. If he knows we're on to him, he might disappear again for a long, long time."

Outside water was dripping from the roof above and falling on the ledge outside Maddox's office window. It froze instantly on the accidental mound of dirty ice the winter process was fabricating.

"Do we agree that we now have a suspect in Goodman's death?" I said.

Maddox thought about it, and it was obvious he had been thinking about it.

"Sure, but we need a motive," he said. "Since he lived downstairs, we'll assume he had opportunity."

"I'll work on motive," I said. "I have some ideas."

Maddox was leaning back in his seat against the wall covered with memos and lists and phone numbers neatly lined up in three rows. His suit coat was without wrinkle, his tie neatly in place.

"I'd suggest you let Phillips worry about a murder case, but I know I'd be wasting my time," Maddox said.

"There's Terri Krug, too," I said.

"Oh, by the way, that little bottle of pills you found in Freddie's stuff?"

I nodded.

"D's," he said.

I nodded again.

"Surprise," I said.

CHAPTER 17

We drove east on Grand River Avenue past Michigan State University and past many of the bars the students parade to in order to find other students parading there. The sun peered over the rooftops into Patty's eyes.

"I must have left my sunglasses in the office," she said.

After we passed Hagadorn, she pulled into the Wonderland Auto Sales and stopped in front of the main office. Wayne Stillwell ran a neat car lot. The entire lot had been plowed clean and the cars put back in trim little rows.

"Follow my lead," I said.

"OK, chief," Patty said.

I got out and began to look over the nearest row of spotless cars. Not much there for me, unless I counted the Isuzu Trooper. I ignored it because Patty had instructed me it was "high time" Stuart Mallory owned a "real car."

On the ramp sat a fairly new metallic blue Cutlass Supreme coupe with $11,995 written on the windshield. It had four decent tires and didn't look repainted along the bottom. It didn't look as though someone had chopped two damaged cars and welded them together. If they had repaired bullet holes or something, it didn't show. I wondered how many miles it had on it. I'd guess 40,000.

I heard the office door close, signaling the deployment of the sales force.

I moved to the next car, a late 1980s Mercury Marquis

four-door. I was poking at the tires when the salesman appeared.

"That's a fine car, there," he said. "I almost bought
it myself, but the boss said he couldn't afford the
salesman's discount on such a car. Hi, I'm Bob James."

"The musician?"

"Who?"

"Bob James, jazz musician," I said, shaking his hand.
"I'm Stuart Mallory, and I intend to drive one of these
cars away today."

"Well, great," he said. "You couldn't have selected
a better place to do business in all of Greater Lansing."

The salesman was older than I would have expected.
He looked wiser and more noble, an appearance I
attributed to the effects of frequent lying.

"How about that Trooper over there next to the
Buick?" I said. "I don't see a price on it."

"Well, let me take a look at the inventory sheet,"
he said. "You interested in a car or a sport utility
vehicle?"

"How much do you want for it?"

"I think we're asking at least 12 for that Trooper,"
he said.

"Not interested," I said. "Woman in the car says I
have to buy a car."

"Your wife?" Bob said.

"No, my lawyer," I said. "And adviser."

Bob took another look at the Mercury and was about
to say something when I spoke up.

"Actually, Bob, I came here to exercise free enterprise with Wayne, the boss," I said. "If he's in, I'd
appreciate if you sent him out here. It's cold."

"Let me check and see if he's in," he said, trotting to the trailer.

"I can see how you'd have to check on it," I said, "the office being so massive and all."

I looked over at Patty. She winked.

Within seconds, Wayne Stillwell was wrapping his coat around him and coming down the stairs.

"Stuart Mallory, Stuart Mallory," he said. "I should've expected you after what I saw on last night's news."

"My misfortune, your profit," I said.

"Something like that," said Wayne, looking over his vast fleet of used cars. He offered a practiced and almost sincere chuckle. "Unless you're interested in some specific car, maybe we should talk inside?"

I pointed at the Cutlass. "Get the keys," I said.

Wayne stepped inside the door and asked someone to find the keys to the "show car" and bring them outside. He came back.

My pointing was Patty's signal. She stepped from her Achieva, closed the door in a gentle but firm fashion, and came to stand beautifully at my side. She punched a few numbers into a small hand calculator, then nodded at me.

"This is Patricia Bonicelli," I said. "My lawyer."

They shook hands.

"I'm sorry I haven't been able to come up with what I owe you," Wayne said. "It's been a bad season in more ways than one. Very tough, very tough. And I'm afraid I won't have it this week, either. Tough season, what with Christmas presents and all."

Bob came out with the keys and handed them over to Wayne. I snatched them from Bob's hand just before Wayne could get them.

"That's alright," I said. "I've instructed Ms. Bonicelli here to sue you for what you owe me, plus court costs, attorney fees, interest, and so on, and she figures you'll owe me about $10,000."

"Actually, about $12,500," Patty said, "if we file immediately and settle immediately."

"Jesus Christ," Wayne said. "Is this a shakedown?"

I was on my way to the Cutlass when I heard Patty say, "No, Mr. Stillwell, we endeavor to negotiate a satisfactory settlement for what you have owed my client, Mr. Stuart Mallory, private investigator, for about five months."

God love her.

I climbed up to the Cutlass and unlocked it. It looked clean inside and smelled good. The peddles looked worn properly and the mileage was just under 20,000. I turned the key and it started quickly, though it ran rough for a few seconds. In that temperature, you forgive any engine for stumbling a few seconds. I backed it slowly down the ramp and stopped where Wayne was listening to Patty. I rolled down the electric window.

"We're going for a spin," I said.

"No you're not," Wayne said.

"Better get a license plate, Wayne," I said.

Patty climbed in the other side. Wayne went into the office.

"You think he's calling the cops?" Patty said.

"Not likely."

Wayne ran out and attached a magnetic license to the trunk door.

"You do good work," I said to Patty.

"Not bad yourself, fella," she said.

Wayne opened Patty's door and climbed past Patty into the rear seat.

"I can't let you take my show car," Wayne Stillwell said. "I've got too much tied up in this car. And I'm not in the rental business."

I ignored him and pulled onto Grand River Avenue. The car accelerated smoothly and quickly. Maybe the V-6 will replace the V-8. I tried various buttons and switches, forcing the dashboard through its paces.

"I don't owe you $12,000," Wayne said, gaining confidence. "You'll owe me cash."

I swung into the Meridian Mall parking lot and made some sharp turns to test the steering's tightness. The Olds stopped quickly on a dry stretch of pavement and changed gears without a "clunk." I found a nice slippery spot and tried to do a 360 "doughnut" in it and almost went into a four-wheel slide into a line of parked employee cars at the lot's edge. I'd have to get used to front-wheel drive.

"Jesus Christ," Wayne said.

I drove it out of the parking lot and headed toward his car lot.

I raised my voice appropriately. "I didn't insist that you pay me in cash when you called me to find out what kind of guy was about to marry your daughter," I said. "And you don't have $12,000 tied up in this car, more like eight or nine, so don't bullshit me. I'm not in the mood. Besides, I saved you the price of a very expensive wedding."

Wayne remained silent, but he folded his arms, probably ready to argue later. He changed his mind when I drove past his dealership.

"Hey, where're we going?"

I thought about it. "I think I'll take it out on the expressway and see if I can get it to do 120," I said. "A detective's car ought to be able to do 120. If it fails, I'll put it back on the ramp. No problem."

Wayne leaned over the front seat to talk to me.

"Alright, that's enough," he said. "Tell you what, you give me $2,000 and you can have this car today."

"No, Wayne, I'll tell you what," I said. "You'll sign over the title to me, which will relieve you of your obligation to me. I'll give you a receipt for what you owe me —"

"Plus six months interest at 18 percent a year," the lawyer said.

"Right. And you'll accompany me to the Secretary of State's office and we'll get all the paperwork straightened out. I'll pay the fees and taxes and stuff."

"Big deal," he said.

He plopped into the back seat to act defiant and hurt, but he was thinking about it.

"And, Wayne, I won't sue you," I said. "More important, I won't have to explain in court what you hired me to investigate. It would make interesting reading for your daughter."

"You'll still owe me for my services this morning," Ms. Bonicelli said to me in a very professional voice.

"I'll take care of that," I told her.

She nodded.

God love her.

"I figure this car has 40,000 miles on it," I said to Wayne Stillwell. "At least 30,000. It says 20,000."

"You accusing me of spinnin' odometers? No way."

"Wayne, you forget who you're talking to."

"Well, this car has precisely the miles on it, it had when it was driven onto the lot," he said. "I swear it."

I stopped in East Lansing at a light.

"If I find out any differently, I'll come back and shove it down your throat," I said. "So, do we have a deal?"

His arms were folded again.

"OK," he said. "But I never want to see you again after today. Ever."

"Promises," I said.

CHAPTER 18

Shortly after 10:00 Phillips' unmarked car pulled up to Dawn Donuts and nosed into a snowbank. Phillips and Maddox got out and scanned the parking lot, then walked inside.

Maddox came directly to my corner table and took a seat opposite me. He folded his lined overcoat twice and set it on the seat next to him. He had the same blazer he had on yesterday, but the shirt was clean and he'd topped it with a different tie.

Maddox said, "What're you driving now?"

I pointed at the blue Cutlass Supreme just outside the window. "My new wheels," I said.

He nodded. "Rental?"

I shook my head. "The car lot owner owed me money," I said. "I just got paid."

A second nod.

Phillips showed up with three glazed and a large coffee. He sat next to me in the booth.

Maddox pointed at my car. "Mallory's new car," he said.

Glancing through the large display window, Phillips nodded, then took a bite from his first glazed. "Didn't know the insurance paid off so quickly," he said.

Maddox explained the nature of the purchase.

"Make sure you tell all the appropriate licensing authorities what you're driving now," Phillips said.

"Gee, thanks for reminding me about the rules, sergeant," I said. "I'll owe all this compliance to you."

"Found Freddie yet?" Phillips said from a mouth full of doughnut.

"Must be 500 cops in these three counties, and you want me to do all the work," I said.

Maddox sighed. "I'm here to get the two of you working together on this," he said. "Now for Christ sake let's caucus on this a little. I'm sure we all have other things to do. I certainly do."

"You learn this approach at some modern management techniques seminar the city paid for?" I said.

Maddox looked at me long enough to tell me he would ignore the comment. He turned to Phillips. "Sergeant, summarize what we have, and then we'll figure out what to do next."

Phillips finished the doughnut. I sipped my large coffee and Maddox just looked into the parking lot outside. It was pretty empty, especially for a Monday morning.

"Danny Goodman burns to death in his room in a rundown tenement house," Phillips began. "His only neighbor, Maurice Ludwig, a.k.a. Freddie Samuelson, known felon and former Illinois prison inmate, was his only known friend, except Mallory here, and was not in the house and disappeared. A Merc registered to Samuelson was parked in the snow in front of the house and rifled by Mallory and searched by LPD.

"Mallory is hired by persons unknown—probably the Goodman family—to prove the fire is not an accident, and he removes various things from the burn site, including a pair of Goodman's pants. In the pants he finds car keys, money, sawdust, and various other personal items. The pants are stolen from Mallory's car, indicating they must have contained something of value.

"Meanwhile, Mallory interviews the neighbor, Terri Krug, who has an excellent view of the destroyed home, and she is found the following morning sticking out of a snowbank along a highway near Holt. Tissue analysis of both Goodman and the Krug woman show they had the painkiller dilaudid, which is also found in a bottle in Freddie's suitcase at his new place on Michigan Avenue. Mallory locates Freddie, interviews him, but Freddie leaps from the building and disappears.

"Mallory here says he believes Freddie and Danny were working for Stone, Inc., the contractor for the new downtown Riverside Mall. Mallory believes they are tied in some fashion to a sort of foremen, a guy named Randall Kowalski, since Freddie was dropped at his new location by Kowalski."

"What do you have on Kowalski?" I said.

Phillips pulled out his notebook. "I have his address and age and all that, but he appears clean," he said. "Never arrested, charged, convicted, or anything. He transferred his car license to Michigan from Illinois last year, but he's clean there, too. We asked around down there and were told he's a union buster, a personal employee of the owners, the Slaters." He shrugged.

"What do you have to offer here?" Maddox said to me.

I told them about my two visits to the mall and the confrontation between Kowalski and me. I also told them I trailed the Bronco back to the mall after Freddie got out of it.

Both nodded heavily.

"You didn't follow them in?" Phillips said.

I shook my head. "I was after Freddie, not Randall," I said.

Phillips seemed satisfied.

"There's more," I said to the two cops. "You familiar with Stewart Meyers?"

Maddox shrugged slightly. "Who isn't? Big-time money man in real estate in this town. Powerful politico."

"Owns the house on Prospect that burned down," Phillips offered.

"And he owns the apartment Freddie moved into, as well as the house Terri Krug lived in, and where her husband, Bobby, lives and where Randall Kowalski calls home."

They looked at me without emotion. They were obviously thinking.

"I smell something," Maddox said. "But I don't know what I smell."

"Meyers' also a financial backer of the Riverside Mall project," Phillips said. "It all ties together."

"Sure," I said. "Let me put it all differently. Two known arsonists are living together in a house on Prospect. One is murdered, perhaps to shut him up about something. A potential witness next door is murdered. Both arsonists are tied in some fashion to the contractor or the chief financier of the Riverside Mall, which is struggling."

"Struggling?" Phillips said.

"You've got to read a newspaper now and then," I said. "The project's behind schedule, in debt, on the ropes. A fire would solve a lot, probably get the big money people off the hook."

The two cops sat silently for a minute, perhaps thinking. I got up and bought a cinnamon doughnut and re-filled my coffee. They didn't appear to have said much by the time I got back.

"Maybe we ought to go down and chat with Leon Slater," Phillips said.

"I thought you wanted to be a lieutenant some-day," I told Phillips.

"What?"

"The chamber of commerce, the mayor, city man-ager, and even half the legislature has been saying this mall is God's answer to the city's decline in the retail business," I said. "Don't you remember all that hoopla on TV and in the paper?"

"Sure, but this is murder."

"Only two murders," I said. "An arsonist, as you often point out, and a down and out from Kentucky. No local store owner, no school principal, or 14-year-old girl. Just two people who didn't vote, didn't count, and didn't spend much money anyway."

Maddox shook his head a little.

Phillips sipped his coffee.

"Besides, your evidence rests on reports from a goddamned private eye," I said. "Or most of your evidence, anyway. You willing to let your reputation swing on that?"

"I'm going to retire in 28 months," Phillips said. "City wouldn't make me a lieutenant before that anyway."

"Maybe you'd better let me go see Slater alone," I said.

"Whatever you two do," Maddox said, "have your fucking act together when you go in there. The surest way to blow this whole case and have city hall come down on us like a shitload of iron ore is to go in there like the two of you are about to go in there. Go together, as investigators, as cops, or don't fucking go at all."

He stood up and began to put his coat on.

"Let's go, sergeant," he said.

Phillips stood and slipped into his coat.

"I'll meet you at your office at 1:30," I said to Phillips. "We'll go from there."

He said nothing as the two walked out, got into their car, and drove away.

CHAPTER 19

The radio news announcer was telling me that Central Michigan was in for a slight warming trend over the next day or so, accompanied by some snow, followed by another arctic blast, although not as cold as the previous gust from the north. The long-term forecast predicted much warmer weather in a week or so. The January thaw might even come a little early.

I was driving west on Grand River Avenue having just visited my auto insurance man. He sold me a new policy and promised a check for $1,945 for my El Camino, and he said he was encouraged that I was leaving the business. I didn't want to discourage him.

Sandra Goodman's house was out near the airport in a 1960s housing development. As I turned off Grand River Avenue, I noted the "Crime Watch Neighborhood" sign and hoped I looked like I belonged there. The street had been plowed only once, right down the middle, but half the homeowners had cleared their own driveways to that path. I parked four houses down the street, not sure what I was going to do next. I let the Cutlass idle, which it did smoothly.

The Goodmans lived in a split-level frame home with yellow aluminum siding and a two-door garage. It had two big picture windows up front and squatting shrubs along the bottom of the upper half. Inside it would have three bedrooms, a breakfast nook with an intimate view of the neighbor's driveway, a half-finished basement, and lots of carpeting, some of it shag. In the backyard would be a small utility shed, a swing set, and perhaps a wooden deck. There was enough room between the homes to drive two Mack trucks side by side, but barely.

It was nearly noon and it would be difficult to stake out a house in a residential neighborhood for very long. There didn't seem to be anyone home. The driveway and sidewalks were shoveled clean. The front picture window curtains hung open.

I eased the Cutlass into the driveway and I walked to the front door and used the buzzer three times. No one came out. No audible alarms sounded. No one shot at me. There didn't seem to be anyone home. I walked to the two-door garage and peeked inside. Nothing.

Finally in the car, I worked my way over to Stewart Meyers' neighborhood, sliding past his house. The street had been recently plowed curb to curb. Meyers lived in a two-level red brick structure which could be easily mistaken for a small suburban hotel were it not for the lack of a *USA TODAY* vending machine near the front door.

The garage was in the rear, although even from the front you could see it had at least three doors. A four-door Volvo—probably the just-around-town car— sat in front of one of the garage doors. The house would have a modern burglar alarm system, cable in every room, at least four bathrooms, and a dining room to seat 20 guests comfortably. The homes next door were barely a stone's toss from Meyers' house.

I didn't intend to go up to the door, but it's a good idea to know where everything is and what it looks like when the sun is shining. It makes it easier to sleuth around in the dark.

Five minutes later I was at a filling station filling the Cutlass's tank and calling the number Sandra Goodman gave me for messages. There was no answer. So I drove to my office where, to my surprise, the parking area behind the building was plowed. I parked near the back door.

Inside the inner door of my office sat a young man reading *Newsweek*, which he probably brought on his own. I opened my inner door with a key.

"Hi," he said.

"Hi," I said.

"May I see you for a few minutes?"

"Sure," I said, letting him go into the office in front of me. He stepped over my mail very politely. I picked it up.

"I'll bet you're Sayre," I said.

"Yes, Tony Sayre," he said. "How did you know?"

"I'm a detective," I said. "It's magic how we figure out some of these things."

He laughed.

"Actually, you're the only one left I don't know," I said. I stuck out my hand and he shook it.

"I've come in the hopes of getting some information from you," he said. "Do you have a few minutes?"

I looked at my watch.

"Actually, I do, but I've got a meeting in an hour and I have to get something to eat before that."

He looked at his watch. "I was about to leave if you didn't show up, so we might just adjourn to lunch," Sayre said hopefully.

"Let's sit and talk and see what happens," I said.

We both sat down. I sorted briefly through my mail, picking out an envelope containing a check for $448. Another contained the $1,000 from the insurance company. Things were looking up.

Then I picked up the telephone and checked my messages. I had one. Patty had made an appointment for me for the FAA physical at 4 p.m.

She works fast.

"You've got to understand that everything we say here today is off the record," I told Sayre.

He was slowly shaking his head and thinking. "Well, I'm a reporter, and I report," Sayre said. "I'd like everything to be on the record, and I ask that you trust me about how I report it."

I shook my head slowly. "I'd like what I say to be background only," I said. "Like that deep background stuff I hear about."

Sayre laughed. "That deep background stuff is only a Washington subterfuge," he said. "It's the only way Washington bureaucrats will talk to the press, and the reporters are so desperate they agree to it."

"That's what I want," I said. "You can think of me as the head of the FBI."

He laughed.

"Well, OK, maybe the under secretary of southwestern interior matters or something. But the rules remain the same."

I threw most of the mail into the waste basket next to the far wall. The basket rewarded me with a "bong." The Detroit Pistons would miss me.

Tony Sayre was balding early, but he looked barely

30. He wore clothes suited to be almost anywhere at any time and topped it off with a dark blue narrow tie of some vintage. His overcoat, which Columbo might have mistakenly taken with him at a restaurant, was over the back of his chair. Sayre had his narrow reporter's notebook out on his knee, but he was considering his options.

So was I. I asked, "What do you report on?"

"I'm a business reporter, a columnist," he said. "I try to dig beneath the surface and get the real stories." He started digging in his coat pocket.

"Don't all reporters do that?"

He shook his head and tried to snicker. He put down his pen and notebook and leaned back a little.

"It says in the journalism textbook that the first thing you have to do when you are interviewing is to establish yourself as the person who asks the questions," Sayre said. "I've failed."

"My textbook says the same thing," I said.

Sayre said, "No, not all reporters do that. Most reporters just cover the surface, do it in four tight paragraphs, and go on to the next story. I was trained by the old school, so despite the obstacles, I'm trying to get beneath the surface." He handed me a card. Antonio Sayre, columnist, *Lansing State Journal*.

"Old school," I said.

"Yup," he said.

"What are you here for?"

"Ah ha," he said, grinning, warming to the situation. Sayre would let me ask questions as long as the questions did his job. "I'm here about the downtown Riverside Mall and the problems the builders are having."

"Like what?"

"Well, labor problems, money problems, weather problems."

"I've read about them," I said.

"What can you tell me about them?" He was glancing around the room at the cardboard boxes.

From across the desk, I studied his balding head and narrow tie and his reporter's notebook.

"I think you'd better lay your cards on the table or go back to your office," I said.

He squirmed, but it was for effect.

"Let's start with Danny Goodman," I said. "What do you know about him, and don't lie to me about it."

The reporter looked around the room a little at the cardboard boxes. "I think I'm in the same position you are," he said. "I almost have to ask you to keep what I know to yourself."

"Sort of off the record," I said.

He nodded.

"You moving?" he said, indicating the boxes.

"Yes and no," I said. "I have to leave because my lease expires. It expires because I gave notice. I gave notice because I was going out of this business, and I packed to leave. Now I don't know." I played with the envelope with the check inside. It was a riddle for me, not for Sayre.

Sayre stood up and stretched his arm across the desk. "I won't tell anyone what you say if you don't tell anyone what I say," he said. We shook hands, and he sat down again.

"It'll make it hard on you to write a story, though," I said. "Right?"

"Probably."

"I promise nothing, but perhaps we can renegotiate this later," I said.

"OK."

"So, tell me about Danny Goodman," I said.

"How did you know I knew something about Danny Goodman?"

"I didn't," I said. "But I do now."

Magic.

CHAPTER 20

We decided we were hungry and would talk better with food in our stomachs. So in separate cars we drove over to Arby's and met in the corner booth.

"I heard about your car," Sayre said. "That have anything to do with all this?"

"Tell me about Danny Goodman," I said. "I'm itching to know."

The reporter took a large bite out of his sandwich and stuffed some fries after it.

"I used to work in Florida," he finally said. "While down there, someone assigned me to do a business story about the high price of arson. It turned out to be a damned good story. I won Associated Press and state press association awards with it. Talked to cops, firemen, arsonists, insurance people, businessmen. You know, everybody, and did a four- or five-part series on it.

"So when I came here, I thought I would try to do a similar story. I looked in the morgue—you know what that is?"

"News clippings," I said.

"Yeah. They call them libraries today. Anyway, I looked in there for a while and found some clippings about some people charged with arson. I looked up a couple. One is dead, one's in prison, and then there was Danny Goodman. It didn't take much to find him, although luck had a lot to do with it. I called some sheriff's deputy who originally had the case and asked him where Goodman was today. He told me. I went to see him."

We ate some of our sandwiches.

"He wasn't very helpful at first, but he didn't tell me to go away and he didn't avoid me. So, I stuck around and asked questions."

"When did this all start?"

He thought about it. "About three weeks ago, but it took a week to get him warmed to the idea."

"So, what did he tell you?"

"At first, of course, he barely admitted he could recognize a pack of matches. But I kept listening, and he began to tell me about some of the things he did. Some of the minor things, all somewhere else or a long time ago. He wouldn't talk about anything current."

"You talk to him in his room?"

"Other than the first time, he never met me there," Sayre said. "We always met downtown or at MacDonalds or even here once. He called me and we'd set up a time and place. That's one of the reasons I figured he would eventually tell me something important. He had to call me just to sit and think about avoiding telling me something important."

Sayre was into his story now, and he had more or less gulped two Arby's sandwiches and his fries without tasting much.

"I stuck with him even though I began to suspect I was wasting my time," he said. "And much of this was on my own time. Evenings, weekends." He shrugged. "Anyway, one day he actually came to the office. No one knew who he was. And right there in the middle of the newsroom he told me he had been hired to burn down the Riverside Mall."

Sayre looked around Arby's and then at me.

"Ever meet a guy named Freddie?" I said.

"You don't seem surprised about the mall," Sayre said.

"I'm not surprised about the mall," I said. "I am surprised he told you in the middle of the newsroom. Why didn't you write a story about it?"

"Well, I asked him if I could quote him on that, and he said, sure, but he would deny it to the gods. Said he had no credibility anyway, and said he was only half the team."

"He say who the other half was?"

"Nope. I asked and he avoided the answer. Said they weren't to do the job until some of the materials had arrived so they could claim that on insurance, too, even though the materials would be removed and used elsewhere before he torched it. Said it would be a few weeks, and he said he was dying anyway and it would only be a matter of months before he died. So, Mallory, have I been open enough for you? You going to cough up your side sometime?"

"Yes, my car probably has something to do with it," I said. I told him the police were now looking for a guy named Freddie Samuelson, which was an alias, and that I was looking for him the night my car was destroyed. I told him that Goodman was probably murdered. I also told him that Terri Krug, the neighbor, was probably a witness to something and she was a murder victim, too.

"Jesus Christ," he said. "I wondered about Goodman, but the woman, too. I hadn't connected them at all, and I should have."

My watch showed it to be about 1:00.

"Ever get through to Lieutenant Maddox?"

"Oh," he said with some surprise. "You know about that, too. Yes, but he was considerably less than helpful, by most definitions. Said he had an investigation going about Goodman, that there was some question about the cause of his death, and that to say anything further could jeopardize the investigation and any trial that may result."

I smiled. "He wouldn't tell you anything more unless he knew you well. You haven't been in town very long."

"Three months," Sayre said. "I'm originally from Pittsburgh. Got my degree at Penn State and worked in Florida for six years. I got this chance to be a regular business columnist and run my own show. I took it."

"I don't think I've seen your name in the paper," I said.

"It's there, business page, twice a week, byline and photo and all. You probably don't read the business page very much."

I shook my head. "I'm talking out of school, but I don't get the impression that the business page tells me the truth very often."

He smiled. "We try," he said.

* * *

I deposited my new-found fortune in the bank, then squeezed into an already dirty snowdrift two blocks from the police department. Since there was no meter, I assumed I was parking at a yellow curb.

Sergeant Phillips was on the phone when I arrived

at his desk at 1:30. He was impressing someone with the cost of motor homes. He ended the call quickly.

"I was hoping you'd forget," he said.

"Bad luck seems to run in streaks."

Phillips shuffled some papers and made some stacks and put some of it into wrinkled and smudged manila folders and those into various drawers. He stood.

"Lieutenant wants us to go over some reports before we go over there," he said, walking away.

I followed him to Maddox's office where the lieutenant and a uniformed, gray-haired fireman chatted in a fraternal spirit.

"Mallory," Maddox said. "This is Chief Inspector Nick VanBuren of the fire department. This is Stuart Mallory." He shook my hand, but his observation of me revealed no fondness. Phillips and I found chairs. Mine was near the far wall to the side of the window.

"I was just telling the chief inspector here about what you've accomplished so far," Maddox said to me. "Now it is time we brought you up to date on what we have."

VanBuren broke in quickly. "I want it understood that it is only because the lieutenant asked me to that I divulge this information to a private investigator, especially one with Goodman as a client."

"I now represent the underwriter of the house Danny Goodman died in," I said. "That company has a very large financial interest in this investigation, a liability in both property and death benefits. I don't give a damn what you think of me, chief—it might even be a mutual distaste—but I suspect the insurance company expects more professional treatment from the fire department."

I got up and started to slip into my coat.

"What the chief was saying here is that—"

"I heard the chief, lieutenant," I said. "When you boys finish trading state secrets, you can catch up to me at Leon Slater's office."

I headed for the door.

"Get back here, Stuart," Maddox said. "Calm down."

I slowed and turned and looked at Maddox and he was looking at me without much fondness, too.

"Let's get along," Maddox said. "We're just trying to solve a couple of murders here. You'd think we could get along for a few days."

I sat down again.

"Tell us about what you've learned about the fire," Maddox said to the chief.

VanBuren opened an executive-style notebook and looked at it through half-frame glasses he produced through sleight of hand from his outside coat pocket.

"The fire came from the furnace," he said. "The house had one of the old gravity feed coal furnaces converted to gas. The fire ran through the interior of the building first—those areas are the most completely burned and most heavily charred—and then into Goodman's room and two others through a laundry shoot, which was probably no longer in use but certainly a functional fire shaft."

"Accidental?" Phillips said.

The fireman shook his head. "We think not," he said. "There seems to have been an accelerant in use, we suspect kerosene, perhaps fuel oil. There was a

Japanese kerosene stove sitting in Goodman's room, and there was a kerosene can in the basement, and even after the fire it still contained some of the fuel. Anyway, something was dumped into the burning chamber to cause a large flare up which would surge beyond the containment ability of the furnace."

"Wouldn't that be a little dangerous?" Maddox said. "Wouldn't whoever dumped the fuel in there most likely be caught in what might become an explosion?"

"Certainly," the chief said. "But it would be put into a plastic bottle or something, something like a one-liter soft drink bottle or a bleach bottle or something, and shoved in there. It wouldn't take but a minute for the plastic to rupture, causing precisely what the arsonist had in mind. By then, he's long gone. Besides, an arsonist is accustomed to taking risks with fire. At least in theory."

Phillips said, "Can we prove this?"

The chief nodded. "Pretty much," he said. "We don't know who did it, but we can show in court how it was done."

"We know that an Illinois arsonist did it," Phillips said. "Mallory had him once, but let him go."

"I just told the chief about that and about what we learned from Freddie's suitcase," Maddox was saying.

"Was there kerosene in the stove in Goodman's room?" I said.

The chief looked through his report for a few moments. "It is hard to tell," he said finally. "It obviously caught fire, indicating it had some fuel, but it expended what fuel was there. We found it on its side partly crushed, which would have dumped the available fuel anyway, right into the fire."

"What's your point?" Phillips said.

I shrugged. "Nothing," I said. "Just wondered. Probably means nothing, one way or the other. It just occurred to me that if I was going to kill Goodman, pumping him full of dilaudid to make it look like an accident, I'd just turn the stove up, set it under a curtain or something, and quietly leave the room and lock the door behind me. Why meddle with the furnace?"

"Would it work?" Phillips said.

"Sure, rather quickly," the chief said. He began looking through his papers again, finding what he wanted. "Says here the door to Goodman's room was a dead-bolt locked from the inside. The fireman kicked it in, of course, but it had been locked from the inside. Tore a hole in the frame as he kicked it in."

Maddox stuck a finger slightly in the air. "Then maybe the idea was to give Goodman the drug—or he took it himself and the killer knew it—and have him lock his own door and lay down to sleep. Then the killer could go to the basement and do his work and leave the building."

"Perhaps Goodman killed himself," I said.

"What?" the chief said.

"He could have done it himself," I said. "Taken the dilaudid. Gone to the basement and fired up the furnace, ran upstairs and stretched out for the big sleep."

"Why?"

"Look at the autopsy," I said. "He was dying, and perhaps it was painful. It's winter, it's a bad winter,

and we all know the connection between hard winters and suicides. His life was a mess and had been
for a long time. Maybe he was between a rock and a
hard place. The point is, he could have done it himself."

The chief examined me with less hostility.

"I'm not proposing that's what happened," I said.
"But it might have happened."

"You're the one who first convinced us it was murder,"
Maddox said. "Are you just touting the line from your
insurance company employer? Trying to get them
off the hook already?"

"No, this just comes from an active imagination," I
said.

"We need more information," Maddox said. "We
certainly need more information before we go charg-
ing over to Slater's office, if what Mallory says here
is true."

Maddox's phone rang and he found himself looking up a file and explaining something to a Detroit
police officer. It was five minutes before the call ended.
Meanwhile, Phillips squirmed in his seat and looked
at his watch. The mannerisms were obvious, and were
intended to be. Maddox ignored him and told him to
talk about the Terri Krug autopsy.

"Died by 3:00 a.m., the coroner says, and most likely
before that. Says the least amount of time it would
have taken to freeze someone solid was three and a
half hours in the 26 below zero we had that night,
assuming she was exposed to the wind. She died lit-
erally of being frozen to death, and she was also up
to her lower lip in painkiller. The plow hit her pretty

good, almost snapping her in half. Broke her spine and several ribs and sliced through her chest."

"Perhaps that was the idea," Maddox said. "Maybe she wasn't dead when she was put there, but the killer intended the plow to do the job for him when it came by. Maybe he didn't know how soon the temperature would kill her. I didn't." He tossed a shoulder a little.

Phillips made a note. "I'll check to see how regular the plow was," he said. "Also check to see if the driver saw anyone. Maybe the killer waited around somewhere to make sure. This wasn't in our territory. Ingham County handled it, so I've got to ask them to check it."

"Are we sure someone killed her?" VanBuren said. "After all, if Goodman could have killed himself, so could the woman."

We thought about it.

"Doesn't seem likely she killed herself," I said. "What was she doing out there in those clothes? How did she get there? Why did she go there? What did she see that caused someone to kill her?"

"Why did she take the same painkiller Goodman had?" Maddox said.

"And if Goodman committed suicide, why did someone steal his pants from my car and kill Terri Krug?" I said.

Phillips was going through his paperwork and he winced slightly as he looked up at Maddox.

"Says here that the woman had a taco or two before her death," he said. "I didn't notice it the first time through."

VanBuren looked around for an explanation.

"Goodman had tacos in his stomach, too," I told him.

Maddox placed both hands on the desk, as though he were pushing away, finishing the meeting. "Like I've already said, we need more information, a hell of a lot more information," he said. "Sergeant, get a couple of men and get some of this stuff nailed down, today if possible. Find out if these tacos came from the same place, if that's possible, and take mug shots and see if anyone in one of the city's 50 taco shops remembers seeing these people."

CHAPTER 21

I disengaged the Cutlass from the snowdrift and drove back to my office. I removed the Nikon and the telephoto from the cardboard box I'd carefully packed them in, picked up the Monday *State Journal*, and drove back to Grand Avenue downtown. I parked about a block from the work entrance to the Riverside Mall and cranked a roll of Tri-X into the camera. I pulled the 200 mm lens from its pouch and attached the lens to the doubler and the doubler to the camera bayonet connection.

Focusing on the entrance, I took a sample meter reading. Too little light. This roll would require "pushing" when I developed it. The telephoto lens and doubler cut the available light so deeply that I would have to shoot it too slowly to freeze the image. I reset the meter and tried again.

It was still short of light—even on a bright wintery afternoon—but it would have to do. The doubler— which effectively turned the 200 mm into a 400 mm lens—presented its own set of focusing difficulties.

I waited, listening to the radio and wondering how anyone could call much of today's sound rock and roll.

An hour later, Randall Kowalski came out with two other men and strolled down the path toward the street. I watched him through the lens, waiting for him to turn toward the camera. He didn't. I took a couple photos anyway as he half turned toward me.

Get what you can get when you can get it. Says so in the detective manual.

Kowalski was talking and pointing back toward the mall with the other two men. Needing to close the distance, I got out of the car and walked north along Grand Avenue. Keeping to the building's shadow, I found an outdoor stairway, which provided what I needed. I climbed 10 steps and sat down, focusing carefully on Kowalski as he moved away from me toward his Bronco. As he moved in and out of my shifting focusing plane, I snapped off a couple of shots as he stopped at his Bronco when the other two men departed.

To be ready for the instant I would need the camera, I focused the lens on the sharpness of his Bronco door handle. As he turned around to shout a final instruction to one of the men, the sun peeked from behind a cloud, shedding the scene in light. I caught three good shots of him before he turned and got into his Bronco.

I climbed slowly down the steps and disappeared behind a plumber's panel truck. Kowalski turned north and left.

Within a few seconds I pulled the Cutlass out of its parking space and headed after the Bronco, but it had already disappeared east on Michigan Avenue. I thought about driving over to where he was staying, but headed north anyway and went directly home.

I got there in 15 minutes and let Basil outside, then went directly to the basement darkroom and turned on the electric heater. In five minutes I had the light out and the Tri-X film loaded into the stainless steel developing tank. It was cold down there, but the heater and warm water flowing through the homemade sink warmed it up OK. Thirty minutes later I had the film drying in a makeshift film locker and was back upstairs petting Basil and making coffee.

I took the phone book out from under the phone near the kitchen, and as I did so the phone rang. It startled me, as such a coincidence would. I ignored it. It fell silent after five rings.

The yellow pages provided a nice list of the fast food places specializing in tacos. I tore out the two pages with the ads and stuffed them into my coat pocket. The coffee finished, I dug out an old thermos and filled it up.

The phone rang again. I answered it on the seventh ring.

"Caught you," Patty said.

"In the nick of time," I said. Whatever that means.

"Why didn't you answer it the first time?"

"If I had known it was you..."

"You are really a strange man when it comes to your relationship with the telephone," she said. "You have a flight physical in exactly 45 minutes. You want me to meet you there?"

"And hold my hand?"

"Or something."

"You needn't worry. I'll show up for it."

"Promise?"

"Promise."

"Your word's good enough for me," she said. "Where do you want to meet for dinner to celebrate your return to aviation?"

"How about some tacos?"

Two hours later Patty met me at the Taco Bell out-
let within a block of the doctor's office.

"So, are you a pilot now?"   She slid into a booth
and opened the first of two tacos.

"That's just the physical," I said. "The flight review comes later."

Patty took a bite out of her taco and gathered the
itinerate crumbs from her lips with a smooth sweep
of her tongue. She sipped her diet drink.

"How much did it cost?"

"Sixty-five bucks," I said.

"I'll reimburse you," she said.

"No," I said. "This was on Danny Goodman."

She ate more taco. So did I. I sipped my Pepsi.

She said, "It's not that I don't trust you, but is there
some proof that you actually had this physical?"

I dug into my wallet and produced the white copy
of the medical certificate. I handed it to her.

"Don't get taco sauce on it," I said.

She examined it, turning it over, reading the fine
print from the FAA. She gave it back and I put it
away.

"I take it you did not fall down when he made you
close your eyes," Patty said.

"I didn't cry when he thumped my knee with a
rubber hammer either."

"Tough guy."

"A regular Duke," I said, squirting taco sauce deeply
into my third taco.

We ate more tacos.

"There's a reason we're eating tacos," I said, and I
told her why.

"You going to run around town tonight winking at

taco girls asking if they ever saw Danny Goodman?"

I nodded, and pulled from an inside pocket a picture of Randall Kowalski still a bit damp from my efforts in the darkroom. I showed it to Patty.

"Randall Kowalski," I said.

"You think he likes tacos, too?"

"Well, the police are looking for Freddie Samuelson and checking the taco places to see if anyone knows Terri Krug or Danny Goodman. There's no point in duplicating efforts. I thought I'd try to see where Randall eats his tacos."

Patty returned the photo, and I checked it for taco smudges.

"I'm not coming with you," she said. "I have other things to do."

"Good. This is demanding and dangerous work, and only skilled professionals should be engaged in it."

"I'm still not coming along," she said.

I stood and leaned far across the booth's table and kissed her.

"I love you, too," she said. "But you'll be alone on this quest. Tomorrow, though, I would like you to drop by the airport first thing in the morning, about 8:30. You can add a certain dimension to the occasion, much like I added this morning at the used car lot. Put it on your calendar."

"Got things figured out?"

"Yup," Patty said, sipping her diet drink. "You ever heard of a sump drain on a gas truck?"

I thought about it. "No."

"Me neither," she said. "But you'll be an expert on it by 9:00 tomorrow morning."

* * *

It was snowing steadily when I began my search for Kowalski's favorite taco restaurant. To improve the odds, I marked off those which were within five blocks of downtown, and that narrowed it to four stores.

In all cases I asked to see the employees who were on duty at the counter during the two evenings in question, and in three of the stores I was lucky to find the same crew.

Nobody recognized Randall Kowalski. One girl thought he looked like a wrestler. One manager called the police, wondering if I should be asking questions like those. Someone at the other end probably thought I was one of the city's detective staff and asked him to provide all due cooperation to the detective working on a murder case.

The manager of the fourth store said that most of the crew that worked that night would actually be in later, around 9:00.

I adjourned to a booth near the front window and figured out which stores might be on major routes into Lansing and which might be on major routes toward Holt. It was a stupid notion. All fast food stores sit on major routes. On a hunch, I mapped out a route to Holt and back and decided to hit those first.

The clerk with a mouthful of braces at the second store recognized Kowalski quickly.

"A big man," she said. "Construction or something. Should I be telling you about him?"

"Does he come in alone?"

She thought about it and wrinkled her forehead. "I

don't remember," she said. "Wait here a minute, will you please?" She abandoned the counter and went into the back of the store where the ponderous secrets of the taco business are safeguarded. She returned with a young man with an "asst. mgr." sign on his shirt.

"Him," she said, pointing at me.

I was ready. I flashed my official looking certificate from the Michigan Secretary of State and dropped two more pictures on the counter, those of Danny Goodman and Terri Krug. Krug's picture was a gift of the police department.

"Seen either of those?" I pointed.

The boss and the clerk both studied the pictures.

"This woman," the clerk said. "She was with the other guy."

The boss looked at her and then at me. A group of people came in behind me and began figuring how many tacos they would buy. I got out my notebook in an official manner and pried my pen from an inner pocket.

"What is your name please?"

The clerk gave me her name, then dutifully added her address and telephone number.

"Could you come back here, officer?" the boss said, indicating how I could come around the counter and enter through the secret door next to the bathrooms. He directed another employee to take the counter and steered the clerk to the back too. I followed him into the stainless steel kitchen area to a very small desk squeezed into a small corner.

Before he could ask questions, I picked up his telephone and called the detective section. I left a message with the duty officer and urged him to get in touch with Maddox or Phillips.

The sergeant showed up within 10 minutes. I was learning from the clerk that Kowalski was in often enough to call him a regular.

"Who's this guy?" said Phillips, looking at Kowalski's picture.

I told him. "Clerk says he was here last week with Terri Krug," I said. "Same night she disappeared."

"Oh, really?" said Phillips, studying the photo, installing Kowalski in his memory. "He's the guy with the Bronco, right?"

I nodded.

"Family friend of the Slaters, the people who are building the mall."

I nodded again. Dutifully.

"You've been busy," he said.

"Just trying to earn the decoder ring."

* * *

I left Phillips interviewing the taco shop crew and asking police questions and drove out to Sandra Goodman's neighborhood. I parked under a tree about three homes from Sandra's house and shut off the Cutlass. It was obvious people were home. Lights shown from about every room and two cars sat in the driveway.

I waited and watched the snow fall. I didn't know what I was waiting for, but I waited quietly in the Cutlass under the tree while sipping coffee from the thermos cup. I had a curious feeling about Sandra

Goodman's last telephone call, and I couldn't identify that, either. It didn't sound like her, although it
didn't sound like someone else. She didn't sound under
stress or at gun point, but she didn't sound consistent. She had gone out of her way in a blizzard to
plop about $10,000 in seedy twenties and tens on the
desk of a private investigator to find out who killed
her father. A few days later she called the private
eye and said she had a change of heart.

Let bygones by bygones, she said.

Sure. I sipped my coffee. Sure we will.

About 45 minutes later I was working on my third
cup of coffee when Sandra Goodman came out of her
house and got into the small Datsun and backed into
the street. I fired up the Olds and followed my client.

She didn't go far. She went about one mile and
pulled into a grocery store parking lot and got out
and went inside and began shopping for groceries. I
parked some distance away, figuring I would hide
my car's identity as long as I could. Then I went inside.

Pushing my own cart, I began to do a little shopping of my own, staying an isle or two away from
Sandra Goodman. I went through the produce section after picking up some Granny Smith apples, a
green pepper, celery, and carrots. In the bakery department I tossed in two loaves of English muffin
bread and a loaf of whole wheat.

Sandra Goodman progressed past the peanut butter and was moving slowly past the deli.

I picked up a pound of bacon and then put it back.

Be nice when there was at least a hint of meat on the bacon. I reached for some country sausage instead. Maybe I would change my mind at the deli meat counter, if it was still manned this late at night.

Sandra Goodman disappeared into the next isle, but her cart indicated she very much needed this trip to the store. I went past the deli section and got a pint of fresh nacho cheese sauce and began to look for the nacho chips which had to be nearby. I skipped the bacon.

My client had loaded soft drinks and canned food by the next time she came around the end of an isle and I worked my way through the cereal gauntlet. I made it to the dairy section and grabbed a half a gallon of two percent milk, some cheese, and eggs.

Sandra Goodman and I met where all the margarine was piled.

"Hi, Sandra," I said.

"Oh," she said, genuinely surprised. "Stuart." She glanced into my cart and then into her own.

"Nice to see you," I said.

"Are you following me?"

I looked around innocently. "I'm not in the habit of following my clients," I said, avoiding an honest answer. "What would I learn if I did follow you?"

I put a pound of margarine into my cart and considered some butter, too.

"So, how are the preparations going for getting out of the private investigation business?" she said, trying to be indifferent about our meeting. She studied the margarine.

"I might not leave the business," I said. "But I do have to leave the office."

"I thought... Oh, well, I thought you were going to work for someone else," she said.

"I was," I said. "And I still might. But the thought of spending the rest of my life writing planning commission reports and research papers scares me."

We moved in unison down the isle.

"So, instead, I'm still on the job, investigating crime, trying to find out who killed your father," I said.

"Oh, God," Sandra Goodman said, stopping in the isle to face me. "Please stop investigating that. I've changed my mind. My father's remains have already been cremated, and there just doesn't seem to be any reason to go into it anymore."

"Has someone threatened you?"

"No," she said too quickly, looking away. "Why would you think such a thing?"

"Would you be in jeopardy if someone discovered us in this grocery store talking, talking almost in a conspiracy?"

"Oh, Stuart," she said, moving further down the isle, but looking around, confirming my fear. Not knowing what to do, not having planned on running into me. "Just drop it, please. Someone could get very hurt if you don't."

Sandra Goodman pushed her brimming grocery cart quickly down the isle, refrigerators filled with ice cream and frozen waffles to her right, shelves of potato chips and crackers to her left. It was a benign atmosphere, but just then it seemed rather threatening.

I let her go. Since I could only do her harm by following her, I lingered in the same department until I saw her hurriedly scramble through the check-out line and exit into the parking lot.

I finished my unscheduled but necessary grocery shopping, cleared through the checkout line, and drove home. I unpacked the groceries, started a fire, prepared coffee, and called Patty, who was getting ready to go to bed and reminded me of our meeting at the airport first thing in the morning.

"Sleep tight, my love," she said. "And don't be late tomorrow."

Once the fire began to push the chill from the house, I arranged my easy chair and lamp in front of the fire, poured a large mug of coffee, and opened the book Henry Bretton gave me at the airport. There were moments that reminded me why I remained single after all these years. I liked doing my own thing among my own possessions, not asking anyone's permission to fart or build a fire. I could operate on my own schedule, act resolutely and alone, and worry chiefly about myself. Still, I wondered about her furniture. I couldn't help but agree with Patty, though, that her furniture—designed for the newer, more formal structures now popular—would not fit in the old farm house. However, her easy chair had to be in far better shape.

CHAPTER 22

The sun was beginning to occasionally poke through the clouds as I pulled into Midway Aviation and found a parking spot next to a City of Lansing Department of Aviation car.

Patty pulled in before I could get to the building. Accompanying Patty was a good looking blond guy wearing a conservative sport coat and tie and looking pretty uncomfortable in it. He wore Ray Ban sunglasses and a beach-boy smile. I knew I didn't have to like him if I didn't want to, and that helped.

"Nice timing," Patty said. "This is my client, Jason Colby, and my friend the private eye, Stuart Mallory." She watched us shake hands.

"Good to meet you, sir," Colby said.

"A pleasure," I said, turning to Patty. "Give me some signals here so I won't stumble through this."

"We've figured out, based on delivery receipts and tank seals, that Midway was being shorted by the independent contractor delivering the fuel. They would bring it in here in big tanker trucks—"

"Five thousand gallons a load," Colby said.

"— Yeah, and dump it into the underground storage tanks. Before they did this, one of the local employees—frequently Jason here—would remove the little metal seal on the truck which would show that it had not been tampered with since it was shipped. Then it would be pumped into the ground and the trucks would leave."

"Why wasn't this discovered?" I said.

She shrugged. "It's not important here, actually,"

Patty said. "What's important is that Jason here didn't steal the gasoline, and I think we can prove that. Someone else did."

Jason was moving from one foot to the other stamping a small pile of snow into ice. He was not dressed to be standing outside in the waning moments of a blizzard, but he was handling it like a gentleman.

"Where's the sump pump fit in?" I said.

"Jason will show us both how it works in a minute," she said. "But it has to do with cleaning tanks on the trucks."

"Actually, removing the moisture from the truck tanks," Colby said. "We must make sure the gasoline we sell doesn't contain water."

"Let's go in," Patty said.

We followed her inside and went straight to the owner's office where he and Henry Bretton, the chief flight instructor we met over the weekend, were waiting for us. Patty introduced me to the owner, Charlie Doan. Bretton glared at us.

"I want it on record before we begin this little conversation, of course, that we did not fire Jason," Doan said. "In fact, we have been very pleased with his work here."

"You accused him of stealing gasoline," Patty said.

"Not really," Doan said. "I just said we were missing a lot of gasoline in his charge and I was beginning to wonder where it was."

"Where do you think I've been hiding it?" Colby said.

Patty touched him gently as a signal to let her do the talking.

"He doesn't have a market for several thousand gallons of gas, or a place to put it meanwhile," Patty said. "But that's not the point right now. We're here to show you where the gasoline has in fact gone, and we want to get Jason's job back."

"We can take care of the second part right now," said Doan, leaning back in his desk chair. "Jason, you're hired."

I helped Patty remove her coat and she opened her brief case and spread papers on Doan's desk, arranging them in a conspicuous fashion. Doan watched with vigilance.

"At first, Stuart Mallory and I figured the underground tanks were leaking," Patty said. "And they might be. We just don't know."

Doan shrugged.

"But that wouldn't necessarily explain the consistent loss of aviation fuel," Patty said, warming to the courtroom summary. "I've learned a great deal about this business during the past week, as you might guess, and I've learned, among other things, that you are willing to sustain some considerable losses in gasoline. You have to, since your line boys sump the trucks once or twice a day."

"We can't allow a massive loss of gasoline," Doan said. "Sure, a little sump waste is necessary, but not the amount we're talking about here."

"Are you sure? Based on the figures we've put together over the past few days, we could explain the loss in fuel simply in over zealous line boys sumping the line trucks."

Doan was shaking his head. "Not that much," he

said. "No way."

"Investigator Mallory and Mr. Colby can show you how that is done after we are finished in here," Patty said. "First, we'll show you where all the gasoline has gone. I think you'll be glad we stopped by. You might even be willing to pay Mr. Colby's legal expenses."

"I doubt it," Doan said. "It's an affront just to hear you say it."

Patty ignored him. She picked up a manila envelope and removed one thin strip of metal which looked like polished aluminum. She checked the date on it.

"Two years ago your supplier sent you 4,000 gallons of aviation fuel by tanker truck," Patty said. "The tank was sealed with this seal. You can see the date and the supplier's name and the amount of fuel stamped into the metal."

She handed it to Doan, who looked at it as though he knew what it was.

"Take a look at the seal and check its width and texture," she said. "Then take a look at the seal removed from the next delivery eight days later." Patty handed him another strip of metal about six inches long and he looked it over. "You can see the new one is a little wider and a little stronger. It has all the correct information on it, and for all practical purposes it is just like the first one."

She looked into her envelope again and removed a third metal strip.

"Here's the seal from the third delivery that month," she said. "Same as the second. And what's interesting about these two deliveries is that together they were 209 gallons short of what you ordered and paid for. Unlike the delivery from some tankers, which I understand are just poured into the ground using gravity, these trucks pumped it into your underground storage tanks. In fact, your records reflect meter readings recording the amounts, which your linemen dutifully kept in your records."

She pointed at his records.

"As you can see by comparing the metal seals with the amounts of these transactions, you did not get what you paid for."

Doan put on a pair of glasses and picked up the ledger in one hand and one of the metal strips in his other.

"Are you saying someone put these seals back on the tanks after stealing gasoline from them?" Doan said.

"No," Patty said. "Someone installed new seals using sealing equipment much like your supplier's sealing equipment, but not the same. I checked with your supplier late yesterday. They've been using the same piece of machinery to seal the tanks for the past six years."

Colby sat briefly in a chair, then stood again.

"Let me cut to the quick," Patty said. "We're all busy here. Your chief lineman and I have gone over your records thoroughly during the past 24 hours and we found that someone between the supplier and you has been routinely ripping you off at the rate of a minimum of 100 gallons a shipment. I think you can figure you lost at least the same amount on those loads just poured into the ground. I especially point to those loads since there would be no pump meter record."

Patty began to cover the front of Doan's desk with little strips of aluminum, lining them up by date from his left to his right.

"Once you compare the delivery ledger with the seals, you'll see that someone out there has systematically stolen almost 400 gallons a month from you during the past 22 months or so. At minimum, I figure that is a net loss of about $13,000."

Patty handed him a neatly typed piece of paper.

"Here's our estimate month by month, seal by seal," she said. "You can make your own comparisons, of course, but I think you'll come to agree that Jason Colby is not only innocent, but a loyal employee as well."

Doan accepted the new piece of paper with what might have been growing enthusiasm. It was the first time he looked up at Patty.

"My client regrets resigning his position," Patty said. "He wants to be reinstated with back pay, and he would appreciate reimbursement for his legal expenses." She handed Doan an envelope with the law firm's name on it.

The owner looked up and slid his chair back a little. The flight instructor walked to the window where he could more rapidly compare the figures from one sheet of paper with those on another.

"We might need a good lawyer here too," Doan said.

"You can hire me after we clear up Mr. Colby's business," Patty said. "But you must realize that when you stop and consider the evidence here, we're talking about something bigger than Midway Aviation. Whoever is ripping you off is most certainly ripping off many other clients of the same company. I'd suggest you let a competent investigator get a handle on the size of this theft ring, then turn the information over to your supplier and the FBI."

"The FBI?" Bretton said.

"Sure," Patty said. "It is an interstate theft of gasoline. That's a federal matter. But to give the investigation the proper time, you'd have to make sure none of this information left this room."

"The investigative plan is a simple one," I said. "We would hire a couple of men to follow the trucks from the supplier and find out where they are going. Once we had the pattern and knew where the trucks were stopping en route, we could put the paperwork together for the federal investigators. We'd make sure it was not shoved under the rug."

"And, you'd be in an excellent position to file for compensation of the lost fuel," Patty said. "You'd have a case against your supplier, although I suspect they would make good."

Doan stood up and stuck out his hand first to Patty and then to Jason Colby. He seemed pleased.

"We'll keep it all a secret," Doan said. "I assume Mr. Mallory here is the man to handle it."

"He's also a pilot," Patty said.

"Not quite yet," the chief flight instructor said from the window. "He needs a biennial flight review."

"I'm working on another case right now," I said. "I can recommend others locally."

"It has waited two years," Doan said, reading Patty's

legal services statement from the sealed envelope. "It can wait until you're ready."

"Fine," Patty said, sticking out her hand to Doan. "Do we have a deal?"

Doan looked at it. "I'll pay his legal expenses, but I won't pay him back pay. He quit, and he wasn't here working. But we'll call it a leave of absence or something."

They shook hands.

CHAPTER 23

From the airport I went down to the office. It's good to start a day right when you're a professional. I felt good about the events at the airport, and I felt it would bleed over into my own work.

I put the Olds in back and squeezed it between a broken down Ford LTD and the dentist's Audi. Two men stepped out of the Ford and came over to my car.

One held a large pistol in his right hand and held it steadily in my direction. "Keep your hands on the steering wheel where I can see them," he said. I did.

The other man slipped around behind my car to the passenger side and tried to open the door.

"Get out of the car," said the man with the gun.

The pistol was pointing fairly expertly at the back of my head, the best I could tell, and the hammer was cocked. I rejected the notion of challenging him.

I got out. He pushed me with his free hand so that I had to lean away from him and against the Olds. He'd done that more than once in his life.

"You carrying?"

"What do you think?" I said.

He began to pat me down through the thick coat and he found the pistol rather quickly. Getting it removed from the coat would be more difficult, even as the second man joined him.

"We're going for a ride," he told me. "You'll keep your coat on and zipped the entire trip. You make one move for the gun and I'll kill you. Understand?"

I nodded.

He pulled me from the Olds and shoved me toward the Ford's back door.

"Keep your hands in front of you," he said. "Together."

I did. The second man opened the door and shoved me inside. Then the man with the gun sat down beside me and closed the door behind him. The other man walked around and sat in the driver's seat.

"Where's the fucking keys?" said the driver. He had the sort of nose you don't forget easily. It looked as though at least two people had applied a heavy fist to it during his life.

"On the seat," said the man with the gun.

The man beside me was a bit younger than me and in much better shape. He had dark black hair cut close and peered at me through dark brown eyes. He needed a shave. He held the gun like someone who had held a few guns in his life. He wore a camouflaged hunting outfit and he would fit in perfectly in a pine grove or perhaps a jungle. The driver wore an insulated outfit much like Randall Kowalski's insulated work clothing. He seemed rather nervous about the arrangements.

The driver got the car started and backed out of the parking lot. We headed downtown, then west.

Then we drove north, past the airport and into another county. We even passed within a mile of my house. I would have enjoyed the ride were it not for the heavy flavor of finality to it. I occasionally glanced to my side to find the pistol pointed at my midsection. It never wavered.

Then we drove off the road onto a newly plowed side-road and went on for a half a mile or so. Then we stopped near the edge of a pine forest which expanded away from the road and up the gentle slope to the north. Kowalski's Bronco idled in front of us, and he sat in the front seat.

The man with the pistol cleared his throat. "I want you to reach carefully into your coat and remove your weapon. Come out with the barrel first and han' it to me gently."

"I'll have to unzip the jacket first," I said.

"Do it."

I unzipped the jacket and then reached inside and got the pistol and twisted it around so that I could remove it with the barrel. If the man with the gun intended to kill me, he would have already done it. My best chance of walking away from this woods today was to play along with him.

There was always the chance Kowalski would kill me instead.

"Now, get out of the car," he said.

I did. It was beginning to snow again, heavily, the kind of snow which falls thickly in big flakes and then disappears as quickly as it arrives. Randall Kowalski was outside waiting with a pistol of his own. He waited for the first man to come around the car and come up from behind me and prod me with the first pistol.

Kowalski pointed to a spot in the trees. After pushing me a little, they led me over the bank left by the recent plowing and we walked through deep snow about 50 yards to where the snow sucked up all sounds. No one from the road could see us, although it would be difficult to pass by without wondering why an aged LTD and a Bronco sat at the road's edge in this weather.

Once in the trees, the two men held me securely by the arms and Kowalski stepped around to face me. He had put his own pistol somewhere out of sight. As he looked at me, the snow fell on his face.

"You don't take a hint very well," Kowalski said.

"Perhaps I misunderstood it," I said.

Kowalski swung fast and put his right fist into my stomach. The air burst from my lungs, and I would have bent further if it were not for the two men holding me up. Kowalski had thick mitts on, not plain fists, but his punch was backed by a body not much smaller than the Bronco he drove to the woods. And he had moved very quickly.

Kowalski watched me and picked a moment he thought I was ready to listen. He had to wait a minute or so.

"We want you to find something else to do," he said finally, and almost with patience. "Leave the construction project alone. Leave the Slaters be. Stop messing in our business. Don't ask any more questions about Goodman or Samuelson. If we stumble over you again, we'll kill you."

Kowalski waited a few seconds for his words to sink in, then he hit me again. I vomited what little I ate for breakfast. Then he leaned back a half step and planted one in my face. I saw it coming and tried to move away from it with meager success. I remember only the sound from inside my head of bones straining against superior force as I pulled unsuccessfully against the two men holding me in place.

Then he hit me on the side of my head. Then again. My face felt like my elbows did when at a full run I fell on them on concrete. The agony went directly to the stomach, and then I lost consciousness.

When I awoke, I lay almost face down in the snow under a pine tree. My body held down one of the tree's branches. This was apparently where I fell or was tossed. I wondered if anything was broken or if I was dead. There was a little hope in the latter.

My right arm and hand responded to my request for movement and pushed along my side through the snow and came to rest near my face, shoving pine needles and a pile of snow into my eyes and against my cheek. I pushed away the snow, which was covered with blotches of blood. I didn't think it was someone else's blood.

I sent messages to my legs and feet requesting movement and was greeted with appropriate responses, although my feet felt very cold and almost numb. A few more minutes of napping among the pines in subzero temperatures and I would have an interesting case of frostbite to deal with, if I was lucky.

Concentrating on such possibilities, I curled upon myself and worked my way into a sitting position. I couldn't see the road from there, but if the two vehicles were there I would be able to see their roofs. I could see nothing on the road, although it was beginning to snow heavily again.

Leaning forward and getting a purchase on the ground beneath the snow in front of me, I worked my way onto my feet and slowly stood up. I swayed, but I stood. My head felt disconnected and barely in charge, but it was not in pain. That worried me. I worked my fist up to my face and examined it through the thick gloves. I could feel very little on my face, but I could feel something.

At my feet was my vomit, sitting at the bottom of

the arch it cut into the snow. I tried to find something good about it but couldn't. Looking at it, though, I found my pistol in the snow. I leaned over to pick it up and vomited again. It was pretty dry, considering.

I remembered wanting to be able to walk out of the woods, and I turned toward the road and managed to make one step after another toward the bank the snowplow had left. I fell once, face down, more the product of being unable to lift my foot fast enough to take the necessary step than a product of the damage done. On hands and knees, I plowed my way up and through the drift, then slid down the other side onto the road. I sat there at the edge holding a pistol by the barrel in my left hand and trying to catch my breath. I knew I had to get to a main road soon. The temperature would not tolerate much waiting.

That's when a Clinton County Sheriff's deputy cruiser pulled up and stopped opposite me. A deputy got out and pointed at the gun in my hand.

"Please drop that," he said.

I looked at it and commanded my hand to drop it, but the gun stayed right there in my hand. I looked at it curiously. The deputy must have understood something because he reached past my face and took it from me.

"Thanks," I said. I at least tried to say it. What came out sounded more like a drunk's exhale.

"Can you stand up?" he said, touching my shoulder.

"Sure," I said, and leaned over to put my hands out to squirm into a standing position. One arm slipped out from under me and I fell into the snowbank again.

CHAPTER 24

The deputy knew his duty. In spite of my advice to take me home, which I explained would not be a long drive, he drove me to Sparrow Hospital where an X-ray showed I had two cracked ribs on my left side, probably inflicted with a swift kick after I passed out. An intern put a few stitches on two or three cuts on my forehead, and she treated various cuts, bruises, and swellings. An X-ray indicated my nose wasn't broken, but it acted like it was broken. A nurse stuffed my nose with cotton twice, finally curbing the bleeding. I was examined for frostbite but determined to be OK. They wrapped my ribs tightly and told me to rest for a few days.

The medical staff assured me I would probably get well, unless the damage to the head was worse than they concluded. They were not encouraged when I explained that most of the damage was incurred after I blacked out. He only hit me four or five times that I remember, and I had a lot more marks than that.

When the hospital was ready to release me, Phillips joined the deputy.

"Does the other guy look as bad as you look?" he said.

"No," I said. "I didn't land a punch on any of them."

He nodded. "Maddox wants to see you in his office if this has anything to do with the Goodman thing," Phillips said.

"This is still a Clinton County case," the deputy said. "We need to make a decision about charges here."

The deputy was a tall, heavily-built black man named

Julius Calloway who had told me his appearance was not an accident. A retired man walking his dog in the country saw two men beating a third man at the edge of the forest. When he got home he called the sheriff's office which promised to go have a look. The deputy had to pick me up and stuff me into the cruiser's back seat, he said, before I froze to death trying to get to my feet.

"Stuart Mallory is a private investigator," Phillips said.

"I know that," Calloway said, rolling his eyes a little.

"He's workin' a case which involves some very important people in this town, and I suspect we'd like to confer on various charges before anyone files against anyone on this, no matter which county we're talkin' about. You go messin' around in this and it would screw things up royally."

Calloway was not pleased with Phillips' assessment of his investigative technique. "Who's the ranking officer in charge of this?"

"Maddox. Lieutenant Maddox."

"I'll check," Calloway said.

Phillips nodded.

The deputy nodded and walked over to the emergency room desk. The clerk handed him a telephone and he punched some buttons. He talked a little.

"Who was it?" Phillips said.

"Kowalski, and two buddies," I said.

He was looking at my face and was actually trying not to wince.

"A warning?"

"He said I didn't heed the first warning."

"Yeah, he probably means your car."

I nodded. "Either warning could have killed me."

The deputy came back.

"I have to file a report with all the details," he said. "Your prosecutor will talk to my prosecutor. Otherwise, we're cool."

Calloway handed me my pistol and showed me that it was empty. "That's the way you handed it to me," he said, pivoting and heading down the corridor.

Phillips nodded.

I bent over to get my coat and my guts coiled in reaction to the pain in my rib cage. I dropped the pistol into the jacket pocket.

"Drop me at my office," I told Phillips. "My car's there."

"Let's go to the office first," he said.

"You'll have to arrest me to get me to go to Maddox's office first," I said.

We walked down the long hall to the emergency room door, which automatically opened at our arrival. Phillips took my arm as we crossed some packed snow and guided me to his unmarked car and made sure I didn't fall getting into the passenger seat.

We drove downtown. He turned north on North Grand Avenue away from the downtown and the police headquarters. I would have looked over at Phillips for an explanation except that it hurt the skin on my face to turn my head in his direction. It hurt to turn in almost any direction.

Phillips swung up to the front door of the small office building and stopped.

"I expect you'll want to go up to your office first," he said.

I unlatched the door and it swung partly open, stopping as it imbedded itself in the pile of snow the plow provided.

"You want a little company?" he said.

I swung my legs out and got them firmly planted in the snow. Phillips turned off the engine and got out of his side. He came around to my side in time to see me stand up without help and try to swing the door shut. Phillips shut the door and reached out a hand to help steady my approach to the building.

I let Phillips take some of my weight, and we staggered inside. As we went through the front door a woman and young girl ventured out into the cold. They both looked at my face. The little girl rapidly turned away. We could hear them chattering about it as they moved up the sidewalk.

Inside we made our way up the steps. The legs didn't hurt, but it was exhausting nonetheless. I unlocked my office door and almost stumbled through my mail, which included at least two magazines. That accounted for the depth of it. The rest was easily explained by remembering that it was a beaten middle-aged private eye trying to step over it.

Phillips stood quietly and considered the piled cardboard boxes.

"I once thought about going into business for myself," he said. "Glad I didn't. This is pathetic."

With some effort, I removed my coat and eased myself into my client's chair. Phillips dialed the phone and waited for Maddox to come on the line. He waited quite a while. Finally he sat in my chair. I stood up and got four extra-strength Tylenol pills out of the small bottle next to the coffee pot and washed them down with a swallow of the weekend's coffee.

Phillips began telling Maddox what I'd told him. He even said I was in bad enough shape to go home and lick my wounds. He listened and hung up.

"Your car outside?"

"That's where it was a few hours ago," I said.

"Maddox wants me to look it over first," he said, holding out his hand presumably for the keys.

"I think the keys are still in it," I said.

Phillips walked out and down the hall. I opened one of the desk drawers and removed a box of .38 shells and loaded the pistol. It was harder work than it looked. The emergency room crew had rolled up my shoulder holster and stuffed it into a little plastic bag. They advised I not wear it for a few days, even if I did not take seriously their medical advice and go home and rest. Reaching for the holster, the therapist said, would cause unnecessary strain on the ribs.

So be it. I stuffed the pistol back into my coat pocket.

"It's outside warming up," Phillips said coming back into the office. "You want any help going back down the stairs?"

"Sure," I said. "Might as well complete the trip."

Phillips looked through the office one more time and this time noticed the city map with the red marks on it. He strolled to where he could look at it directly. He nodded toward it, which meant he wanted to know what it was.

"Those are the Stewart Meyers properties," I said.

"At least some of them."

"Jesus Christ," Phillips said. His finger traced two or three of them, confirming at least what I said about Freddie Samuelson's place on Michigan Avenue and the homes on Prospect.

I dropped the insurance materials into a large brown envelope and shuffled toward the door. Phillips followed. I locked the office up and we went down the hall and then slowly down the steps. Phillips guided me to the rear parking lot and watched me get into the Cutlass.

"I'll be OK," I said.

He nodded and disappeared around the front of the building. With some effort, I strapped the seatbelt on and backed out.

I headed downtown past the capitol building and then down by the river. I parked the Cutlass near the new mall and got out. There was a little effort involved. Kowalski's Bronco crouched in the far edge of the parking lot. I took a deep breath and walked down the sidewalk trying to stay in the path where I could keep a good firm hold on the concrete. I worked my way up the path to the trailer and went inside.

Staci looked up at me from her desk work.

"Oh?" she said, recoiling. "What happened?"

"Excuse me," I said and went past her cluttered desk and down the hall toward Leon Slater's office.

"Can I help you?" Staci was saying behind me. Then I heard her clicking the keys on her little telephone.

I got to Slater's office and it was shut. It was one of those modern, thin balsa hollow plywood doors and I thought briefly about kicking it off the hinges for the drama of it all, but as I turned to get into position my ribs told me not to be so damned dramatic about it. I couldn't kick much of anything.

I opened the door and went inside. Slater talked on the phone making notes on a large legal pad and looked up as I came across the small trailer office and grabbed the phone from his grasp. The phone intercom was buzzing repeatedly. I gave the phone a yank and pulled the wiring out of the cute little modern wall socket. The plastic connections went flying across the desk and spread across some papers.

"My God," Slater said, pushing his chair back and springing to his feet.

I slapped the phone down hard on the desk, which broke the glass on the desk. The glass shattered into hundreds of lovely pieces.

"What?" Slater said.

I came around the desk, cornering Slater between his desk and a filing cabinet. I grabbed a handful of his sweater and pulled him to me much like Batman did in his movie.

"Remember me, Slater? Remember? Take a careful look. If you send Kowalski and his friends to do this to me again, I'll kill them and then come back for you too."

"I don't know what you're talking about," Slater said. "Kowalski? He wouldn't—" Sweat already beaded on Slater's forehead, and he'd turned two shades lighter since I entered his office. He looked pretty frightened, hanging there in his sweater.

"Tell me you understand or I'll start pounding on your face," I said.

Slater was nodding enthusiastically but without much knowledge. "I really don't know why you're here about—"

I shoved him against the hall hard enough to knock the photo of the Mackinac Bridge off the wall. It went clattering into the growing pile of glass on the floor. Slater twisted so he could see the photo on the floor and he seemed as distressed about it as he did his own life.

I turned and circled the desk. My muscles and ribs were killing me. Then I heard Kowalski's voice back up the hallway. I reached into my jacket pocket and got out the pistol and cocked the hammer just in time to shove it into Kowalski's left ear as he came through the door.

"Just one excuse," I said. "Just one fucking excuse."

Kowalski backed away rapidly and smoothly as I pushed. He stepped through the broken glass on the floor and came to rest near the wall atop the bridge photo and stood next to the window. Kowalski watched me intensely, waiting for my first mistake.

"Randall?" Slater said. "What do you know about this?"

Kowalski shot Slater a side glance filled with hostility.

"Sit," I said to Kowalski. As expected, he just looked at me.

"You wouldn't," he said. "Not here."

I took the pistol out of his ear and fired one deafening shot at the plaster model of the Riverside Mall, hitting it in the largest building. At that range it was an easy shot. Like the pistol, the mall exploded, launching bits of plaster, plastic, and various tiny construction materials throughout the office. I put the pistol's barrel back in Kowalski's ear and it must have burned a little. I cocked the hammer.

The big man must have seen something in my eyes because he sat down in the glass. Slater sat down too.

"Big mistake," I told Randall Kowalski. "This was just another case. You made it personal."

"I'm calling the police," Staci said in the hallway.

Kowalski almost barked. "Don't."

"What?" Slater said.

Staci disappeared back toward the reception area and front door. I followed her and passed her as she was dialing 911 at her desk. I told her the detective section's number as I passed.

Kowalski erupted into motion close behind me, but I ignored him and rushed the front door, staggering down the steps outside. I succeeded in getting to the Cutlass and got in and fired it up. A small crowd of workmen had stopped their toils long enough to watch my exit and Kowalski's abbreviated departure from the office trailer. I recognized one of the workmen as the man who drove the car to the woods. His nose stood out.

Kowalski did not follow me to the car.

I drove away and had to stop for the light at Michigan Avenue.

Then I started laughing. It hurt like hell to laugh. My face ached and my ribs pushed tears into my eyes and my nose pumped pain into my head that I cannot describe.

But I laughed. At least it seemed like laughter.

CHAPTER 25

Maddox used Patty's key and opened my back door about four that afternoon and came in and looked around. He found me in my easy chair in front of the woodstove either asleep or in a drugged stupor. Patty came in then and did her own looking around, then they both left.

I learned all that later. But from the moment Maddox and Patty Bonicelli arrived, a conspicuous Lansing PD cruiser sat in my driveway just outside the back door, though my farm sits in Clinton County's jurisdiction, not Lansing PD's.

Patty awakened me about the time the sun went down. She waited until my eyes opened and I focused on her, and she didn't wince when she looked at my face. That was not her style.

"They beat you up pretty good," Patty said.

"I'm sorry," I said. "I should have called you and warned you not to come by tonight."

"Sorry, hell," she said. "You'll have to get better before we can honestly have a discussion about this, but you should have called me. I shouldn't have needed to find out from Maddox." She told me about his afternoon visit with her.

I shifted a little in the chair, enough to remember that I shouldn't shift a little in the chair. Patty was inches from my face when she leaned carefully down and kissed my forehead.

"This is the sort of thing that scares the living shit out of me," she said.

"Me too." I thought about not saying it, then said

it anyway. "I'm also scared for you."

"That's not necessary."

"Sure it is. We wouldn't have an honest relationship if I didn't tell you this could hurt you and that it concerns me."

Patty stood up and looked down at me with some apprehension, and perhaps some annoyance too.

"Let's argue about this after dinner," she said. "I'll bet you're hungry."

"I haven't eaten since breakfast," I said. "And I think I lost most of that."

"How?"

I told her.

"Jesus, Stuart," she said, heading for the kitchen.

I listened to the domestic sounds of utensils and tried to picture her furniture in the farm house. But I think Patty was right about the combination.

"You'll have to come to the table like an adult type person," Patty said. "I'm sorry about your wounds."

She was leaning over me, though, hand extended, ready to help me from the chair. I carefully retracted the extension for my feet and eased the chair into a regular sitting position. I knew the standing up part would be interesting. I had gotten stiff and ineffective from sleeping in the chair. I put out a hand and she helped me to my feet. The ribs ached and the muscles pulled, but we were both startled when the automatic hit the wooden floor with a loud, solid jolt. It had been sitting in my lap.

Patty started breathing again, then leaned down and picked up the automatic between two fingers by the barrel, just like women in the movies do. She handed it to me.

"Put this somewhere where I don't have to think about it," she said.

We sat down to a traditional Midwest dinner. She had fried a large round steak and baked several large potatoes in the oven. Steamed broccoli rested at the side. I ate like an animal until I pictured the scene, then I slowed down and just ate like a starved human being who was awakening from a severe beating. I told Patty about the taco shop discovery last night and about the beating in the morning. I also told her about my visit to the Stone headquarters following the trip to the hospital.

"Maddox told me."

"How'd he know?"

"Some sergeant went down there just after you did. I guess he walked in during their confusion about what to do about you. Maddox says they probably won't file charges."

I smiled. I'll bet they won't file charges.

"He's going to stop by this evening, by the way," Patty said. "Just to check in on you."

"I'll bet," I said.

"He brought me here. He wouldn't let me drive my car out here and leave it in the driveway where somebody could put a bomb in it or something."

We ate some more. I hollowed out my third and last baked potato and picked up the broccoli bowl. I casually presented it to Patty, who shook her head. I finished the broccoli. Sometimes there's no substitute for it.

"Feel better?"

"Yeah. I feel better," I said. "Thank you."

She patted me on my hand. It looked like the only safe place.

"You might want to sit in the tub for a while, too, with some Epsom salts."

"Later," I said. "Perhaps after Maddox leaves."

Maddox showed up fifteen minutes later. He looked more relaxed than he does normally. He wore only a sport jacket and a sweater under his overcoat, and it wasn't apparent that he'd shaved since he went home.

"I'm told that the secretary down at Stone's head-quarters—some dark-eyed honey in a skin-tight sweater—was almost in hysterics when Phillips walked in to talk to Randall Kowalski," Maddox said. "She isn't used to having scab-faced private eyes come in, pistol in hand, threatening her boss."

"What do they teach in business colleges nowadays," I said.

Maddox sat on the hearth by the woodstove.

"That was really foolish bravado," he said. "Going in there like John Wayne, ribs strapped in place, just to let them know you aren't going to be spooked."

"I had to do it," I said.

Patty shook her head and drank more of her rum and Coke. She was sitting on the corner of the couch watching us play tough cops.

"Yeah, I know," Maddox said. "You stay here for a day or two and let us clean this mess up now. We'll find this guy Randall Kowalski and get some evidence and put all these bastards behind bars."

"Where's Kowalski?"

"He's gone," Maddox said. "He wasn't there when

Phillips got there. He'd apparently followed you out of the building and never came back. He's not at his apartment, such as it is, and he's nowhere to be found. You stampeded the herd, looks like."

"Slater?"

"Called his attorney and they're not saying much," Maddox said. "We don't seem to have much on him right now, but we're asking a lot of questions."

"He's the boss." Or so it would seem.

"I think our best chance is finding Samuelson, or whatever his name is," Maddox said. "Then we'll have a witness to connect all of them."

"I think if you find him, you'll find Kowalski," I said. "But I suspect Samuelson's gone."

"We've got a van down the street from Kowalski's place, but we don't expect much," he said, standing up. "We have men out stirring things up here and there. Maybe we'll get lucky."

"There's something I haven't told you because I think it would be a violation of a trust," I said. "But you need to know."

"Spill it."

"Well, let me put it this way. It would seem that Goodman was hired to burn down the new mall."

Maddox stared at me. "I don't really think that's news at this point," he said. "Goodman. Fire. Arson. Stone. The mall. What else would he be doing there?"

"OK."

"So, how do you know this?"

"Can't say. Maybe I can soon."

"Maybe a subpoena would help."

"Now you're beginning to sound like Phillips."

He rebuttoned his coat and began to put on his gloves.

"Time to go," he said. "I'll look in on you tomorrow morning when I come for Patty. Meanwhile, the prosecutors have conferred and want you to file the charge against Kowalski in Clinton County. It would give us something to hold him on if we found him."

Patty followed him to the back door and locked the door behind him.

"Coffee?" she said.

"Yeah," I said. "Maybe the caffeine will cut the headache."

"I was thinking of decaf so you can sleep."

"I've been sleeping," I said. "Anyway, caffeine won't keep me awake. Not tonight. Not with the pills I'm taking for the pain. Make it leaded, please. My head demands it."

Within a couple of minutes I heard the coffee pouring through. Patty came in with a plate of cookies and some napkins and set them out of my reach. She disappeared into the kitchen again.

Then she came out with two cups of coffee.

"If you're going to be awake, so am I," she said. "I brought plenty to do anyway."

She patted a pile of papers and books. I worked to ease the chair back into a normal sitting position and took the coffee and sipped it. It seemed to immediately make me feel better. People who don't drink coffee don't understand its effect. Sure, it might be all in our heads, but there's no harm in that. Besides, chemists agree it's not all in our heads.

"I need to talk about this case," I said.

"Fire away."

"First, I need a cookie or two to clear my head," I said.

She handed me the plate of cookies. They were from the bakery in our favorite grocery store and they were loaded with chocolate chips.

"I'm treating you to cookies because I want to hug you and love you and say, Jesus I'm sorry they beat you up, but I'm afraid to hold you, Stuart," Patty said. "You look pretty breakable right now, and god knows I don't want to hurt you."

Patty looked like she wanted to cry. She looked worse than I felt. She held my hand in her two hands and knelt in front of me. She was studying my face and my head. Carefully.

"They beat you up pretty good," she said.

"Yes, they did," I said.

"Does it hurt a lot?"

"Not as much as it looks like it should," I said.

"Maddox says you're lucky," she said. "The damage could have been a lot worse."

"I think they meant to hurt me worse," I said. "I think Kowalski wanted me hurt badly enough that I would be unlikely to crawl from the woods, and if I did crawl from the woods, that I wouldn't be able to pursue the investigation and I wouldn't want to. He had that look."

"Maybe you're too hard-headed or something."

"I'm just lucky."

She got up and sat near me on the couch. "So, my man Colby showed you the sump pump this morning. Tell me about it."

"Yeah, he did," I said, sending my memory back

to the morning's gathering at the airport. Seemed like two or three days ago. "Well, as you know, they get their gas from the underground tanks out there. They pump it into the trucks so they can drive around to the planes themselves and pump the fuel into the planes, rather than have the planes come to the pump."

"Sure," she said, almost weary of my oration.

"Well, every time they pump gas into the trucks, and every night when they fill each truck, they drain a gallon or two right out of the tank, at the lowest point, in order to try to remove the moisture from the tank."

"The moisture from the ground," she said.

"Sure, but more than that. As you know, the air contains moisture, and when the temperature drops, the moisture condenses and falls out of the air. We call it dew when it falls on our grass."

She nodded. Still weary.

"When the 500-gallon tanks on the truck are almost empty and the temperature drops, you get a lot of moisture," I said. "Then you go and load maybe 400 gallons into the truck from the underground tank and have to sump the moisture out. Colby showed me that you can sump anywhere from a half a gallon to five gallons. Whatever you have to sump in order to get a clean sample."

"They pour the gasoline there on the ground?"

"No," I said, warming to the lecture. "The EPA would have a fit. They pour the sample into barrels and someone eventually comes and takes the barrels. The point is that you could sump one bad gallon, get a clean tank, and then sump yourself four or five good gallons and dump them into a separate barrel for your own use."

Patty was watching the fire and thinking.

"Earth to Patty," I said.

"Do you think Colby is actually stealing gasoline, doing like you suggested?"

"No," I said, pretty certain of my answer. "He showed me how it could be done, but it would be pretty difficult and messy to accomplish. Too easy to get the barrels confused, besides."

"Good."

"By the way, Patty, you were magnificent this morning," I said, and I meant it. "I was proud of you. You managed a difficult jury like a pro."

"Thank you," Patty said, smiling. "I got paid, too."

"But you must share it with the firm," I said.

"Of course," she said. "The firm pays my phone bill, your FAX bill, and it provides a desk. And I'm proud of you, too."

"I didn't do much for you this morning," I said. "You didn't leave much for me to do."

"I was talking about later, in the woods," Patty said. "And at Slater's office later."

"Thank you."

"Stuart, I don't want to encourage that sort of macho bullshit," Patty said. "But you hire yourself out as the last chance for justice, and unlike so many, you follow through on the promise."

I smiled. "That's a sentimental way to say it."

"Sure it is," she said. "Just you make sure I don't have to put it on your headstone."

CHAPTER 26

About 5:00 in the morning a passing motorist saw what appeared to be smoke coming from under the eaves of one of the structures of the new Riverside Mall. At first he thought it was steam rising from the Grand River flowing behind the mall. But it smelled like smoke, so he called 911 and got the Lansing Fire Department down there. The building burst into flames before the department could get five pumpers and two ladder trucks in place, and the buildings burned into the early morning traffic, which slowed as drivers gazed at the downtown commercial dream turning to ashes, the thick, black smoke rising into the December daybreak gray. The traffic, in turn, sparked at least three auto accidents, sending a young woman to Sparrow Hospital where surgeons were trying to put her face back together.

I learned most of this from Maddox, who arrived promptly at 7:00 to get Patty and who said he soon would be hot on the trail of whoever torched the mall. I suggested that Danny Goodman was innocent. He told me to find a sense of humor.

An hour later I was learning more details from an occasional live report from local television when *State Journal* reporter Tony Sayre called to tell me about the fire.

"We can easily see the fire from here," he said. "In fact, there are about 10 people lined up at the windows in the newsroom here, avoiding their work."

"I thought fires were the work of reporters."

"Reporters yes, not editors," he said. "The copy desk

is lined up at the window. That's about as close as those introverts wanna get to real news."

"Is that why you called? To tell me about the copy desk?"

"No, I'm putting together a story down here," Sayre said. "I don't know if they'll run it, but I'll write it and see what happens."

"What have you got that's new?"

"I don't have much that's new, but this morning's fire puts everything else in a new light," he said. "Suddenly everything that Goodman told me is more important. After all, Goodman told me they hired him to burn the building down in the first place, and I have it in my notes."

"Who hired him?"

"The owner, I guess," he said. "Well, let me find it in my notes here. Goodman died under questionable circumstances, and then there's the murder of the woman next door. Then there's the disappearance of the other guy who was living in that building."

"Are you going to quote me on that? We agreed that you wouldn't."

"No, but I'll get somebody at the cop shop to confirm that story," he said. "Not to worry. Let me see here, I have the notes ... let's see, no, Goodman never said who hired him."

"Too bad," I said. "It would be handy to know. Certainly you asked him that question."

"I can remember asking, but I don't remember Goodman answering," he said. "And my notes certainly don't indicate he answered. I assume the owners hired him, and I suspect you do, too. Who else?"

"I don't know, but certainly he has to say who hired

him or it is useless," I said. "Don't you remember anything he said on that subject?"

I could hear Sayre going through his notes. "You knew him. You can guess what he was like. He comes in here all fired up, in a way, to tell me something we need to know. He wants to be brave about it, to tell me, to brag about his knowledge, and he tells about the fire, but once he hears it come out of his mouth, he hopes to god he won't get found out. He wants us to know there'll be a fire, but he's reluctant to say how he got into it. I listen, try not to take many notes because it scares him, and then he gets frightened and leaves."

"Too bad," I said. "I would love to know what Goodman would have said about that. There are a lot of Indians in this, and the chief could have been any one of four or five of them. I'm not a journalist, and I know nothing about the news business, but I would hold the story a little while, especially if that's all I had."

"I've got to run with it," the reporter said. "This is the sort of thing they hired me for. Besides, the damned thing's burning down right now."

"If you wait, you can get the answers to some of those questions," I said. "Besides, if you run what you do know, you'll just give your competition a chance to beat you to the real story."

"Mallory, this is really the only newspaper in Lansing. We have what we quietly refer to as a monopoly."

"There's TV," I said. "And maybe the *Detroit Free Press* or *Detroit News* will send someone over. The burning of a downtown Lansing mall ought to be news, even in Detroit."

"That's just my point. I have to beat those papers

to the punch. And I don't worry about television as competition on an enterprise story."

"Enterprise? What's that?"

"A story you do all your own work on from the idea through the final story, more or less. TV doesn't do much of that."

"Well, Detroit reporters or no, whoever, they won't have much to work with if you don't give them a starting point," I said.

Sayre was silent for a few seconds.

"Well, I've got to see what I can get from the cops anyway," he said. "I promise nothing, but if I don't get much more information, I might hold it. Do you get something out of it if I hold it?"

"Nothing," I said. "But you might scare away some people who would become harder to find."

"That's the traditional cop shop argument for keeping something out of the paper," he said. "I've heard it before."

"Maybe it was true then, too."

"It's always true, but there are other considerations, and other arguments, such as the public's right to know. The public also has a need to know what kind of assholes represent the immediate threats. But, I'll do some callin' and we'll see."

"Let me know," I said.

"I'll give you a call. You'll be in your office later, right?"

"Not today," I said. "I've come down with something and I'm staying home."

"Just as well," he said. "It's colder than hell outside."

"I know."

"I'll call you at home then."

He hung up. I didn't believe him about what he had, but I knew that I've held my cards close at times too. Maybe he had a blockbuster story waiting for page one. Maybe not.

Before Sayre's call I had been considering climbing into the tub and letting hot water absorb my pain. Patty urged me to do it, knowing I preferred showers to baths. But now I had to string the telephone line from the bedroom to the bathroom so I wouldn't miss any calls, and it wasn't an easy thing to do for someone who couldn't bend over without fighting a sweaty urge to scream or cry. But finally I got the line to the bathroom and got the tub filled and Epsom salts into the water and the straps off my ribs and eased myself into the water. I soaked two wash cloths and draped them over my head, occasionally pouring water over the wounds on my face and head.

It felt good to do that. My body needed it and deserved a little pampering. It would do little for my psyche, though. Less than a month ago I had decided to leave the private detective business, following a job offer from the county planning commission. I had lived through a two-week stint of having no client and had become an expert solitaire player. I owed money in several places and the refrigerator was frequently empty. The office building's new owner, inspired by the canons of urban renewal, terminated my lease and offered to help me move if I left two months early. He wanted to modernize the building and fill it with medical clients.

I agreed to move early.

Then a blizzard pressed Sandra Goodman into my office and I became able to satisfy most creditors. An insurance company offered a fat reward and sent a respectable retainer. I found myself unpacking a box.

But Randall Kowalski liked the first plan. He wanted me out of the business. He made sure I would spend this day carefully sitting in my tub pulling cotton wadding out of my nose, sponging a bloodied face and scalp, and hoping to God nobody would beat me up like this again.

The bastard had left me humbled, wounded, and a little afraid, and no amount of silly bravado at the Stone office had changed how my guts felt about that.

*   *   *

Basil began to annoy me about an hour later because he hadn't been fed properly in about a day. His disappointment in the person he'd appointed for this task showed thoroughly. Besides, the water was getting cold. I crawled from the tub, toweled, and reinstalled the rib press and got dressed. Downstairs again I poured out the old coffee and made new, this pot one of full strength, and picked up yesterday's *State Journal* and turned to the classified ads.

It was time to get my life in order. Some people go to a shrink. Others divorce their mates. Some point their cars at distant points and watch the miles roll by. And there are times we just clean our houses in order to reimpose ourselves on our existence.

If Stuart Mallory Investigations was to continue in business, it needed a new home.

I circled the prospective locations and began to call. Within 30 minutes I had two good prospects, one only two blocks from my present location. Both agreed to let me examine the offices before noon.

I called Sayre, but he wasn't there. I left no message. I called Patty and she wasn't there, but I left a message. I called Maddox and he was there, but was in a meeting. No one asked me if I wanted to leave a message.

It was very difficult for me to reach down and put on my tall leather boots, but I did. I always felt a little like Paladin when I put them on, but then that was part of the benefit of wearing them. I strapped the .38 into an old waist holster and got my checkbook. I took four generic ibuprofen tablets and shoved the bottle into my jacket pocket.

Ready.

It took about 15 minutes to drive to the first location, the one further from my office. It sat on the ground floor and from what remained on the front window you could see that at one time it had been a tire store, a wig shop, and a "this-n-that mart." Some of these and those remained in boxes in the rear. The bathroom in the rear still had running water, but it had been a decade or two since it had maintenance. Both faucets dripped continually and the toilet listed to the west.

It wasn't for me.

On a leg of Grand River Avenue no longer accustomed to heavy traffic sat a two-story brick office building housing a real estate lawyer, a coin dealer, and two empty offices. Owner Jack Vanderveer took one look at my face and reconsidered. I could tell.

"My lord," he said. "What happened to you?"

I told him, more or less. I also told him how it came that I was looking for an office.

"My face is not as repulsive as it was yesterday," I said. "I look pretty good today."

"My lord," he said.

"If I take the upstairs office, then when someone comes in and shoots me, the stray bullets won't harm your other clients or passers-by," I said.

Vanderveer looked a bit aghast.

"I'm just kidding," I said. "It was a joke."

Vanderveer led me upstairs and showed me the office with two windows, one overlooking Grand River Avenue and the other the roof of the closed bakery next door. There was no sink, but the bathroom was clean and just outside the door. The walls were painted a flat gray with a touch of blue and the rent included heat and utilities. It was an honest looking office and I told him I would sign a year's lease if he knocked $50 off the monthly rent. He said he needed the extra for the improvements.

I offered to install a modern burglar alarm system on all windows and doors if he forgot the first four months rent. He said it was worth three months rent, perhaps, if I did it within 30 days.

It was Christmas Eve, he said, and he'd even give me the rest of December gratis.

His office was three blocks away and we signed the agreement within an hour. Using his phone, I got the current landlord to agree to have a subcontractor haul my stuff to the new location by 5:00, then I went through the stupid song-and-dance routine with Ma Bell to get the phone service moved before year's end. They'll never learn how to be something other than a monopoly.

I called Patty to announce my new address and left a second message.

Back at my old office I put everything back into the boxes. Downstairs the dentist's drill whirred away in someone's head while I sat with my feet up watching the sun fall on the snow outside. I felt better about things and about myself. I also felt hungry.

That's when the workmen arrived to move my office. Within an hour I was sitting at the same desk looking south on Grand River Avenue and putting away a Wendy's double with fries. It didn't look like enough food to satisfy my hunger even when I bought it. That's why I bought a half dozen donuts to go.

CHAPTER 27

As I finished the second donut, the telephone company called.

"I just noticed the paperwork is actually dated today, Mr. Mallory," the clerk said. "So I thought it best to call and confirm line ownership first, if possible."

"I'm here," I said. "And amazed."

"I think someone got the paperwork downstairs faster than expected," she said. "Probably because of Christmas."

"Probably."

"This was a dead line, and all we had to do was activate it," she said as she made computer noises at the other end. "I'll just amend the original order's start date, and we're in business."

"Just in time for my Christmas shopping by mail," I said.

She made more computer noises.

"Most of us are going home in a few minutes," she said. "You should knock off early, too."

"I should," I said.

"Merry Christmas," she said.

"Merry Christmas," I echoed, trying to put some feeling into it. I was always a late starter at Christmas, and this season seemed particularly slow.

When the clerk was gone, I called Patty again.

"What the hell does this note mean?" she said.

"Just what it says, probably," I said.

"You've moved?"

"Yup."

"Why aren't you home?"

"I got bored, and well, I got to feeling sorry for myself and needed to do something."

She shuffled paperwork at the other end.

"Sorry for yourself, eh," she said. "Where are you now?"

"My new office." I told her about the fast telephone service.

"Amazing."

"That's what I said."

"Well, I just got off the phone with my mother," she said. "I just told her I'd be spending Christmas here instead of there. I lied. I told her I was sick, although actually I figured I was going to stay and take care of my honey."

"I'm fit enough," I said. "But the last part's still true."

"Fit enough to drive to Birmingham and deal with my parents?"

"If they can look at me, then everything should be OK," I said.

"There's that," she said. "Perhaps we should spend Christmas Eve in front of the soapstone, and then drive over there tomorrow and have the big dinner."

"Probably a better decision. Maybe I'll heal by then."

"Sure," she said. "How long's your lease for?"

"Six months, renewable thereafter for six-month lumps."

"Does this mean, Mallory, that you're going to continue to be a private investigator?"

"I guess."

"What about the planning commission?"

"I don't know," I said. "I haven't thought all this through yet. Say, are you wrapping things up down there or what?"

"Well, not really, but I can quit anytime, I guess.

You have to remember, I have a full-time job here."

"You being critical?"

"Not really," Patty said. "I just thought you were safe at home, healing, perhaps entering a safer profession."

I didn't know what to say to that, so I said nothing.

"Let me call you back in a minute or two," she said. "You have the same number, right?"

"That's what they told me."

I strolled around my new office a little, looking, then unpacked all my books and put them into the built-in bookcase on the window facing the roof next door. I restocked the desk and put my banker's desk lamp where I liked it, adjusted the modern thin style venetian blinds, and sat down again.

Then I pulled an adjustable wrench from my office tool kit and started hanging up the various things for my walls. I used the wrench as my hammer because I couldn't find my real hammer. The phone rang when I'd hung my license on the west wall. Patty told me she'd be over in an hour to see my new office and provide decorating advice.

I hurried a little. I drove to the branch post office and had my mail transferred, picked up a bottle of champagne and a box of trendy wheat crackers at the liquor store, and bought a small table cloth from the soon-to-be-out-of-business-dime store on Grand River Avenue, then dashed to the office. There I half filled the coffee pot and fired it up. I took my empty cardboard boxes down to the dumpster to the building's side and then waited at my desk with the champagne sitting outside on the window ledge and mistletoe over the door.

* * *

Patty came through the door saying, "Woooo, what digs," and appraising my new office. She was right on time. I took her coat and hung it on my corner coat rack post.

"Not bad," she said. "Actually, it's a noticeable improvement over your previous office, unless you consider the ambience of your profession, at least that presented by Hollywood."

"Yeah," I said. "I did lose the bay window and the outer office."

"But you gained clean carpet, decent heat, and a better address. There's hope for you."

I told her about the arrangements will help keep my rent low at least for a while. "And he owns some other properties I can probably provide security equipment for too."

"You can do that?"

"Sure," I said. "I'm a security analyst. Haven't you read my yellow pages ad?"

"You don't have a yellow pages ad."

"No? Why those creeps. That explains my business failure."

"Stuart, there's a bottle of something outside the window here," Patty said.

"Didn't take you long. A real crackerjack snoop, you are. Trained by the very best," I said. I opened the window and removed the champagne from the make-shift chiller. I examined the bottle's temperature. "Just right."

Patty found the crackers and the dime store tray they were in.

"This is sort of sweet," she said. "Champagne and crackers."

"And a tour of the facilities for all invited guests," I said, then indicated the mistletoe. "And me, of course, too."

Using my thumbs, I popped the bottle's top and it flew appropriately across the desk and smacked into the window. Patty watched it go and munched a wheat cracker. I filled two plastic glasses and gave one to her.

"So, did you drive down and see the fire scene yet?"

"No," I said. "I didn't want to see it. It would remind me what a failure I've been on this case."

"Failure?"

"Sure. I should have been able to prevent that. We knew all along—or most of the time anyway—that Goodman was hired to burn down the mall. If he wouldn't do it, then someone else would do it."

"God, Stuart, take a look in the mirror. Look at your face. I think you gave it the college try."

"It wasn't good enough," I said.

She thought about it as she strolled through my new office, looking at my few belongings. "I don't want to hear this bullshit," she said. "You don't have the power of arrest. You aren't permitted to investigate murders. You can't guard a building the size of that mall. You expect too much of yourself."

I shrugged.

"And besides, this is Christmas Eve, and I don't want to talk business anymore."

"Fair enough," I said. "But you asked about the fire."

"I did," Patty said, moving toward the center of the room. "And I won't again. Get your butt over here and make me forget what I need to forget."

First I refilled her champagne glass and made her sip from it after linking arms with me. Silly, but honest. Then I took her into my arms and delivered Stuart Mallory's best, considering the cracks in his ribs and the lacerations on his face. I could tell it was working. She was forgetting even as I eased up to take a breath.

Then I unbuttoned her business suit and began to work on the buttons of her blouse.

"Somebody ought to shut the door," she said.

I completed work on the buttons and began to kiss her shoulders and the tops of her breasts.

"The door, Mallory," Patty said.

"It's the risk that makes it seductive," I said through her lips.

She was kissing me aggressively enough that it would be difficult for her to respond. Besides, she was working on my belt, getting into the holiday spirit.

"This won't hurt you, will it?" she managed to say.

I shook my head. I had my hands under her skirt working the pantyhose toward her knees.

In a few seconds we were on the floor, squirming, panting, kissing, and initiating the carpet to the more stimulating activities of its new tenant. Anticipating what this would do for my ribs, Patty got on top where she also could keep an eye on the door.

"God damn you, Mallory," she said. "If anyone sees us."

No one did that I know of, but it would have been something to see.

CHAPTER 28

We went to Birmingham for Christmas and Patty's parents didn't seem to be amused by my face and rib protector. In fact, her mother seemed concerned for my safety, and indirectly for Patty's safety, and wondered perhaps if I should go into "industrial plant security" or "police work" instead. I smiled and bantered and chattered and kept the wisecracks to myself. Everyone was behaving especially nice, so no one mentioned my face. It would have been easier if everyone had pointed at me and staggered back in horror. Patty enjoyed the drama, or said she did. The Christmas turkey dinner was delicious, except for the oyster dressing. About 9 that night, with family waving in the window and urging us to drive carefully, Patty and I piled into the car and headed back to Lansing, about an 80-mile trip. Patty reclined the seat to "rest her eyes" and fell asleep before reaching I-96.

We stopped at her apartment where we had coffee and a turkey sandwich from the Christmas day dinner. I drove out to the farm and got there around midnight and went directly to sleep.

I awoke just after sunrise feeling out of place and lost, but much of the soreness had abandoned my body during the night. More blood seemed to pour through my arteries, and did so at a better pace. The need for ibuprofen did not come immediately to mind, although caffeine did. The ibuprofen desire followed shortly.

I stopped at Denny's on the way to the office and had a Denver omelet and an extra order of toast and read the *Detroit Free Press.* Other than the weather, there seemed to be damned little going on in the world that was unusual, although the Lansing mall fire did make the outstate news page with a full picture and comments from the mayor and the governor.

Neither seemed pleased.

At the office I started a full pot of coffee and checked my messages. I had two from the insurance company. Maddox left a third message saying he was just checking in to see if I was still alive.

I left a message for Maddox, who was in a meeting with his detectives, and called Melody.

"It appears that while we were watching the barn, lightning struck the house," she said. "I've got two appraisers up there right now."

"Tell them to look carefully at the bottom of the rubble," I said. "Some of the construction materials that are supposed to be in the building were probably carted away before the fire."

"You know something?"

I told her what Sayre said that Goodman said. While I was at it, I told her about my trip to the woods and the fact that Maddox says the principals seem to have scattered here and there since the fire. I also told her about moving the office to Grand River Avenue.

"It'll all be in my written report," I said.

"The cops are right," Melody said. "File the charge, and for God's sake, nail some of this down. You're on a retainer, you know."

"I've been busy," I said. "I forgot."

"And, Stuart, be careful."

"I will, but remember, you're paying me to take

the risk so that no one there has to take the risk."

"Probably."

"And we'll get 'em," I said. "I promise."

"I hope so," Melody said. "We'll take a major loss on all this if we don't."

I called the Clinton County Sheriff's office and offered to file an official complaint. The deputy said he would get in touch with Calloway and have him hunt me down. He came on duty in mid-afternoon.

I filled my thermos and called Patty.

"I'm sitting right here at my desk staring at The Place on the carpet where we inaugurated my new office," I said.

"I have someone here, so can I call you back?"

"Sure, but I'm going to slip out of here in a few minutes and go see Stewart Meyers," I said.

"Oooo," she said. "He has a heavy hitter attorney."

"He might need one soon, too."

"You have an appointment?"

"No. I figure he'll see me, though."

"Good luck," she said. "Call me."

I wasn't sure what to expect by visiting Stewart Meyers, but there didn't seem to be much to lose by such a visit, either. They'd already beat me up.

Meyers' office was downtown in the same building the Michigan Chamber of Commerce called home, and that was probably no accident. Kindred spirits. It was clustered among the massive structures housing the bureaucrats that run the State of Michigan by making most of us fill out forms and then storing them somewhere no one could find them without providing a two-day notice and paying an annoying copying fee.

I parked in the snow next to a frozen parking meter and walked one block past the Lansing Civic Center to Meyers' office, taking the elevator to the fourth floor. I stood before the receptionist with coat in hand. She smiled, trying not to wince at my bruised and healing face, and said, "How may we help you?"

"You can help me find a competent, trustworthy governor," I said. "The search will be a tough one, unless we agree to exclude all the politicians."

"Pardon me?"

I sighed a little. "You can also help me by letting me speak with Stewart Meyers," I said.

"Do you have an appointment?"

"No," I said, showing my disappointment. "I'm here representing the insurance company for the Riverside Mall. We need to talk." I gave her my card.

"Please take a seat," she said, reaching for the telephone. She was tall and dark haired and scrubbed clean and obviously spent very little time in the sun. Ever.

I sorted through the medical waiting room type magazines and found the *Wall Street Journal*, then settled into an imitation leather chair facing the receptionist. I was reading about the rising value of gold coins when the receptionist gained my attention.

"Mr. Meyers is seeing someone right now, but he says he can give you a couple of minutes as soon as he leaves."

I nodded and said, "That would be nice."

Other front page *Journal* stories covered the price of crude oil, the dreadful effects of peace on the military-charged economy on the East Coast, and a near recession in the publishing industry.

"Mr. Meyers will see you now," she said, pointing at the door.

I put my coat over my arm and went inside. Two walls were paneled in deep mahogany, and Meyers sat behind a mahogany desk. He stood as I came in. Another man, probably an attorney, sat at the edge and rose more slowly. He was dressed in a dark blue wool suit and if he carried a lead pipe or an assault rifle, he hid it well. He kept his eye on me, though.

"Mr. Mallory, this is Paul Holland," Meyers said, shaking my hand. "He's a lawyer, and I've asked him to sit in on this discussion."

I took Holland's hand and looked at him.

"Are you a heavy hitter?"

"You'll have to pardon me," Holland said. "I don't understand."

"I was told that Meyers was represented by a heavy hitter," I said. "So, are you a heavy hitter?"

He smiled, and part of it was honest. His recovery was complete.

"I'd like to think so," said the lawyer, "although I'm not sure I've ever been described as a heavy hitter. Do you think the situation calls for one?"

I put my coat across the back of one of the two visitor chairs and sat in the other.

"Yes, it does, and you know it, or you are not the heavy hitter they claim you are," I said.

"If you're going to be contemptuous, we can bring this discussion to a close right now," Meyers said, sitting down and putting some considerable distance between himself and the desk. Sitting conspicuously

on the desk's corner stood a photo of Meyers and
the governor shaking hands and smiling into the camera.

"You're right, I'm contemptuous," I said. "Take a
look at my face and you'll see that I'm entitled to be
insolent."

"All right, I'll bite," Holland said. "What happened
to you?"

I told him.

"What makes you think that this violence—which
most certainly is common among peepers like you—
has something to do with my client?" Holland said.

"Gee, your client could tell us real clearly," I said,
turning the room's attention to Meyers for a moment.

Meyers shrugged and looked at me and then at his
lawyer.

"Do we have any other item of business?" Holland
said.

"It's up to you, I guess," I said, addressing Holland as though Meyers was barely in the room. "I
came here to have a chat with Mr. Meyers—not you—
because I believed that we could all save some time
and probably a little of his money. Silly me. We can
get all this out on the table and I can be on my way,
or I can continue to dig around and get beat up now
and then and finally, perhaps in a few days, we can
go east a few blocks and talk with the police and the
arson investigators and probably the press. I cannot
calculate the damage to Meyers' reputation and credibility,
which must be the foundation of his business. But if
you prefer that route, Mr. Holland, that's fine. But
it's damned inept legal advice. You must be a corpo-
rate attorney, Mr. Holland, because a criminal lawyer is smarter than that."

"That's just extortion," Holland said, almost shouting. "And insolent to boot."

"No, that's conjecture, inference, speculation. A guess, and a good one. There's considerable evidence that Stone and its backers hired two arsonists to burn down the mall because it was in financial trouble. There's growing evidence that one of them was murdered. It is painfully clear that the fire in your property on Prospect was arson, and the men who beat me up work for Stone, too. The police are now typing up subpoenas to get financial records—they might even come see you very soon—to begin to put all of this into one pile.

"I can tell you one thing for sure," I said. "Your insurance company won't give you a dime on the Prospect property, where the two arsonists lived and one died, and are not likely to give you a cent on the mall, either, until and unless you begin to cooperate."

"We will cooperate in every way with a proper, professional investigation," Holland said.

I pointed at my chest. "I'm a professional investigator, and this is the professional investigation," I said. "You'd better look at the fine print of your insurance contract. It says if you don't talk to the cops, you get nothing. If you don't answer the firemen's questions, you get nothing. If the authorities want you to take a polygraph and you respectfully decline, you get nothing. If you fail to cooperate with the company's representative, you get nothing. I'm the company's representative, and I've been beaten and left to die, so don't insult me again on that point. It's counterproductive."

I stood up and dropped my card in the middle of Meyers' desk, then put my folded coat over my left arm.

"Time's a wastin'," I said to Meyers. "Two company appraisers are digging around in the rubble right now. When they find what we expect to find, you not only won't get a cent, but your options will be gone. You see, I don't think you're as guilty of the felonies here as perhaps Leon Slater and Randall Kowalski, but if you want to wait for all this to hit the grand jury and the *State Journal* first, then go ahead and stall. I don't care, really."

I headed for the door.

"I need to talk with my attorney for a few minutes," Meyers said as I opened the door. "Could you wait outside?"

"No, but you can find me at my office for the next hour," I said. "Then I'm going to Clinton County to talk about filing some charges up there."

CHAPTER 29

Holland called about 45 minutes after I walked out of Meyers' office.

"Mr. Mallory, Mr. Meyers wants you to come back," said the heavy hitter. "He wants to cooperate as best he can."

"It's hard to find a parking place downtown among all those important buildings, and I get a little queasy just being among those powerful people," I said. "Why don't you have Meyers stop out at my office? It's on his way home and the parking's plentiful."

I knew he wouldn't come to my office, but it was fun just insulting the two of them.

There was a slightly audible sigh, and it was meant to be audible. "It would be a lot easier for all of us if you returned downtown," Holland said. "He'll make it worth your while."

"Give me twenty minutes," I said.

The sun seemed to be making a difference in the day when I parked about a half block closer to Meyers office than I had the first time. The temperature felt as though it might be higher than zero. Balmy by Michigan December standards. It is amazing that you can actually begin to get accustomed to subzero temps, and it is noteworthy that this bit of truth surprises me almost every winter.

I found Meyers and Holland seated much as before. This time they had a thermal coffee carafe, cups, and bran muffins on a chrome mobile serving cart. In the middle of the desk sat a small battery operated tape recorder.

"We believe it prudent to tape this conversation," Holland said as I noticed the tape recorder. "I hope you don't mind."

I shook my head. "I don't mind, not as long as I get a copy," I said.

They looked at one another. "We thought you might ask," Meyers said. "We agree to have a copy made."

It wasn't what I had in mind, but sometimes you just grab what you can get at the moment and move the hell along for fear of losing your grip on everything. This was such a moment.

"I want it delivered to my office today," I said. "By 5:00. I'll file it."

"OK," Holland said.

We sat down. I got out my pen and my notebook and looked at both of them. Meyers had removed his tie and looked a bit older than he had an hour earlier. Holland looked richer.

"The man who was burned to death in your property on Prospect Street was a fellow named Danny Goodman," I said. "Police consider him a known arsonist, although he has never been convicted. Did you hire him for the project or are you aware that someone else did?"

Meyers looked at Holland, who nodded.

"I must start a little earlier than that," Meyers said. "The project was in trouble almost from the beginning. The land cost too much. The architect's fees came in higher than expected, and then the plans had to be substantially altered. The legal fees to obtain variances and whatnot exceeded our estimates and took longer than expected. The project started in the wrong season, pushing some of the construction which should be done in warmer weather into colder weather."

Meyers threw up his hands. "Then two union contracts came up for negotiation and they started to slow down on the job. The materials seemed to cost more than Leon estimated. It was a fucking mess."

"Leon, you mean Leon Slater?"

"Of course," he said. "Anyway, Leon said he'd call in someone to deal with the unions, and this guy Kowalski appeared. I gather that you've met him."

I nodded again.

"I'm sorry about that," he said, and he even appeared sincere. Such a performance must come from all that practice at being a financial adviser. "Anyway, Kowalski took things pretty much in hand. He was bringing in a lot of people, and so I offered my office and our properties to put them up here and there. We own a lot of properties on the other side of the river there, and it seemed convenient."

Meyers stopped and thought a little.

"About Danny Goodman," I said.

"Well, I was not aware of Goodman's talents," he said. "I didn't hire him, and I'm not sure Leon hired him."

"Was he alone?"

"I don't know," Meyers said. "I just don't know."

"Tell him," Holland said. "He needs to know."

Meyers stood up and walked a few steps and then returned to his seat, probably realizing too late how unnecessarily dramatic the gesture appeared. "About a month ago someone in my office, the real estate management wing, got some information—overheard a conversation or something—that indicated Slater's people, this Kowalski fellow and his friends—were up to something seriously illegal. My employee told me about it, and I called Leon and talked to him about it. He thought I was crazy and that my employee had misunderstood something.

"That night I got home and pulled my car into the garage, using the automatic garage door opener. Before I could get out of my car, Kowalski and another man stepped out of the shadows and told me it would be to my benefit to cease to have any real interest in the Riverside Mall. That way I would not know anything about anything, and if a fire started someday, I could be totally surprised and take the check to the bank."

Meyers looked across the desk, then at Holland, and then at me again. "Right there in my own garage," he said. "God, it was unnerving. He said if I called Leon about it that he would come back sometime, perhaps when I wasn't home."

"Did you call the police?" I said.

"And tell them what? I thought about it, then realized that all that had happened was that a man working for a construction project I helped to finance had visited me at my home to discuss some problems."

Holland poured more coffee and attacked a bran muffin. They were beginning to look better.

"I'll admit that if I followed his advice that I would benefit," Meyers was saying. "The mall was becoming an architect's drawing to pour money into, and we would lose our shirt if things kept going the way they were going."

"So you followed his advice."

"Yes, I did," Meyers said. "I stayed the hell away. I never went down there again, and I haven't the slightest bit of personal knowledge about the players. If, as you say, Goodman was an arsonist, obviously someone else burned the place down. I know nothing about anything."

"Have you ever ordered anyone to burn down any of your properties?" Holland said.

"No."

"Have you been aware that anyone else has done the same thing?"

"None other than what that Kowalski fellow said," Meyers said.

"Ever meet a man named Fred Samuelson?" I said.

Meyers thought. "He's one of our tenants, isn't he?"

"I believe so," I said. Perhaps Samuelson still was a tenant.

Meyers shook his head. "I think he also lived in that Prospect home, so are you saying he is an arsonist, too? He's the guy who torched the mall?"

"I'm not saying much at all," I said. "Samuelson lived there, and he might have seen something, known something. He now lives on Michigan Avenue over a pharmacy, and he's disappeared. I wondered if you met him."

Meyers shook his head. "I don't think so," he said.

I looked at my notes, and corrected some of the words here or there.

"So what you're saying is that you were never in a position to hire any of the people who might have burned the mall down or committed any other crime relating to this," I said. "You're as innocent as a financial adviser can be."

Holland spread his hands.

"Heavy hitter," I said. "Congratulations."

Meyers looked on blankly. Perhaps there was a lot of truth in what he said.

"Leon Slater is now hiding behind a lawyer, and Kowalski is nowhere to be seen," I said. "The cops are looking everywhere for Kowalski. Has your real estate office arranged other suitable accommodations for Kowalski?"

Meyers shook his head.

"Can you give me a list of those people Kowalski brought here and you put up?"

Meyers looked at Holland. Holland nodded.

"By 5:00 at my office would be fine," I said.

He nodded again.

"Do you get the impression that Leon Slater is behind all of this, that he arranged it?"

Meyers shook his head a little. "People surprise me all the time, I'll admit, but I don't think Leon Slater is capable of some of the things you—or even I—are beginning to suspect of him," he said. "He's a good contractor, solid, good worker, but he's a wimp, like me."

I thought about it. "If Slater brought in Kowalski, then he's responsible for something. I don't think Kowalski works for Slater."

"He has a sister," Meyers said. "I've never met her, but Leon speaks of her constantly, saying he'll check with her on this, 'Check with Sis,' he says, or, 'I've got to call Sis.'"

"Her name?"

Meyers shrugged. "It escapes me right now, but I can get it for you."

Holland picked up some papers and sorted through them one sheet at a time. "Darelle Slater," he said.

"She lives on the island," Meyers said.

"Mackinac Island," I said.

He nodded.

I leaned forward in my seat and looked at Meyers.

"I can't think of much else to ask right now, so I might have to get back to you," I said. "But I have a suggestion. You can take it or leave it. I would spend a long lunch with Mr. Holland here and figure out what you're going to tell the police. Then I would go down to the detective section—about a three-block walk, if you go around the Capitol Building—and have a long chat with Lt. Maddox and Sgt. Phillips. I'd clear the air, and clear your name as soon as you can."

Holland looked at a common office phone message he had.

"I have Phillips' name here," Holland said without more comment.

"We're talking two counts of murder, arson, conspiracy to commit both, and probably some other things, perhaps insurance fraud," I said. "Go to them so they don't have to come here and mess up your carpeting."

I stood up and slipped into my coat. Holland turned off the tape recorder.

"Thank you, Mr. Meyers," I said. "You've been a great help."

Meyers sat looking at his desk, probably wondering how much longer he would have it. It was a nice desk.

Holland nodded and finally grinned.

* * *

I drove downtown and passed the Riverside Mall, or what was left of it. One fire truck still lingered watching a pile of smoldering wood, brick, and steel. There was nothing left of the mall, and the next big contract would go to the company able to cart it all away and clean it up. A crowd of about 200 people, probably enjoying some time off for lunch, wandered nearby watching the firemen and thinking about the mall, what it could have been to them, what it could have been to Lansing.

Downtown shoppers ranged through the streets in groups and individually, probably returning Christmas presents or taking advantage of after-Christmas sales. One woman staggered across the street carrying two large bags filled with rolls of Christmas wrapping paper. It wasn't a heavy load, she just couldn't see where she was going.

I squeezed the Cutlass into one of several parking spaces in downtown Lansing and went into Dimitri's for some fast lunch, sitting in a corner where shoppers wouldn't have to look at my face and wonder where I got it. There seemed to be a lot of them today, more than before Christmas, and there was more to my face than there was before Christmas, too.

Mackinac Island.

It wasn't the first time the thought had occurred to me. Ever since I found the map of Mackinac Island in the Prospect Street Mercury I'd wondered what Goodman or Samuelson, or both of them, were doing up there. The island is not a place an arsonist or a convict selects to spend a few days cooling out. It is a family place, a summer vacation spot of the highest caliber, and in the winter it floats at the Straits of Mackinac in a growing sheet of ice.

I remembered that I had promised Patty the next time I went to Mackinac Island I would invite her, so I used a pay phone just outside the restaurant door to give her a call. She wasn't there. It was, after all, lunch time.

Back in the Cutlass, I drove back to the office and poured myself a cup of coffee and moved the Royal from its august place atop the filing cabinet to my desk and rolled in some paper with a carbon.

Melody always liked my report style.

CHAPTER 30

Patty called back right after lunch. I told her about my two conversations with Stewart Meyers and his attorney.

"Holland's a master," Patty said. "He'll guide Meyers to the shortest path out of that mess."

"So, do you want to go to Mackinac Island with me?"

"Are you kidding? They have real winters up there. Besides, they don't open that island in winter, do they?"

"I don't know," I said, considering. "But people live there year around. Some people do, anyway, and you must be able to get to the island in the winter either by air or water. It isn't in the Arctic, for God's sake."

"Damn near."

"Well," I said, beginning to get the picture, "I promised you I'd invite you next time I went."

"That was a couple of summers ago, and I was talking about a summer invitation," Patty said. "This is winter, Mallory. It has been below zero for damned near two weeks, and may be below zero from now to June, for all I know. And it has to be colder up there than it is here."

"Lot more snow, too."

"If I could, I probably would go on up there with you," Patty said. "But I can't. Work is beginning to pile up around here. Someone left the firm today and we've divided up the clients and cases."

"Who?"

"Johnson."

"About time," I said, remembering him. "Was he

sober when he left?"

"It was sobering for everybody else, but we don't think it sobered him up much."

"You'll be glad he's gone."

"Yeah, everybody says things like that until the time comes, and then you have to do all his work, too. No, I can't go. Why don't you call Matt?"

Matt Wiley was my life-long friend and occasional confederate.

"I'd like to see you before you go, though," Patty said. "I'd be wasting my time to urge you to stay put, wouldn't I."

It wasn't a question.

"Probably," I said. "But you are the only person who could make me stay."

"Heavy responsibility," Patty said. "No, you go if you must, and be careful and do what you must do."

When we had hung up, I looked up Matt Wiley's number. I used to know it without looking it up, but the last couple of times I called I got some woman out of bed on the other side of the same county. I got the last two digits confused.

Wiley answered on the second ring.

"You snowed in up there?"

"Hardly," Wiley said. "I got my new four-wheel drive. Did I tell you about that?"

"No," I said.

"Well, I got it in November and it has kept me out of trouble ever since. To what do I owe this call?"

I told him briefly about the case and then told him what would take me to Mackinac Island.

"I think I ought to talk to Darelle Slater," I said.

"Mackinac Island is about my last lead in this case. Want to go?"

"Oh, I guess," Wiley said. "I've come down with a pretty good cold, as you can probably tell, and I'm just about to turn the corner with it. I was sort of looking forward to a couple of days in bed. I deserve them."

"I'll drive," I said, "and provide the entertainment."

"You'll probably need a guide up there anyway, your having become a city boy," he said. "We'll take my wheels. I can just sleep in the back if I have to."

"Good," I said. "How are the roads up there? Can I get into the place and leave my car?"

"Oh, sure," Wiley said. "We have plows and everything up here. Even trucks to push 'em. Eddie, a neighbor, you remember him?"

"Nope."

"He's the tall guy who doesn't say much. About 50, bright white gray hair. Anyway, he swings his Chevy through here with his plow once a day, so you'll be just fine."

I looked at my watch.

"Patty wants to see me before I leave, and I've got to go home first," I said. "So it will be probably 5:00 before I get there."

"I'll try to get some sleep so I'll be good company," Wiley said. "And I have a contact or two up there and I'll try to get us a room. Save some money if we're lucky."

"Good man," I said.

* * *

I had my Eddie Bauer bag out and was stuffing it
with two extra changes of clothes, some heavy winter clothing, and some odds and ends. I tossed in the
flight paperback at the last second. Maybe I would
get stuck in a drift somewhere and have to do some
serious reading. I fed Basil before I left, making sure
he had enough for a couple of days. I changed his
litter and patted him on the head. He followed me
around the house making noises and complaining,
knowing I was leaving.

Basil gets moody whenever I get the luggage out.

"I won't be gone long," I said.

Basil meowed, the Doubting Thomas.

That's when the Clinton County deputy pulled into
the driveway and walked through a lot of snow to
get to the front door. I waved to him to go to the
back door, and he did.

"You called?" Calloway said when I let him in.

"I'm willing to file the official charge whenever you
can put it together," I said.

He unbuttoned his coat and reached inside and removed a brown envelope, opening it.

"I thought you might, so we took the liberty of
filling everything out just as you said it to save the
taxpayers some gas money," Calloway said, unfold-
ing the official charge and spreading it out on a corner of the kitchen table.

I signed it after a brief glance.

"Thank you," he said. "I hope we find him."

"So do I," I said.

He buttoned his coat again, almost tediously.

"You are healing up nice," he said, looking over
my face.

"Thanks," I said.

Then he was outside, in his car, and gone.

Dashing downtown, I had a fast mid-afternoon snack with Patty. We shared a very small pizza. Then I headed north on U.S. 27 on clean, dry pavement, despite a constant dusting of snow, which blew across the highway in little streams. A Jackson Browne tape from one of his earlier albums gave my trip its cadence. I cut west just past Alma on Michigan 46 and within 30 minutes I was pulling into the plowed, bumpy driveway leading to Matt Wiley's A-frame cabin on the lake. Parked next to it was a dark green Jeep Cherokee, his new four-wheel vehicle.

Wiley didn't answer his door, but it was not locked. I went inside and found Wiley very much asleep on his living room couch surrounded by influenza paraphernalia, an opened magazine, and a cold but full coffee cup. I would feel real guilty waking him up.

So I turned on a couple of lights and looked in the refrigerator to see what I might be able to prepare and didn't find much in the way of dinner things, but I found what I needed to make pancakes, bacon, and toast. I used his microwave to thaw the bacon and started that in one pan and got out his electric skillet and prepared the pancakes for that. Being as quiet as I could, I cleaned off his table and covered it with silverware, plates, butter, and syrup.

Matt Wiley began to stir when the eggs hit the grease.

"Jesus," he said, stumbling about the room and stretching and massaging his face. "Jesus, is it morning?"

"I think that after we eat here that you ought to go to bed and sleep the night through," I said. "Don't worry about coming to Mackinac with me."

Wiley continued to look around in his own living room, finding his bearings, thinking, waking up the head.

"I think I was sleeping with the dead," he said through an obvious nasal sound. "It felt real good."

"Take a seat," I said, shoving pancakes and eggs and bacon on his plate.

He sat and looked at his plate, shaking his head a little. Then he settled into an eating routine more like the Matt Wiley I was familiar with. After three cups of coffee he became rather talkative and actually sounded better. He told me he had reservations for us at a motel in St. Ignace and that I could walk to the island across the ice, pay to have a plane fly me over, or borrow a snowmobile.

"I think I have a line on a snowmobile," he said, finishing his second egg and fourth pancake. He was feeling better, but I still thought he should stay in bed, and I told him so.

"Naw," he said. "I need to get out of here. I've been using the recent bad weather as an excuse to stay here and work on this book about the controversy of Indian fishing rights. I haven't been farther than the corner grocery in more than a week."

"How's the book coming?"

Wiley thought about it, then snickered. "I need to get out of here for a while," he said.

I got up and assembled the dishes.

"While you do that, I'll get my things," Wiley said, disappearing up one of two sets of stairs to the loft. Wiley's A-frame was traditional in shape but twice

as large as those you see along most inland lakes.
When he designed and built it, he thought of the structure
as his permanent home, so he'd installed thick insu-
lation, two sets of stairs, and divided the rooms upstairs into two bedrooms, a bath, and a study.

Still the place looked like the home of a bachelor,
and I found myself looking it over as a way of sort
of turning up the corner of a page of my own life.
He needed some color and some softness in the place,
and he probably knew it.

I had finished the dishes and cleaned up the table
when Wiley came part way down the near stairs.

"You armed this trip?" he said.

"Yup."

He went back upstairs, then returned with two bags.
He stuffed his influenza tools into one of them and
carried them out to his Jeep. I went out behind him
and put my bags into his Jeep, too. Back inside he
attached a couple of lights to automatic switches, turned
down the thermostat, and escorted me outside.

Wiley climbed in the passenger side and handed
me the keys. Before I could get my seatbelt fastened,
he had reclined his seat and closed his eyes.

"I trust you can figure everything out," Wiley said.
"Wake me when you're ready to tell me about the
case."

CHAPTER 31

Michigan is a state of two peninsulas. The Lower Peninsula, the chunk of land most people think of when they think of Michigan, is the shape of a left-hand mitten. Matt Wiley and I were driving north right up the middle of that peninsula toward the tip which is called the Straits of Mackinac. There the Upper Peninsula joins the lower by virtue of the Mackinac Bridge, the only bridge of its kind already paid for.

Once you pass Mt. Pleasant—which sits dead center in the middle of the Lower Peninsula—you start to see several forests, and although they are impressive, you have to remember the trees are only a century and a half old at best. More likely younger. The early settlers stripped the state of its forests, which were extensive, cutting the lumber from which they built the region in the first place, and making it possible for Grand Rapids—like other cities—to become a leading international producer of furniture. Outside the Cherokee I could see the forests fairly clearly only because of the remarkable moonlight which drenched the terrain to the sides, giving everything a black and white look with nothing in between.

The miles had been pleasantly flowing by in very light traffic when Matt Wiley woke up on his own just as we passed Houghton Lake. He leaned his seat forward and smacked his lips, looking around. It is difficult to get your bearings in such a situation, and much harder to do when you are sick with cold and drugged with cures.

"We're passing Higgins Lake now," I said. "Hungry?"

He glanced over at the gas tank. "Beautiful lake," he said. The tank was still around half full, time to fill it in the winter.

"I'll take care of that when we stop," I said.

"OK."

"Hungry?"

He shook his head. "I ate a hell of a breakfast this evening," he said. "I think it's still with me."

He reached below his seat and removed his own thermos, pouring himself a cup.

"So, tell me about your case," he said.

I did. I told him everything from the beginning. Somewhere in the midst of the conversation we pulled off the interstate into Gaylord and filled the tank at a Shell station and returned to the expressway. The crisp but befitting air at Gaylord left us very much awake as we pulled back onto the highway. We were slipping between Burt Lake and Mullet Lake when I finished telling him what Stewart Meyers said that morning.

"You figure the woman's behind it all?" he said.

"I don't know," I said. "I just know the cops are looking everywhere in Lansing for these guys, and Leon's not talking, and I've got to do something. I can't help remembering Leon Slater's face when I smashed the glass to the photo his sister took of the Mackinac Bridge. He appeared horrified, as though he was immediately in fear of what she would think, what she would do. I think he forget I was there momentarily."

"And you said there was a map in the car, too," he said.

"Yup. I don't know what to make of that. I really don't. But I figure either Freddie Samuelson or Danny Goodman—or both—had been to Mackinac Island, and they weren't there to eat the fudge or ride the horseys."

We sipped our coffee and aimed the Jeep at the north star, shining clearly and steadily directly over the hood. The snow was gone for the moment. The digital clock on the dash said it was 11:30 and we hadn't passed a car in half an hour. Every other car on I-75 was either traveling at precisely the same speed, or we were the only fools on that road at that time of night in that temperature.

"You going to hunt down the men who beat you up?" Wiley said.

I shook my head, then shrugged. Decisive. "I suspect somebody will find Kowalski, and I'm not sure I would recognize one of the other two. But, yes, if I ever find either of the other two, he won't see me coming, and he'll remember me when I'm gone."

Wiley laughed.

"You remember that captain in Saigon?" Wiley said. "You know, the guy with the pimples and the pearl-handled .45 caliber. I think he remembered you when you were gone."

I had to grin. I had forgotten.

"It's been a long time, Matt," I said.

"Seems like it, doesn't it," he said.

We drove some more, two enduring soldiers going gently into our night. In the distance, occasionally between the trees, we could see a light or two from the Mackinac Bridge still 20 miles distant, but it meant we had descended into the shallows of the original Great Lake, Lake Algonquin, the giant puddle formed as the wall of glacial ice thawed and shrunk as it retreated north about 11,000 years ago. In geological time, it is a current event. Fewer than 4,000 years ago the glacier stretched east and west just north of what is now Lake Superior and was by then a seasoned author of the Great Lakes script.

"Do you remember a winter as cold as this one?" I said.

Wiley was sipping his coffee and holding his cup in both hands to warm his fingers.

"Sure," he said, finally. "But I don't remember many in my adult life that were this cold this early and this long. Maybe I'm just getting old."

I finished my coffee and leaned down so I could see the stars to the northeast.

"When I was a kid," I said, "I remember playing in the snow until what had to be very late hours. I mean young, maybe ten or so. My parents must have been crazy."

"Or appreciative of the winter."

"Perhaps," I said. "But I would sled down the hills in the moonlight and eventually get tired or bored, and I would sink into the snow somewhere, like it was a giant bed, and stare up at all those stars. God it was a wondrous sight, and I know it was colder than hell, but at that age I guess you don't feel it."

"I remember swimming in 50-degree water, too," Wiley said, "but I wouldn't do it today." We drove on some more. "You can still see those stars, but you have to get out of the cities anymore. You can see them at the farm, and up here you can still see them, but sometimes I wonder when we won't be able to

see them here either. Maybe I'll do some homework
on that and write an article about it. Stuart, we should
find some place and get something to eat and then
find someplace else and do some serious drinking."

"I don't think they would be quite as tolerant of us
up here at this time of year," I said.

"You never know," Wiley said. "The people in this
area are a little unsophisticated, somewhat by choice,
but they're pretty tolerant sometimes. This region re-
spects those who work hard, play hard, fight hard,
fuck hard, and die hard. They have to. I'm not sure
where we fit in that, but we used to be damned formidable."

"We still are," I said. "Genuine tough guys."

Wiley sneezed just then. "Well, we used to be anyway," he said.

After a wide and gentle slow curve in the interstate, we arrived at the long entrance to the bridge.
The City of Mackinac passed gently to our right, marking
the top of the Lower Peninsula, and as we climbed
the gradual slope of the bridge we could see Mackinac
Island hunkered down in the ice to the northeast. The
lights from its small tourist village and frozen harbor blinked at us.

* * *

We did not set an alarm, basically because we didn't
have one, and we slept past 9:00 in the morning. I
awakened to the sound of Matt Wiley taking a shower.
But within 35 minutes we managed to both get cleaned
up and prepared for a cold day. We walked across
the street from the downtown St. Ignace motel and

had a hefty breakfast with plenty of fresh coffee. I hoped it would help prepare me for a day that looked a little gray and windy.

Wiley and I had been talking about Michigan's summers and how good the summer fishing is in the Great Lakes when he turned the subject to the day's duty.

"You don't want me along, do you?" he said.

"No, you stay here," I said. "I rented the room for two nights, so you can stay warm and nurse that cold."

Wiley looked through the restaurant windows—which were sweaty with condensation—across the street and between the buildings at the ice which now connected the Upper Peninsula and Mackinac Island.

"Normally," he said, "I would argue that, but this cold has me by the balls. I'm just beginning to feel better, and I'd like to continue on that road."

"No problem," I said. "Since I'd have to take care of you all day, you'd just be a pain in the ass anyway."

"Thanks," said Wiley, looking at his watch. "Speaking of which, if you're going to get a free snowmobile, we'd best dash down the street. He said he'd be gone by noon."

We got into his Jeep and Wiley drove three blocks along the harbor, turning into the Wonder of the North Boat Rental-Cruise Agent. He had explained that the owner, who was only hours from leaving on a three-month venture to Florida, would lend us his snowmobile if we put it back into the garage, removed the battery, and locked up.

Leaving the Jeep, we walked down toward the water's edge, which was now crusty, sandy ice. Occasional slabs or blocks of ice ruined an almost perfect surface. I followed Wiley as we turned up our coats and

held parts of our arms across our faces as protection
against the unobstructed wind. He led us to the lake
side of the building and then inside where he and a
gray haired man almost as tall as Larry Bird shook
hands.

"This is the guy I told you about," Wiley told the
man. "He's the private eye, Stuart Mallory, a life-
long friend, war buddy, and fellow Casino player."

The man grabbed my hand and pumped it warmly.
"Paul Petersen," he said, smiling, looking me over.

"Good to meet an old friend of Wiley's," I said.

"I owe one hell of a good summer of business to
this guy," Petersen said, indicating Wiley. "I'm too
embarrassed to tell you about it."

Petersen moved back and pulled a tarp away from
a snowmobile aimed toward the water. "Me and the
missus plan to leave today and take advantage of
the clean highways," he said. "We hope to get to Cincinnati
by tonight, so I'd like to get started here."

It looked in good shape and fairly new.

"You ever ride one of these?" he asked me.

"Yes, a couple of years ago," I said. "It operates
much like a motorcycle, except there's only one gear."

"That's right," Petersen said, obviously pleased, and
leaning over to show me things. "You start it here,
and make sure to give it a little twist, it wants a little
gas when it's cold. And the tank's full, although you
won't need it I expect."

He was moving away from the snowmobile and
heading toward the window. I followed, and Wiley
followed me.

"Now, do you see those trees out there in the ice?"

I looked. He was right. There was an identifiable
row of what looked like small pine trees planted in

the ice, and they led off in the direction of Mackinac Island. I hadn't noticed them before.

"I see them," I said.

"Good. Now, you just follow that row of trees over to the island, and follow them back, too. You won't get in trouble if you just follow the trees."

"I'm not likely to get lost," I said. "I can see the island from here."

Petersen laughed. Wiley chuckled.

"You can right now," Petersen said. "And you probably will be able to see the island all day long, too. But sometimes a little snow comes up and, added to the wind and all, you can get a little disoriented out there. So follow the trees."

He pointed to the south, toward the Lower Peninsula.

"Over there is a shipping lane. The Coast Guard cutters keep that open all winter, so stay the hell away from that area. You can't trust the ice anywhere in that direction."

"OK," I said. "I should be back here well before sundown, and you want it right here, locked up?"

"Yeah, right here," he said, returning to the vehicle, pointing behind the big two-cycle engine. "And the battery is right down in here. Just take it out and put it on the floor over here where I can find it in April."

"Will do," I said.

"One more thing," he said, brushing past me and past Wiley. "You'll need some proper gear out there. So put one of these suits on." He looked at me again. "You'll want to cover you face and your legs, anyway." He was looking me over again.

"I'll dress warmly," I said. "I've got to go back to

the motel and make a couple of calls before I leave, and I'll dress warmly."

"He grew up in Hamlin," Wiley told Petersen. "He'll survive."

"I've got to ask," Petersen said. "Who did that to your face?"

"I got on the wrong side of a few men," I said.

"I'll bet you did," he said.

Back at the motel, I put on some long underwear and boots and a heavy but loose-fitting sweater. Wiley sat at the little motel table by the window and played Solitaire and listened to a small radio he brought with him.

Finally properly attired, I turned to the telephone and looked up the Slaters' number on Mackinac Island. I thought a moment before I dialed it, getting my thoughts in one pile. I still wasn't sure why I was here. Then I called.

"The Slaters' residence," a woman said.

"My name is Stuart Mallory," I said. "I'm in St. Ignace, and I've come a long way to visit Darelle Slater. May I speak with her?"

"Please hold," she said, and then I listened to silence for about two minutes. Then someone picked up the phone.

"Mr. Mallory, this is Darelle Slater," said another voice. "You have come a long way. What can we do for you?"

"I suspect you are familiar with recent events at the Riverside Mall in Lansing," I said.

"I am," she said pleasantly. "And I've heard your name once or twice, too."

"Good. I'd like to come over to the island and talk

with you for a short while. I believe it is important."

"It is important," Darelle Slater said. "Can you make it over for lunch?"

"Oh, that won't be necessary," I said. "I certainly don't want to trouble you for lunch."

"It's no bother," she said. "In fact, we get so few visitors at this time of year we like to take advantage of those we do get. Shall I expect you by, say, 12:30?"

I looked at my watch. "Sure," I said, "but you'll have to give me some directions."

"Of course," she said. "Are you walking or driving or flying?"

"I have a snowmobile," I said. "So I guess that's driving."

"Well, some people do drive cars across the ice this time of year," she said. "I've already seen several. Anyway, are you at all familiar with the island?"

"I've been there a couple of times," I said. "And I have a map."

"Good. Let me see. You'll reach the island at the north end, not down here, and then follow the road along the shoreline, Lake Shore Road. When you get to the town, the main street is actually Huron Street. Follow it around to the southeast corner, take the first road up hill to Huron Road, and follow it to the point. You'll see it on your map. Our place is the only white cottage to your right."

"Thank you for seeing me," I said. "And lunch is really not necessary."

"No bother," she said. "And I look forward to talking with you. We probably have a great deal to say to one another."

CHAPTER 32

Universal Studios filmed most of *Somewhere in Time* on Mackinac Island because, essentially, the filmmakers needed an elegant 19th century hotel, and they needed a place where shifts in time would be easy to depict. Mackinac Island and the spacious Grand Hotel were perfect. Sure, the filmmakers had to ferry automobiles to the island to depict modern America because such mechanized vehicles are not normally permitted on the island. Tourists and locals get around by horse-drawn carriages and bicycles, and the town itself appears to be carved from the turn of the century, but it's the real thing. Universal had to change little at the Grand Hotel to enable the site to furnish passage to Jane Seymour and Christopher Reeve for their journey through time. The Grand Hotel is indeed the jewel of the north, and make your reservations about two years in advance, folks, or you won't get in.

Mackinac Island is steeped in North American history, too. Legend tells us that its location between the larger bodies of land and its uncommon beauty encouraged some Indians to believe the island to be enchanted and inhabited by, among others, a magician who once trapped young men from the mainland to serve as suitors for his daughters. Later the French Jesuits established a mission on the island, as they did just about everywhere else in the Great Lakes, so they could show the Indians the correct god.

About 200 years ago, the British, not to be outdone by the Algonquin Indians or the roaming Jesuit priests, erected a fort on the southern bluff above what would later become the town of Mackinac Island. The fur trade—and those associated with it—required professional regulation. The fort commanded an excellent view of the only shipping route into Lake Michigan from Lake Huron, and it was supplied in winter by wagons pulled by teams of oxen across the very "ice bridge" I would be using by snowmobile to get to Mackinac Island to see Darelle Slater.

I would be riding into the wind on the way over, but I was properly dressed in my own clothing plus the snowmobiling suit from Petersen's closet. My face was covered in a helmet with a plexiglass shield, and my gloves went all the way up to my elbows. I felt warm.

I had picked up the ice bridge trail immediately and took aim at Mackinac Island. It would not be a lonely crossing as at least two other snowmobiles rode the ice, and I could pick out at least four fish shanties on the land side and two toward the fishing lanes.

At the island I went "ashore" and took the road south along the shoreline. On my left, I passed what had to be a very expensive summer resort. It took about 20 minutes or so for me to work my way down to the vicinity of the Grand Hotel, which waited atop the bluff, majestic on its lofty perch. Christopher Reeve would not have been as comfortable napping on that porch in December as he was in early summer in *Somewhere in Time*.

But if you were waiting for Jane Seymour, it would be worth the trouble.

The road carried me around the southwestern edge of the island and into the town. In summer, the town swells with tourists seeking refuge from the heat and the oily machines in the cities to the south. They come by ferry boat, yacht, and airplane, and they spend a great deal of money in the three months considered summer. Some come for the sailing races, which can begin anywhere, but inevitably end on the island because sailers know a good place to celebrate most anything.

The snowmobile purred up main street, passing closed bed and breakfasts, hotels, restaurants, souvenir shops, clothing stores, and a couple of bars. A few seemed to be open, but I saw only two or three people. The street had been plowed, more or less, showing there existed at least one mechanized vehicle heavy enough to push winter's best aside. I didn't feel so badly about riding a smelly two-cycle vehicle.

As I passed under the guns of the fort, I found the road leading up the hill to the bluff. The snowmobile felt no challenge, needing only more power to get the job done. At the top I turned right and immediately saw the Slater house set against a growth of pines. I pulled the snowmobile up to the white gate and shut it down. It was a relief on my ears, especially after I removed the helmet and let in winter's stillness.

Cottage is a word only the rich would use to describe such a building. It had at least three stories set under a cedar shake roof and carried an assortment of gables, bay windows, and columns on field stone pillars, most of which supported a first-floor porch or veranda that encircled the building. Hundreds of finely turned white balusters held the rail in suspension. At the corner nearest the water was a three-story turret, and the view from any of the floors had to be inspiring.

Crouched on a gentle ledge on the southeast corner of Mackinac Island, the Victorian gothic Slater house had a dazzling perch to watch the sun rise over Lake Huron and assess the scope of the Great Lakes shipping. The house was no bigger than an airplane hangar, but probably more comfortable. There were no tracks or indications of tracks along the path. I didn't expect any.

I pushed at the gate hard to move some drift aside, then began plodding up the hill through the two feet of packed and drifted snow. The wind had prevented snow from accumulating on the wooden porch, which gleamed from a recent application of blue enamel. I knocked on the door.

Without a wait, Darelle Slater opened the inner door and reached and unlocked the storm door. She let me open the outside storm door and bring myself in. She stood well to the side, then eased the door back in place with her shoulder. It fit snugly.

"Good afternoon, Mr. Mallory," she said. "You've arrived just in time. Our lunch awaits us in the dining room."

Darelle Slater wore an angora sweater-dress in pale pink with a matching cardigan sweater edged in soft gray. They complemented her pewter hair.

I began to remove the various layers of winter gear. A black woman arrived from a side door and quietly took my snowmobile garb and other winter wear and disappeared again.

"I didn't want to impose on you for lunch, Mrs. Slater," I said. "You needn't —"

"My pleasure," she said, turning away and walking up the hall. "As I said, we don't get many visitors. Follow me, please. I think you'll like the view from our dining room."

It was a Michigan house. In the hall, wooden floors joined knotty pine walls decorated with paintings, quilts, and small unique pieces of driftwood, parts of sailing ships, and other beach artifacts. Woven throw rugs, which looked Native American in origin, amply covered the wooden floors.

The floor didn't even squeak or sag.

"If you want to freshen up first, Mr. Mallory, the bathroom is right through there," she said, pointing down a short hallway.

"Thanks," I said. "Perhaps later."

The oak dining table was stationed in the center of the first-floor turret room. A battery of spacious windows spanned from Lake Huron to the east and to the Straits of Mackinac to the west.

As expected, the view was extraordinary.

Darelle Slater smoothly signaled me to the chair facing Lake Huron. She stood behind the chair where she could see the Mackinac Bridge in the distance, a view which looked much like the one on her brother's office wall. The black woman appeared as if by wizardry and ushered Darelle into her seat.

I sat down, too.

"Thank you, Charlotte," she said.

Leafy salads awaited us, and we began to eat.

"Do you live here the year around?"

She nodded. "I have for the past five years or so," she said. "It was merely a summer cottage, you understand, so I had to make some changes in it. It wouldn't have been able to stand up to this kind of weather."

"It seems pretty able now," I said. If you turned your back to the windows, you would be unaware of the season.

Darelle wore no make-up on her aging but flawless complexion tanned in either Palm Beach or Aspen. Though small-framed, she would never go unnoticed. Her posture royal, her gaze steady, and her eyes certain.

"You are a private detective," she said.

"Yes, I am," I admitted.

"What kinds of cases—is that the right word?—do you normally handle?"

"There doesn't seem to be a normal case," I said. "There's always a missing person case or two around. I do some security for various corporations, and then there are a growing number of insurance companies with a growing number of problems."

It was not lost on her, but she only smiled and ignored it.

"Does it pay well?"

I shrugged. "No, but if I wanted to get rich, I would have gone into something else," I said. "It's what I do, and it appears it's what I'll do for the foreseeable future. I like it."

"You are the adventuresome sort, I expect," Darelle Slater said.

I shrugged. "It's better than sitting behind a desk somewhere managing data or counting beans."

"You seem a little old for this," Darelle Slater said.

"It's just the beatings you have to take now and then," I said.

I ate some salad. It was fresh and crisp, and the dressing was not the sort of thing I'd find on my grocery store shelf.

"You are the ranking executive in Stone," I said.

She nodded. "I'm the first child, and I was trained by my father, Stone Slater," she said. "When we incorporated, I named it after him."

"Was Stone his given name?"

"Nickname," she said. "He earned it. My father worked hard throughout his life, and he built from almost nothing a rather large organization. His given name was Leon."

"Then your brother is a junior."

She nodded her head and looked at her plate. "My father wanted a son when I was born, and said so on occasion," she said, snickering a little inside herself. "I've tried not to disappoint him, especially since his passing."

"Then Leon, your brother, is sort of Stone Junior."

She smiled, but it lacked any sugar.

"The alias doesn't automatically apply to progeny," Darelle Slater said.

Charlotte slipped into the room and delivered two plates of sliced turkey, spring potatoes, and fresh green beans.

"Thank you," I said.

Charlotte nodded and left. Wizardry again.

"It was my father's wish that his son manage this company upon his death," she said. "It was in the will. After two years of that, we decided that I should resume the position. Leon's strengths are not in management, as you probably saw yourself. He's an architect, and an engineer."

"Mrs. Slater —"

"Darelle, please. I never married."

"Darelle," I said. "Though you are the company's executive officer, is it safe to assume, though, that your brother was in charge of the Lansing operation?"

"Mr. Mallory—"

"Stuart, please," I said. "People call me Stuart or Mallory. 'Mr. Mallory' makes me think my father has entered the room."

"Stuart, understand the nature of this family," she said, putting down her fork and looking at me. "The Slaters are very much a part of the history of this state. This very cottage was built of virgin timber from the Northern Peninsula more than 150 years ago. It was the summer home of the lumber company manager's family. My family acquired the company around the turn of the century, and since then we have refurbished, modernized, expanded both this house and the company that built it. Our lumber is the fiber of thousands of homes and structures throughout Michigan and much of Indiana and Illinois and Wisconsin. This was my father's legacy to his children, Leon and me, and we have built upon it. Our origins are in lumber, Stuart, but today we construct commercial buildings and shopping malls all around the Great Lakes." She pointed at Lake Huron to illustrate the point. "And we do first class work."

I ate some turkey. It was excellent, too.

"So, what do you suspect me of?" she said.

I finished that bite of turkey and looked at the ice on the near side of Lake Huron.

"Two people have been murdered, and there have been at least two cases of arson, one rather major," I said. "Three men from your company took me into the woods and beat the hell out of me and left me for dead."

"That was a mistake," she said.

"It sure was," I said, going on. "It made the whole cause rather personal. I've met your brother in rather tense circumstances, and I don't think he's capable of ordering such things. I've also met and talked to Stewart Meyers, and he's certainly capable of cheating on his taxes, probably a lot, and buying housing inspectors and using insider information to make a fortune. He might even dabble in a little arson, or think about it a lot, but he's no killer. So, I'm looking for a principal who is capable of arranging murder, arson, and an occasional convenient thumping. I'm looking for someone who's a family friend of Randall Kowalski, and I think I'm getting warm."

It was her turn to eat and listen and think, and she did it well. She was not the sort of person who would be easily shaken.

"Let me ask you this, Mr. Mallory, Stuart," she finally said. "If you find this person, what do you intend to do?"

"I'm going to find all the evidence necessary to have this person arrested and locked up," I said.

She laughed a little, but it wasn't an evil laugh, just a little arrogant.

"If you mean me, keep in mind that Stone is a powerful force in this state," Darelle Slater said. "We have a payroll in the millions, providing thousands of people—hundreds of families—with incomes. We pay enough taxes to pave an expressway from Lansing to Grand Rapids every few years, and we give generously to charities and political campaigns."

"Does that mean that if you give sufficiently to charities and pay enough taxes, we should permit you a murder or two?"

She looked at me and ate some more of her turkey.

"I wouldn't put it that way," she said, "although some might think it an apt manner. No, I just mean that it would be an uphill battle. A very uphill battle. We have done an awful lot for Michigan, and there are a wealth of people in positions of authority—such as the governor—who would do their best to run your investigation off course. I don't think your investigation could deliver the goods, but I guarantee you that we could."

She smiled.

Charlotte arrived with two cups and an insulated pitcher. She filled both cups with coffee and left the room again.

"Did you order that I be beaten?"

Darelle Slater looked hard at me. Some of the glitter in her eyes was gone.

"I don't think you're getting the point, Mr. Mallory," she said, pouring cream into her coffee. "People like me don't get involved in such things."

I sipped my coffee. Like everything else, it was excellent.

"Let me tell you what I'm going to do, just so that we won't have any misunderstandings," I said, looking her in the eye. "I'm going back to Lansing. I'll find your brother, Leon, and we'll have a friendly caucus about his future as an inmate in Jackson, and then we'll talk about what would happen if he turned state's evidence and wouldn't have to live among ax murderers, child-beaters, professional sex offenders, and the like. Maybe just for fun I'll let him meet a couple people—just a couple regular o' guys—who are recent residents at that penitentiary just so he can get a first-hand testimonial.

"I suspect Leon will come apart as though he were hit by a Patriot missile. Leon needs to have a choice he can understand, if I'm any judge of moral character. I don't believe I'll need to have the same talk with Stewart Meyers because he's already back at the Lansing Police Department making sure his comments are on tape. Then we'll see whether people like you get involved in such things, and we'll see what the state might do about it."

All the glitter was now gone from her eyes, but she held steady, certain of her past, certain of her future. She sipped her coffee without a shake. So did I.

I wasn't done yet.

"Win, lose, or draw, it will be interesting to see how many state and municipal contracts you get in the Great Lakes region if an Ingham County grand jury files two or three murder indictments against two affluent owners of a major contracting corporation. Why, the press coverage alone will make eyes water from Toronto to Denver. What member of the family will pull this company from ruin when that sort of publicity messes with the ledger books?"

Darelle Slater put her cup down and it missed the saucer. Some of it spilled into the white table cloth, and I was sorry about the table cloth.

"You are no longer welcome here," she said. "I want you to leave."

I sipped my coffee.

"I'll finish my coffee first," I said. "I've got what I came for."

Darelle Slater got up and carefully put her chair in its proper place, pivoted on her right foot, and left the room. Just me and the soiled table cloth and the magnificent view of the shipping lanes.

Charlotte came in with her hands folded and looked at me.

"May I show you to the door?" she said quietly.

I finished the coffee in a gulp and got up.

"Thank you for lunch," I said.

"My pleasure," she said, and smiled.

CHAPTER 33

The western sky was darkening a little as I stood at the gate and strapped on the helmet and worked my hands and arms into the long, black gloves. I was getting used to the dark sky. The sky had been doing that off and on for two weeks now. Actually, the weather had been like that in the Great Lakes as long as I could remember. The snowmobile started almost immediately, and instead of dropping back into and through the town to return to the ice bridge along the shoreline road, I opted for the inland trail that would take me past many of the homes of those who actually live on the island. Besides, according to the map, it was shorter.

I swung the snowmobile around and glanced at the Slater house. Darelle Slater stood inconspicuously in the shadows a few feet from a second-floor window, and from there she watched me depart. I thought about waving, but knew it would be a thoughtless gesture. I waved anyway.

The route took me past Fort Mackinac, built by the troubled British shortly after the series of skirmishes we remember as our Revolutionary War, and then I turned toward the center of the island and moved respectfully past the many cottages which house natives in summer and some of them still in winter. A light showed here and there and the path was well used, although not plowed.

As I turned past a road pointing to "skull cave" to my left, I noticed another snowmobile behind me, a dark red one. It was fairly difficult to casually keep a watch behind me because the helmet blocked much of the vision, and snowmobiles are not equipped with rearview mirrors. Finally, at a turn, I slowed to get a better look at the large helmeted figure behind me, and I knew who it must be.

I gave the throttle a twist and began to rocket up something called Garrison Road, which obviously emptied behind me at the fort. Ahead I was not sure, since I had intended to take another glance at the map when I got further inland. Randall Kowalski certainly was not much of a sporting competitor, so he would not permit me a glance at the map. It also would be difficult to reach inside four layers of clothing and remove the revolver. It would take 10 minutes just to shed the gloves, especially while riding, and my hand could not hold a pistol with the gloves in place.

Kowalski kept pace about 30 yards behind me and didn't appear to want to gain ground. Perhaps he wanted to pick his spot. Perhaps he was not really aware that I knew of his presence. Perhaps it wasn't Kowalski, just a vacationing linebacker from the Detroit Lions. I had to believe it was Kowalski and assume that his intentions were unfriendly.

At the next intersection I took a gentle left turn. It seemed like the thing to do, and it was the easy thing to do, but I knew immediately I should have taken one of the other two alternatives. Now I was heading toward the airport, and I doubted the snowmobile could fly.

The red snowmobile stayed behind me.

At the next intersection I knew the road to the left would return me to the village of Mackinac Island, and the one to the right took me to the airport. I went to the airport, and within seconds I was dashing through the gate and onto the apron. Three airplanes were parked on the field, but there didn't appear to be anyone around. Probably a good thing, too, since there was no point in getting a bystander hurt.

I headed toward the runway and turned west, running parallel to it long enough to see Kowalski gaining ground behind me. He held something in one hand which glittered but did not look like a gun.

Kowalski liked the openness of the airport.

I gave the snowmobile all the gas it had, shooting forward, and quickly reached the runway's end and bolted into the woods. Immediately I had to slow down for fear of running into trees. Navigating a snowmobile through a forest was a discipline I needed more practice in.

Behind me Kowalski was having similar problems, but as I glanced at him, I saw a cliff ahead too late to stop. The machine skidded to the edge, then we went over the edge and down a steep embankment. Although I missed a tree on the way down, a branch caught me squarely in the forehead and removed the helmet and some skin off my neck.

Don't try this at home.

Having been warned by my rapid disappearance, Kowalski worked his way along the edge until he found a better path down. I regained control of the snowmobile and dashed across the Lake Shore Road and straight onto the ice. I poured the gas to the machine and spurted away from the island as fast as the machine would go, the wind cutting at my face.

I had come onto the ice somewhere midway between the bridge and open water. Off to my left, light glittered from the water of the straits. Further in the distance an ore boat sat low in the water and plowed

its way toward Detroit or points south. Kowalski, having
moved further toward the bridge, cut off my best route
back to the bridge by staying north.

I decided to gamble and try to draw him onto thin
ice. I had to hope that the combined weight of Kowalski
and his machine topped my combined weight. It was
a ridiculous risk, but it was about the only chance I
had other than stopping, devoting 20 seconds I did
not have to removing my gloves, allotting another 10
or 20 seconds to plowing through my clothing and
removing the revolver, and then successfully shooting a man who could have arrived meanwhile and
beat me to death.

I aimed the snowmobile at the open water a half
mile away and slowed down a little, especially after
I hit the snow-covered ice. Kowalski's red machine
followed, rapidly closing the gap. As he approached
I let the snowmobile take its own heading and worked
at removing my gloves. I finally removed one glove,
but I dropped it. Kowalski saw it and added more
power, seeing that he needed to hurry. I was working my way through the zipper and buttons of the
snowmobile jumpsuit when he got close enough to
spit at me.

"I told you," he shouted, and raised a hand holding an ice pick or a very sharp screwdriver.

I grabbed my handlebar and veered away to the
right, and he turned to meet my turn but his momentum carried him past me.

Then it happened.

Perhaps it was the centrifugal force of his turn that
did it, and perhaps it was just the combined weight.
But the ice broke somewhere under his snowmobile.

At first it didn't produce a gaping hole, just a significant, deep fissure which began to send Kowalski's snowmobile out of balance and out of control.

Its runner seemed to snag on the edge of something, perhaps the crack itself, and Kowalski was propelled to his left, away from the sharp turn he had been taking and skidded away from me.

I slowed and continued the easy turn I was already in. Within seconds I was headed back to the ice bridge and I feared that the very ice below me, provoked by the cracking ice directly behind me, would begin to crack too. But as I regained 100 yards of what appeared to be solid ice, I stopped.

Behind me the ice had developed several large fissures which were encircling Kowalski. As though it had been waiting for a witness, Kowalski's snowmobile tipped then skidded sideways, disappearing into Lake Huron.

Kowalski lay flat on the ice a few yards from where the snowmobile sunk, but he was floating on what appeared to be an island about 20 yards in diameter. A long pool of water six feet wide had opened between him and me, and the water was oozing onto the ice Kowalski hung to.

I found myself running back toward Kowalski, and it seemed ridiculous. Somewhere deep in my soul I suspected I could do something and should do something. Perhaps my own death by drowning—or the more merciful freezing to death after the onset of hypothermia—would serve justice.

"Help me," Kowalski was saying, holding his position on the ice with the ice pick he still held in his right hand.

I stopped 30 yards away and got down on my stomach to distribute my weight better and pulled myself toward him with my elbows. I had the revolver out of my clothing and I held it securely in my right hand, although it seemed terribly out of place and unnecessary now.

I stopped and measured the distance and considered the thickness of the ice and the depth of my resolve.

"Did you kill Terri Krug?" I said, my words carried to him by the favoring wind.

"Help me, you son of a bitch," Kowalski said. Even though he had to shout against the wind, his voice carried well.

"I can wait," I was saying to him.

"Get some help," Kowalski was saying. "Get some help." He was lying face down on the ice and raising his head occasionally to shout at me. His ice flow was drifting away ever so slightly, widening the oscillating pool of dark green water between us.

"Did you kill Terri Krug?" I said again.

"Oh Christ yes," he said. "Freddie and I. She saw too much. Now get a fucking boat."

"Did you kill Danny Goodman?"

"No," he said. "Freddie did."

He laughed. Perhaps the seriousness of his situation was getting to him. There's a point when laughter is the only possible response to death, especially when it whispers in your ear.

"Danny knew what he was going to do, so he demanded the drug," Kowalski said into the ice at his face. "He died in peace. He was sick."

"I'll go for a boat now," I said.

"OK," he shouted.

"You might move about four or five feet backward," I said. "That should put you in the center of the ice flow, away from an edge."

Kowalski snickered, then used his ice pick to drag himself forward, not backward.

"No, no, no," I said. "Backward."

It was too late. Gouged by the ice pick and weighted down by a large man, the ice broke again. Kowalski slipped quietly into the water almost as though he had never been there. Then he surfaced and used his ice pick on the ice again.

"Help me," he said. His face was white and dripping.

I crawled toward him, closing to within 20 yards.

"Your best chance is for me to get some help," I yelled, but I knew that Kowalski was a dead man. Hypothermia would set in within a minute or two, and he would never be able to stay afloat long enough for me to return. I looked over my shoulder at the fishermen who seemed miles away, and raised my revolver in the air and emptied it one chamber at a time. The blasts seemed to disappear into the empty sky, but someone had to hear them.

Then the ice under me began to disclose its stress with the hushed roar of millions of tiny fissures opening up. I turned so that I could roll back and away from the open water as fast as I could, but it was too late.

The ice gave way directly under me, dumping me into the frigid water. I kept my hands flat on the ice sheet in front of me, maintaining enough of a grip to stay afloat. The useless pistol lay nose up in the snow nearby.

The water's effect is difficult to describe. Immediately the body learns it is cold and throws the heating system into full service, but it cannot deal with how rapidly the body loses heat. Pain disappears in seconds, which is most certainly a gift, and that is followed by the certain knowledge that death is very near, and that this is real.

Kowalski was less than 10 yards away holding on and watching me. I think he tried to grin, but it was impossible to say. I began to wish I had just shot him, needing to believe that I had finished the job.

Finished something.

Neither of us could secure a grip on the ice to pull free of the water. We kept trying. He was having better luck with his ice pick.

We struggled together.

"I torched the mall, too," Kowalski said.

It was my turn to laugh, and it came out in a spurt, sounding like a choke. I think I took in some water. God it was cold.

It seemed ridiculous to talk. The discourse of the dead may be honest, but it is certainly a curious thing.

"Did you work for Darelle?" I said, knowing the answer, and even noticing my use of past tense.

"Always," he said.

Back toward the ice bridge there was activity. People seemed to be coming. I could hear a snowmobile, and there appeared to be something large being towed behind it. Maybe a boat.

"Hold on," I said. "They're coming."

There was a grunt in answer.

"They're coming," I said, but I was losing my

contact with the ice in front of me. That was becoming the most difficult part. The wet ice offered no grip.

And I was losing any feeling in my body.

My legs didn't seem to be attached.

My chest was shutting down.

My stamina was vanishing, being replaced with certainty in the still and icy silence.

"God, hold on," I said to the ice. "Hold on."

I allotted a moment to glance behind me. Kowalski was gone. It had been only a moment, I was sure of it.

Gone where?

Good riddance.

I began to think of Patty Bonicelli.

My dead weight seemed to be pulling me under.

I could hear them coming.

I could actually feel them coming, their vibrations in the ice obvious to anyone.

Oh, Patty, I'm sorry.

CHAPTER 34

Matt Wiley stood at the foot of the bed and watched the sun set behind the venetian blinds. Shimmering orange rays brushed across his face.

"They haven't found him yet," he said. "But I'll keep calling them if you want me to."

I was under a couple of blankets and they didn't seem necessary anymore. My body seemed to be on fire, and the doctors had informed me that was good.

It felt good to me, too.

"I think they're off conferring about my condition," I said.

"Yes, they are," Wiley said. "They're down in their lounge in a little huddle, actually, making jokes about southlanders falling into the water. One of them said something about calling a psychiatrist."

"I think a psychiatrist would have a better sense of humor anyway," I said.

Wiley just smiled. I had the feeling that my hollow bravado was squeezing his patience a little thin.

"I want to get the hell out of here," I said.

"You'll probably get your wish," said another voice, and it was coming from someone in a light blue doctor gown.

"Nice outfit," I said. "Where do you buy those?"

He looked down for a second, then back up at me.

"I don't really know," he said.

A real joker.

"So..."

"There's no real reason to keep you," the doctor said. "We should, I suppose, just to keep an eye on you. We could put you up for the night, but there are truly sick people here, people we can actually cure, and we should be worrying about them."

Maybe he had a better sense of humor than I did.

He was taking my pulse again. He seemed satisfied.

"Does he have dry clothing?" the doctor-type person asked Wiley.

Wiley pointed to my Eddie Bauer bag.

"You may take him away," the doctor said and left the little cubicle in the emergency room.

I was shaky, but I stood on the floor OK. I quickly got into a dry set of clothes and wished I had dry boots. That was one of the things I didn't pack.

Wiley saw my difficulty.

"I'll drive right up to the door," he said. "Your body's in overdrive anyway. You'll never feel the cold outside."

I did, though, and like the memory of Kowalski's beating in the woods outside Lansing, the cold sent a different sort of chill up my spine. Never again would cold water just look like cold water.

Wiley drove me back to the hotel where he dumped me and disappeared. When he got back a half an hour later, I was watching the news about me on TV.

"Big news," I said, pointing at the TV. They didn't have film, so their report lasted only 15 seconds.

Wiley handed me a heavy box. I opened it and found a pair of dark brown insulated boots.

"I took the money out of your wallet," he said. "Merry Christmas."

"I need to go back to the island," I said.

"You need to call Patty," he said. "She shouldn't hear about this any other way."

He was right.

I dialed her number and talked to an AT&T opera-
tor and dialed again. Someone at her office picked it
up and said she'd just left. I told him to catch her in
the parking lot, and he said he would.

Patty came on the line in a minute or two. I told
her who I was.

"You home already?"

"No," I said. "Just wanted to bring you up to date
on the goings on up here. They just fished me out of
Lake Huron."

"What?"

I told her briefly about my visit with Darelle Slater,
and then I told her about falling through the ice. Then
I told her that I was thinking of her during what I
assumed were going to be my last moments.

Then my voice broke. That's when I heard Wiley
shut the door behind him.

"Oh, Mallory," Patty Bonicelli said.

It was good to hear her voice, but rather suddenly
I couldn't tell her that.

* * *

Wiley returned with an enormous bucket of fried
chicken and some Pepsi. We ate as though we'd skipped
lunch.

"Cops are coming to see you," Wiley said, looking
at his watch. "State cops. Should be here any time
now."

"How'd you learn this?"

"Who the hell do you think I've been calling to
find out if they fished him out yet? Which they haven't,

by the way."

He was right. I was working on my third chicken breast when two state police troopers in uniform arrived and came inside. Sgt. Preston and Officer Hills. Hills, the younger of the two, leaned against the door and took notes and Preston sat in one of the two chairs motels provide and took some notes on the small round table. Spread across most of the table was the drying contents of my wallet.

"I know you talked to the deputy sheriff," Preston said once he got settled and introduced at his table position.

"Does anyone ever ask where your dog is?"

He looked at me. "Pardon me?"

"You know, Sgt. Preston of the Yukon," I said. "I think he had a dog."

Preston smiled. "Nope," he said.

I shrugged. Too bad.

"Let me see if we have this right," Preston said. "You went across the island on a borrowed snowmobile to visit with Darelle Slater, a resident there."

Preston looked at me.

"Is that a question?"

He nodded.

"Yes, I did."

"And on your way back, this other guy —"

"Randall Kowalski."

"Kowalski. Right. He chased you across the island and onto the ice, and then you purposely went for the open water."

"Actually, I was going toward the weak ice," I said. "Not the water."

Preston made a note.

"Somewhere in there," he said, "you got out your pistol and fired six shots, which got the attention of the three fishermen who rescued you. Mr. Kowalski's snowmobile went under, and he did too. That about it?"

"We had a conversation while we were in the water," I said. "You want to know about it?"

"Sure," Preston said, using his thumb to reactivate his ballpoint pen.

"Let me put it this way, Sergeant," I said. "He didn't say anything which is pertinent to your investigation. I suggest you contact Lt. Maddox or Sgt. Phillips of the detective section of the Lansing Police Department. They can tell you about Kowalski, and the fact there's at least one warrant out for his arrest, one from Clinton County. Unless you want to get into a messy investigation involving one of your richer local residents, you might want to keep your distance."

Preston looked over his notes, and he looked over the contents of my wallet. He picked up my soggy permit to carry the pistol and examined it, making another note. "Well, for the moment, I'll take your word on that. But I have more questions. Do you mind if I ask them?"

"Of course not."

"Did you push or otherwise cause Mr. Kowalski to fall into the water?"

"No, and I didn't go over and step on his fingers as he tried to save himself, if that's what you mean."

"I don't know what I mean," the sergeant said. "I'm asking you."

"If I had been able to get my pistol out before he got to me, I would have killed him," I said. "But I couldn't, and I didn't."

Hills shifted from one foot to the other. Wiley began to eat his chicken again.

"Do you think you'll find him?" I said.

Preston disabled his ballpoint pen and put it away.

"Someday, maybe," he said. "There are a dozen or so bodies out there—people who've fallen in over the years—that nobody's found. But sooner or later, somebody finds most of them. Our divers found his snowmobile, but he was no where to be found. We haven't found your pistol yet either."

"Ought to be about 20 yards this side of the snowmobile," I said.

"Ah eh," Preston said. "By the way, do you know where Randall Kowalski's family is?"

I shrugged. "You might ask Darelle Slater," I said. "He worked for her. I assume the deputies gave you the information about her."

The pen was out again and he made a note of it.

"I'm going to have to talk to her anyway, I guess," he said. "I hope this isn't a lot of trouble. Anyone I can call for a reference about you?"

"Maddox," I said. "There's a trooper named Whipple at the central state police post. And now there's an instructor there, guy named Emery Frost."

"The sheriff?"

"Yup. I'm told he's in Lansing, he hasn't come over for dinner or introduced the missus. I haven't talked to him in a couple of years, but I hope his memories of me are fond memories."

Hills eased onto two feet. "You two sticking around a couple of days, or are your duties going to take you back?" Hills looked at Wiley, then at me.

Wiley was licking his fingers.

"We're paid through tonight," I said. "We'll be gone early in the morning."

"Say we manage to find this guy's body, and the medical examiner finds a couple of bullet holes in him," Preston said. "Say we then begin to wonder where you were aiming your pistol when you fired it to get the attention of those who rescued you. Where can we locate you to check your story against that development?"

"Lansing," I said. "I live there. You have the addresses."

Hills looked at Wiley long enough to get his attention.

"What's your role in all this?" he asked.

"I'm conversation," Wiley said. "He was afraid to come up to the north country without a guide and company. I let him go to the island by himself because he needs the experience working alone."

"Next time, go with him," Preston said.

CHAPTER 35

I woke up once in a sweat and went quietly to the window where I pulled the shade just enough to look outside and give myself some sense of place.

At 4:00, after having slept better than eight hours, we both got up and showered and left the key in the night box and left. Matt Wiley said he felt a lot better than he had two days ago and insisted on driving his own car. The Cherokee fired up immediately and bolted toward the highway.

As we cruised south over the Mackinac Bridge I glanced over my shoulder at Mackinac Island's early morning lights and wondered what secret they held. I also tried to examine the frosty waters of the Straits of Mackinac, but the concrete of the northbound lanes was in the way.

It would have been too dark anyway.

In Mackinac City, we sat down to a stalwart breakfast. It was the sort of country restaurant where the middle-aged waitress calls everybody "honey" and means it, and where they serve breakfast on large platters carrying mounds of extras like home fries regardless of what you ordered. The locals were in the restaurant drinking coffee and planning their days and wearing heavy coats and flannel shirts and thick boots. We had been talking about Wiley's new writing career for the State Department of Natural Resources.

"I drive all over the state writing reports, taking photos, collecting mileage money," he said. "They seem to like everything I do, but I don't understand it." He shrugged.

"You deserve it," I said.

Wiley shrugged again. "I made enough money to buy a new computer," he said. "My old one was just fine, of course, especially after I'd updated it. Hard drive, more RAM, and so on. But, you go into a computer store, you get the urge for something faster, fancier, loaded with software you'll never use. Pretty soon you take it home."

"Never saw you as the computer hacker type," I said. "Matt Wiley. Wonk. Techie."

He shook his head and admired this third cup of strong coffee.

"Well, it's just a tool," Wiley said. "And if you're really going to stay in the business, you ought to have one to write your reports on, correspondence, and so on."

"Yeah, all that correspondence is getting me down," I said.

"You can have my old one," he said.

I thought about it while I held up my cup for the waitress to see.

"I can't afford it," I said.

"Tell you what," Wiley said. "I'll let you have it for a couple of months, then, if you want to keep it, we'll settle on a disgustingly reasonable price."

I shook my head. "Stuff's expensive."

"The used market for that stuff is ridiculous. Something that cost $3,000 two or three years ago you can barely get $300 for it used."

"Is that your price?"

"Cheaper."

Thirty minutes later we were slipping on our sunglasses and peering into the sun as it began to rise into a crackling clear sky. Wiley was driving. We were going through very green pine forests, the kind that make Michigan the lovely state that it is. I was reading an official state map, the kind with the governor's picture on it, even though I knew where we were. I like maps.

"She going to get away with it?" he said.

"I don't know," I said. "I tried to scare her, but she's a tough one. I think she went elsewhere in the building and told Kowalski to go out there and kill that damned detective and do it neatly and right now. I'm sure he wasn't shivering and waiting in the stable on the off chance I'd stop by."

We passed an old car that the salt had turned to junk, but it was running and doing at least 60.

"She sounds a little scared to me," Wiley said. "Otherwise, why kill you?"

"It also didn't work. I'm here, on my way to Lansing, ready to hunt down her brother and squeeze him. She knows it, and her brother's a wimp. And that has got to worry her something fierce."

"You really going to talk to her brother?"

"Sure," I said. "Leon and I are old friends, especially now that Kowalski has met the big chill."

"A little lame, but it's a colorful way to put it," Wiley said.

"I know, but I just thought of it, and I had to say it to somebody."

* * *

It was still early in the day when we pulled up next to Wiley's cabin on the lake, and I jumped into my Cutlass and headed to Lansing. The sun was up high and a delight to see, and it seemed actually to be warming the air. In fact, the radio weather report called for temperatures near 20, perhaps higher.

Spring arriving in Michigan and New Year's hasn't arrived yet.

I went home first and patted Basil on the head and let him outside for half an hour. He said he had things to do out there. I put more cat chow into his bowl and freshened his water dish and brought my pile of junk mail in from the mail box and tossed it into the soapstone where it doesn't burn very well but makes me feel better.

I donned something less appropriate for the wild north and more appropriate for the serious portion of the state and headed to my new office. On the way from Mackinac, I'd made a list of things I had to do, starting rather soon with updating my security bond if I were to stay in business and calling the planning commission and giving them the good news.

I opened my new office and found a pile of mail at my feet. Most of it had the yellow mail forwarding stickers on it. One item, a large white envelope, had not come through the mail and it was from Holland's law firm. It had been delivered by a local courier so Holland would have proof.

I had forgotten it, and it suddenly seemed like good news. After spilling the rest of the mail on the desk's corner, I opened Holland's letter and found the tape and a list of people Kowalski had brought to Lansing. Two of the names already had been crossed out as having given notice and disappearing. There were eight others.

I started my phone calls with the planning commission.

"We've already heard," said the executive director.

"At least that's what we concluded from what we've heard."

"I'll do whatever I can to help you find someone else," I said, feeling a little remiss.

"Actually, we've decided to find someone part-time for the job now."

"Part-time, as in maybe 20 hours per week?"

"Yeah, about that," he said, beginning to think along the same lines. "It may vary a little here and there, but we'd like to just peg it at 20 hours and hope it evens out."

"Maybe this person, such as a private investigator, could work, say, at his own office sometimes, on his own computer, showing his deep sense of commitment to community planning and being as reliable as hell."

"Sure. Sounds about right. Today I was going to run our want ad announcement over to the *Journal*. You think I should consider the position filled?"

"Yeah, save the taxpayers the cost of the ad, too," I said. "When do you want me to start?"

"Next week OK with you? No, why not right after the holidays?"

"Sounds perfect."

"I'll prepare the paperwork and have it ready for you to sign this afternoon," he said. "And, by the way, Stuart, I'm glad you're on board."

That done, I called the bonding agent's secretary and promised to deliver the premium. She didn't get excited about it, but said she would notify her boss.

Then I called Maddox who was busy in some high administrative meeting. Phillips was there, though.

"We all heard about your stunt up at Mackinac," he said. "In fact, I've had to handle two calls from the troopers already this morning."

"Anything going on?"

"You mean up there?"

"Yeah. Why the phone calls?"

"Nothing," he said. "The trooper says he had an interesting chat with the woman, Darelle Slater, last evening, late, and she barely remembers talking to you but confirmed your visit. Admitted, though, that Kowalski worked for her as a labor consultant."

"Labor consultant," I repeated.

"Anyway, we haven't found Freddie yet, or whatever his name is, and we haven't arrested anyone. The lieutenant's been chewing ass and he's in a fine mood. We're running out of cops around here. The city's getting a little tired of all the overtime we're putting in and not getting anywhere."

"Did Meyers come over?"

There was some noise in the detective section and Phillips had to wait until things calmed down. Typical noise for a squad room.

"What was that?" he said.

"Meyers. Did Stewart Meyers come over?"

"Yeah. Interesting. But not a lot there which would help me fill out a warrant. At least not all by itself."

I told him what Kowalski told me when he was in the ice, and Phillips thought about it.

"Gee, that doesn't help us nail the owners," he said. "We could charge Kowalski and Freddie, but Kowalski's dead and Freddie's probably in Idaho or somewhere. Are the owners going to walk?"

"Don't they usually?"

"You'd better come down here so we can get your statement on the record," Phillips said. "You never know, somebody might nail you yet."

"I've got one more hunch on a way to find Freddie," I said. "Want to come along?"

"With you? I'll have to think about it," he said. "Come down here and make your statement, and I'll think about it."

When Phillips was off the line I called Melody Price and left a message to call me. I said I had some good news. Before I could leave the office, though, she called back. I told her about my visit to Mackinac Island and Randall Kowalski. I also told her what Kowalski said. She listened without interrupting.

"Those were his dying words?" she said.

"Pretty much," I said.

"But you're the only one who heard them?"

"Yeah, for Christ sake, we were sort of alone out there," I said.

"Sounds pretty good, though," she said finally. "We should be able to deny any claim. No claim has been made yet, though. Did you talk with Stewart Meyers?"

"We had a nice chat a couple of days ago," I said.

"His lawyer, guy named Holland, says his client won't be making a claim on the Prospect property. I made him put it in writing, and we got it this morning."

"Covering his client's ass," I said. "He's making sure Meyers can't be charged with defrauding an insurance company."

"Unfortunately, this means you get a percentage fee," Melody Price said. "You could buy me a hell of a dinner with it. After getting that message from your friend Patty, I deserve a nice dinner."

"What'd she say?"

"You don't know?"

"Would I ask if I knew?"

"Then, we'll just keep it between us girls," she said.

CHAPTER 36

Phillips typed up my statement and I signed it. He said he'd been assigned a "shit-load" of post Christmas burglary complaints from prestigious neighborhoods and didn't have time to come along. I don't think either of us was deeply disappointed.

Maddox signaled me to come into his office, and I did.

"I really dislike austerity," Maddox said, sitting down, examining something far away outside his window. "It makes me feel as though we've not been serious about things, that we've been slackers. It destroys your dignity and pride."

"I take it that they've discovered you're making too much money."

Maddox ignored me. He was good at that.

"I guess I just liked it a lot better when the city grew rapidly, streets were paved regularly, families shopped downtown, and American motorists bought Oldsmobiles by the millions."

"When was that?"

He'd put his feet on his desk, and now he put them back on the floor.

"Thanks for killing Kowalski some place else," he said.

"I didn't kill him."

"Well, that's what's on the street," Maddox said. "Or so I'm told. I don't get to the street much these days, unless you count driving to and from work."

Maddox took notice of my face and grimaced and made like he was examining my facial scars from a distance. "Whatever prompted you to go to Mackinac Island in the first place?"

"Hunch," I said.

"You getting those again?"

I nodded.

"I used to get those," he said. "Now I get hemorrhoids." He moved some papers on his desk, touching them as though noxious germs might live on the tops and bottoms but not on the edges. "So, what are you up to now?"

"I'm going to find Leon Slater and explain to him what a good time he'll have in Jackson," I said.

"Why Leon?"

"I went to Mackinac Island," I said. "It didn't take long up there to see that Darelle Slater's pulling the strings. She hired Kowalski. She had to tell him to follow me and kill me. I think Leon's our best chance—your best chance—at getting some testimony you can use."

He shook his head. "I'd stay away from the Slaters if I were you," he said. "You'll have the whole legislature on your ass, if not the governor, too."

"And then I'm going to find Freddie Samuelson," I said.

"You mean that we've been looking for him for several days—and even Ingham County has looked, too—and now you're going to find him?"

I held up a finger. "I have a plan."

Maddox snapped his fingers. "Damn. I knew we needed some plans. They keep telling me we need to establish plans, prioritize our needs, direct our personnel—excuse me, our human resources—into the appropriate activities. Then we're supposed to develop pre-plans and action plans. We need a shit-load of plans these days."

Now I knew Phillips had heard at least part of the

same speech today. "Is there some message in all this for me?"

"No," Maddox said. "I just had a meeting with the city's financial people—financial human resources, excuse me—and I'm struggling to learn the terminology. The lingo. You see, someday I'll want to be promoted to their station in life, so I need to talk like them."

"But you're just a cop," I said. "What do you know about that stuff?"

"Right," he said. "That's the problem."

"Back to my plan," I said. "Do you want to come along and justify what I'm going to do?"

"Me? A professionally trained, highly decorated police officer? A lieutenant in charge of all the detectives?"

I shrugged. "Of course."

"No," he said. "I've got more important duties. I'm supposed to put together a contingency plan about how we can operate the department on nine percent less money. I'm supposed to have it on the captain's desk at noon tomorrow."

I got up and made for the door. One can expect certain kinds of depression-inducing experiences at the detective section—murder, fraud, assault, arson, police coffee— but not this. I had to get away.

"If you go see Leon Slater, we had nothing to do with it," Maddox said.

* * *

I drove through Wendy's and got a double with mustard and pickles and some fries and drove to my previous office out of habit. Good thing, too. Freddie Samuelson's Mercury was sitting across the street from the office building in the little parking lot that used to be a dry cleaning shop, and he was sitting in it.

Maddox would never believe my luck.

Freddie, or Maurice Ludwig, didn't see me go by because he obviously didn't know what I was driving. All he remembers is the El Camino he torched. Or someone torched.

One block away I swung into a side street so I could get turned around, all the while trying to gobble the Wendy's double burger. The fries would have to wait. I swung through the pharmacy parking lot and parked behind a dark blue Dodge Shadow about a half block from Freddie. I could see his head between the edge of the building and the car in front of me. I sat there still chewing the burger and tried to decide what to do.

Sure, I could go right up there and grab him. But I could do that anytime now. I could wait and see what happens, hoping for something better. I could finish my lunch, then decide what to do, or go to my new office and call the cops. They could get Freddie and the credit. Maybe it would cheer up Maddox, make him feel like a cop again.

I decided to wait. Maddox could solve that problem himself. Besides, waiting gave me a chance to finish my lunch in peace, which I accepted. I kept a constant eye on Freddie, or Maurice Ludwig, while I ate. Freddie kept a pretty good watch on my former office building, only occasionally looking from one side to the other.

What I couldn't figure out was why he was watching what he thought to be my office, unless he was doing something for someone else. Perhaps Darelle Slater wanted to know when I returned. Perhaps he was operating under even older instructions. It was apparent he had not gone to my office because I taped a sign on the door to route

the dozens of expected callers to the new office. On the
other hand, perhaps Freddie was not alone and he was
waiting for someone else who was at my other office.
Maybe Freddie had a dental appointment downstairs.

It did not make sense.

I waited some more, and I found myself glancing occasionally and expectantly and almost longingly at the
window which used to be mine to watch the world from.
There didn't seem to be anything going on up there.

It started to get cold in the car, which made me realize I could spend all day out there with very little to
show for it. I got out and pulled up the hood on my
coat, figuring Freddie would remember me in another
coat, the coat which almost went with me to the bottom
of Lake Huron. I pulled the ties fairly snug and headed
up the same sidewalk and in the same direction Sandra
Goodman used when she braved a blizzard to get me
involved in this case. I walked past Freddie's Merc to
make sure he was alone, then back to it.

I pulled open the door and grabbed a wad of coat in
my hand and pulled him out into the snow.

"Don't even flinch," I said.

"Mallory?"

"Are you carrying?"

"No," he said, offering a feeble effort to cover his head.
"Don't shoot. Please don't shoot me."

I pushed him against his own car and checked him
anyway. There seemed to be more coat than man there.
Freddie looked as though he hadn't changed clothes or
shaved since I saw him disappear into the bathroom in
the apartment on Michigan Avenue.

"I won't shoot you," I said.

"You killed Kowalski," he said.

Such a reputation didn't seem to be such a bad thing.

"The Lansing police want to talk to you," I said, considering slapping him around a little for killing Danny Goodman and Terri Krug and burning up my car, but I was afraid he would just break into pieces.

"Everybody's looking for me," he said. "Everybody wants to kill me."

"Look, Maurice," I said, noticing a new glimmer of fear in his eye. "You murdered two people. Why are you so surprised someone is looking for you?"

"I didn't do all of that," he said. "I wasn't alone."

"Come with me," I said, getting another hunch. "We're going for a ride."

"Where?"

I rapidly escorted him toward my car where I pushed him toward the passenger door. "Get in, and don't get grease all over the seat."

Maurice Ludwig got into the Cutlass and I pulled a U-turn a few doors down and headed back. My passenger eyed the remnants of my lunch, but he could see nothing there.

"I'll buy you some lunch after our appointment," I said. "Meanwhile, tell me why you are lurking outside my office."

"I want to deal."

I drove some more, passing my office, heading to where Leon Slater was living while in Lansing. I hoped he was home.

"Let me tell you the deal," I said. "We're going to drive over to Leon Slater's house, and you're going to tell him what it's like in a state penitentiary. You'll tell him about the 'buddy' system. Tell him about how someone will pick out his ass and promise to take care of him, and about the midnight stabbings and the drugs. You're going to convince him to run straight to the police as though his ass were on fire and become a real mouthpiece. It shouldn't be any stretch for you, Maurice."

"What's in it for me?"

I looked at Freddie while we sat at a red light waiting for a green one. I reached over with both hands and lifted him off the seat and slammed him against the door. I took a wad of his coat just below the throat and pulled him back and looked in his face.

"I won't kill you if you do this little job for me," I said. "And then we'll talk to the detectives downtown. You face two murder charges, a parole violation, and probably some narcotics charges in Illinois. You'd better start being nice to people like me, Freddie."

I tossed him against the door again. He rattled, but the car didn't make a sound.

Someone behind my car gave me a little beep as a reminder of the current traffic laws and the traffic situation. We drove on.

Leon Slater lived in an upscale apartment on the city's west side. He had a suite of rooms in the lower floor of an apartment and office building off Waverly Road. I told Maurice to stand in front of the door alone and ring the bell. I stood at the side and watched as Leon Slater answered the door himself and opened it fairly wide to let Maurice Ludwig into his home.

I went into the apartment right behind Maurice.

"Oh, you," Slater said to me. "You can't come in here."

"I'm already in, Leon," I said. "I'm going to stick around, too."

"I'll call my lawyer," Slater said, keeping his distance.

"You do that," I said. "And tell him that you glanced

outside through your peephole, and finding only a friendly drug-pusher, killer, and arsonist outside, you let him in, but you wouldn't let me in."

He looked at Freddie. Freddie said nothing.

"I brought Freddie here to talk with you," I said. "No one's going to hurt you."

"You killed Kowalski," Slater said.

"No, Leon, your sister killed him by sending him after me," I said. "Your sister is going to kill you, too, if you don't wise up. You'd better start thinking of me as your friend, Leon, because I'm here to help you."

I pointed at two chairs in the living room and Freddie moved quickly to one of them. Leon Slater wasn't sure what to do. I unbuttoned my coat deliberately and took it off. My shoulder holster stuck out like a smear of orange paint on a white shirt. Slater remembered the incident in his office. I pointed at the other chair and Slater walked in and sat down.

"Your sister is hanging you out to dry," I told Slater. "When the police finish talking to her, you'll have hired Kowalski, ordered Danny Goodman's death, maybe even killed a couple of people. Remember that."

"Darelle wouldn't do that."

"She's already doing it," I said.

"Now?" Freddie said.

"Now," I said.

CHAPTER 37

Freddie turned to Slater and began to tell him things. He started by describing what happens when three men come into the shower with you and one drops the bar of soap on the floor and tells you to pick it up. He told about how the other two men stand at the entrance, making sure the other inmates find other shower stalls on that shift, and he told how the third man makes sure you pick up the soap and that you know how to use it and that you belong to him for as long as he wants you. He told about the beatings and the knifings and the drugs. Then Freddie told Slater he never wanted to go back, and would die before he went back.

I began to feel like an awfully lucky man. It's not everyday the man you are looking for waits at your doorstep for you to find him. Then to have him step into such an important role without much coaching is almost too much to believe.

I could see that it might work. I told Slater I would be glad to give him a ride to the detective section and that we could pick up his lawyer on the way, too, if he wanted. I told him that he'd better get his side of the story on paper damned soon or somebody would beat him to it. All this time I kept a careful eye on Freddie who might want to take a leak.

That's when Darelle Slater, accompanied by the man who held me at gunpoint in the backseat of a car, came to the front door and pushed the lighted doorbell. I could see all this through the peephole.

Freddie stopped talking and Leon Slater stopped listening.

"Visitors," I told them.

I opened the door and stood behind it, protecting the warm inside from the cold outside, just like Darelle Slater did at the cottage. She came in first and walked past the door toward where her brother sat with Freddie Samuelson and Maurice Ludwig. She never glanced in my direction. The man followed Darelle Slater. I kicked him in the small of his back and sent him flying against the entry way wall. He hit hard enough to crack the dry-wall in two places and knock a picture off the wall in the next room.

I shut the door.

"Now," I said to the man sprawling on the floor. "Spread 'em." He knew what to do, and he did it. That says a lot.

I put my pistol into the back of his head and quickly checked for weapons. He had a nice little .32 caliber automatic stuffed in his back belt, and I took it. I took his wallet, too. Nice to know who you're beating up.

Darelle Slater had been surprised. Score another for me.

"Mr. Mallory, Stuart," she said from her standing position in the living room.

"That's all you can muster?" I said. "Mr. Mallory? You send a man out on the ice to kill me and come visit your brother with amateurish muscle, and that's all you can say?"

She was working on ignoring me.

"Sit down," I said.

She sat.

"Leon, we need to talk," Darelle said. "Come sit down." She patted the seat next to her.

Leon turned to sit, but he stayed on his feet. Maybe

he was still thinking about what Freddie had said to him.

"You do that, Leon, and you'll spend the rest of your life in prison," I said. "A wonderful place."

"Don't be absurd," Darelle said. "No Slater has ever gone to prison, and never will. You'll not prove a thing against my brother. It is time you leave this home. Leon and I have things to work out."

Freddie didn't know what to do. I pointed at a chair near me and he came over and sat in it. Freddie smelled like a man who'd been on the run for a few days. Leon's eyes followed him, so he ended up looking at me as Freddie sat in the corner chair.

"There are some things you need to know, Leon, and there are some things you need to think about," I said. "Your sister thinks you are an incompetent hack. With a sneer, she's going to lead you out to the gallows. You'll hang all by your lonesome, and we both know she hired Randall Kowalski and his dirty little men. She'll have the company, the cottage on Mackinac Island, and all the love your father never gave you."

"That's nonsense," Darelle Slater said.

Leon Slater was still facing me, but he was worrying a hang nail on his left thumb. I couldn't sympathize with him, but I could appreciate some of life's pressures he was enduring.

I gave the vice another turn.

"When you're in Jackson Prison next summer learning how to be lovey-lovey with crack dealers and killers, who's going to be sitting on the porch on Mackinac Island enjoying a cool breeze and saying, 'Poor Junior, he was just a wimp, and such a fool.'?"

"Leon," Darelle said.

"What's at stake here, Leon, is whether you offer your version of events to the police before your sister happens by the detective section and tells some understanding cop what a hardship it has been to carry her helpless little brother all these years, the wimp she says who was never worthy of his father."

Leon turned around and looked at his sister.

"Don't listen to this," Darelle said. "Come here and sit down." She nodded subtly at the seat.

"Is that your sister or your mother?" I said.

"Leon, I've come a long way to clean up this mess, now, dammit, get over here," she said, still holding her voice steady, her tone even. "I've had enough humiliation for one day."

"You?" said Leon, who was not having his sister's success at keeping his voice steady. "You've had enough?"

"Come with me, Leon, I'll get your coat," I said, and looked through the closet with one hand while I held the gun on the guy still on the floor with my other.

Leon turned to follow me. His steps were labored. It was not easy for him.

"What would your father say about what you're doing?" Darelle said, raising her voice. "He had so much hope for you, and for this family."

"Father?" Leon said, turning. "He NEVER had any hope for me. He was NEVER allowed to have any hope for me. Big Sister was always there, filling in, always belittling me, condemning me, blocking me off from Father."

Before I knew it, Leon had run across the small living room and was pointing his finger into his sister's face. He was almost in tears.

Although Darelle was losing her composure, she stood

and took a deep breath.

"Leon," she said, almost clicking her tongue. "Don't you see what this man is trying to do to us? Settle down. Get a tissue and blow your nose."

Leon slapped his sister hard. The blow caused her to lose her balance, and she fell over the arm of a stuffed chair.

Freddie leaped to his feet and was half way to the door before I stopped him by taking a handful of his coat in my fist.

Leon Slater turned to help his sister, but she was working on making herself erect. Leon stood up and backed away.

"I'm sorry, Darelle," he said. "But you begged for it."

"You bastard," she said, dabbing at her lip with a handkerchief. "You're a disgrace to the family. When I get done with you, you'll wish you'd never been born into my family."

"You're not going to send Randy after me," Leon said. "Not anymore. Never fucking again."

Leon Slater took the coat I offered him and walked out the door. I let Freddie follow him.

"I've cleaned up your messes all your life," Darelle shouted. "I had to do this because you're inept."

Leon stopped momentarily on the sidewalk out front, then he walked on.

I put my office pistol back into my worn out but still serviceable holster and considered the man on the floor, the man who had held me at gunpoint, the man who held my right arm while Kowalski beat me unconscious. Without more thought, I kicked him in his side and immediately despised myself for it. He sucked air and groaned weakly.

"You can pick up your wallet and gun at the Lansing

PD," I said. "If you run, I'll find you."

Then I followed Maurice Ludwig and Leon Slater to my car.

CHAPTER 38

Flight instructor Henry Bretton said he was pleased with my first flight in about 15 years. He said he had students with 300 hours of flight time in the last two or three years who flew airplanes far worse. After he encouraged me to brush up on "radio talk," he said many older pilots handled radio communication so poorly they were an embarrassment to the majority of pilots and were usually encouraged to stay clear of controlled fields, if not out of the air entirely. Bretton shouted most of that over the roar of the 160 horsepower of the Lycoming engine of a Piper Warrior as I performed steep turns, stalls, slow flight, and chandelles about 20 miles northwest of the Lansing Airport.

Then Bretton suggested we return to the field where he guided me through four consecutive landings, the last two worthy of the name, and practiced some short-field and soft-field take-offs. As we climbed out of the field after the fourth landing, Bretton leaned over to talk against the sound of the engine at full throttle.

"Make this the last one," he said. "I think I'm wasting your money now. If after a few hours of flying you want to pursue a CFI ticket, you come back to me."

I shook my head. "I've got two jobs now," I told him.

On the down-wind leg, Bretton suggested I make the last landing an "accuracy landing," one where the pilot pulls the engine back to idle and then, using the altitude with precision and care, makes what he hopes to be a perfect landing within 50 feet of a line near the end of the runway. It's how pilots learn to manage speed and altitude for the day you've got to land in a cornfield when you'd rather not.

An accuracy landing is one of the more interesting things for a pilot to do, but it's also a maneuver which contains great opportunity for embarrassment. The idea is to put the plane on the ground at a precise spot without adding power or "landing" earlier, and it is harder than it looks. An airplane won't land when it has enough speed to fly, and it won't fly when it doesn't have speed enough to produce lift. So, the pilot has to make things work.

I pulled the throttle back to idle and slowed my speed to 80 knots, immediately beginning a shallow turn for the runway. It felt good, very good, like bringing in a moderately loaded Huey. At a half mile from the numbers, I eased on some flaps, feeling the ship sink a little. I held the speed steady at 70 knots.

Over the runway's threshold I pulled on all the flaps and waited for the Warrior to stall on the line, but I was disappointed. It floated farther than I expected, gliding at least 100 feet before it would permit the wheels to touch with a little thump.

Bretton laughed. He was already signing my logbook.

"You're still remembering the old Piper Cherokees. You'll find these new Cherokees have more float in 'em," he said. "You get the feel of a Cherokee but the lift of a Skyhawk."

I taxied the Warrior up to Midway Aviation and shut it down. Patty Bonicelli stood just outside the building with her face in the wind, her cheeks red, in her classic gray goose down jacket, looking every bit the successful lawyer and sexy woman.

My luck was holding.

"Well?" Patty said as we sauntered up.

Bretton handed me the logbook. "Piece of cake," he

said, turning to Patty. "You sure this guy's not been in the air for 15 years?"

"That's what he tells me," she said.

"Well, he's just fine," he said, turning to me. "If you two want to take her up, you still have it another two hours."

I looked at Patty. She looked at me.

"I didn't come out here just to breathe fresh air," she said, taking me by the arm. "So, what you been doing the past three hours?"

Bretton disappeared inside the building.

"We spent the first hour on the ground going over rules, maps, navigation, stuff like that," I said. "Pilot stuff."

"Pilot stuff," she repeated.

"I've forgotten a lot."

"You're all up to date now, though, right?"

"Sure," I said. "And there's been this rush of new gadgets. I learned all about something called a loran, and the radios now are digital, and each has about 800 frequencies."

"You're an expert now," she said, looking out at the Warrior which moved lightly as it was hit by a gust of wind, almost like a sprinter would lightly shrug a shoulder.

"Sure you want to do this? I'm still a little green you know."

Patty began to lead me back to the Warrior. She had to go around a large, shallow puddle. The temperature was finally above freezing.

"I'm ready, and so are you," she said. "If you grinned any wider, your face would go into labor. You are disgustingly pleased with yourself."

She was right.

"You going to buy one like this?" She tapped the Warrior on the nose, the spinner.

"Buy one?"

"Sure," she said, reaching the tip of the left wing. "With all that insurance money you're making these days, you can buy one. This one's real cute."

"Cute," I repeated.

"What's this?" she said, touching the lights on the wing tip.

"That's a strobe light," I said. "I think."

"You think?"

"Yeah," I said.

"Are pilots supposed to say things like, 'I think.'? Would Chuck Yeager say that?"

"We didn't use strobes when I last flew. But that has to be a strobe light."

Patty was walking around behind the airplane, touching the stabilator, running a finger along the fuselage. She stopped at the step leading onto the wing and into the cockpit and turned to look into my eyes.

"You'll treat me well," she said.

"Of course."

"You'll fly safely and brilliantly."

"Uh-huh."

"You'll make me a member of the Mile High Club."

"Today?"

She shrugged. "Well, maybe not today," she said, looking around the apron. "But soon. When we're ready. Besides, after that crap you offered on New Year's, you need a New Year's resolution with substance."

"OK."

"Take me up, flyboy," Patty said as she reached for the step.

I did, too.